THE EXILE EMPIRE

JOSHUA DONE

THE EXILE EMPIRE

This book is a work of fiction. The characters, places, incidents, and dialogue are the product of the author's imagination and are not to be construed as real, or if real, are used fictitiously. Any resemblance to actual events, locales, or persons, either living or dead, is purely coincidental.

THE EXILE EMPIRE

JOSHUA DONE

Thanks to my brother, David, who has always been my staunchest supporter and sounding wall, and without whom this book would never have been written.

THE EXILE EMPIRE

JOSHUA DONE

12/14/2453

Location: Unknown

Fleet Admiral Hancock awoke in a cold sweat, his dream still echoing through his mind. It was the same thing every week. The same horrifying memory of killing an entire world, followed inevitably by the death of his own. The alien world had died by his orders. He tried to console himself with the justifications of war, rationalizing that the authority of the Harvester War Charters validated the slaughter. Every morning he tried to convince himself with the cold logic that it had been necessary. It never worked.

Each time he dreamt about that battle, he was in the same pristine blue world he had watched for days, weighing the options. But it was covered in corruption and death; the Harvesters had reduced the few remaining humans to little more than cattle.

Shelkin Reefs dominated the planet, providing the Harvester Hoards shelter and supply throughout the battle. They were more entrenched here than on any world thus far. There was no other choice; it had to be done. Still, the thought of burning an entire planet by carpet bombing it with plasma, atomic, and antimatter weapons did not seem any less horrible then, as now. What made the devastating victory all the more hollow was the fact that it was the last victory mankind, as a whole, had experienced to date.

None of the allied strategists had known, nor cared, why the Harvesters' advancing forces had suddenly stopped, nor did they question why they never tried to save thousands of their own besieged outposts and bases, which had been built over the brutally subjugated remains of human colonies and civilizations. He knew that the war was just; it was a war for survival.

The name Harvester was aptly given. They harvested everything for food and pleasure, including humans. Until it had met them, mankind had boldly surged forward into the galaxy, building and adapting everything to humanity's vast needs. In only a few hundred years, the human species had grown to more than thirteen trillion. Eventually, however, the same enthusiasm and vitality that had allowed humanity to prosper led to their downfall. They met the Harvesters, fought the Harvesters, almost lost to the Harvesters, and after decades of war reached the Harvester Home world. To their eternal horror, they found out why the fortune of war had swung so vastly and dynamically in favor of mankind. The entire planet, the Harvester Home world, was covered in a blanket of dark warships larger than any they had ever seen, brutal and powerful. As Hancock's fleet arrived, a Harvester ship attempted to run the blockade, trying to use the confusion generated by the human arrival to escape. It never had a chance. Before it had gone twenty clicks from the planet's surface, a lash of light from one of the black forms cut the ship in two, leaving it to die in its own flames, debris falling back to the planet.

And then it happened. It was the only atrocity that Hancock could fathom worse than the Battle of the Burning: they destroyed the planet. The first moments of the attack turned the green world into an ocean of crimson fire. After a few minutes, it was rendered no more than a charred rock, the atmosphere burned from its surface. When those black ships turned away from the dead world, focusing now on the human armada, Admiral Hancock remembered wondering if the old axiom, "The enemy of my enemy is my friend," would hold true. It did not. The black fleet sent only one message that took months to translate. It was the coldest and most confusing message ever received: "We have destroyed your home, your fleet is too late, now you die. We will take your worlds for our nests." They had thought humans were Harvesters! Or allied with them at least. They attacked, and humans died. Human ships and weapons were outclassed, overpowered, and outnumbered. The battle lasted only minutes; two-and-a-half million men and women were dead along with ninety percent of the forward assault fleet.

The Exile Empire

The Harvesters had been brutal, but the brutality of the Death truly transcended human understanding. Battles raged at the Harvesters' dead world, and humans died; humans fought them at the Second Battle of the Burning, and they died; they fought them at Tarsus colony, and they died. Within one month, the black fleets of the Harvesters threw their gruesome shadow over Earth herself. Most did not survive, and none who had experienced that final battle would ever be the same. Every last human warship, mercenary vessel, and private cruiser capable of fighting had drawn themselves together for one last battle, the Battle of Fallen Earth.

They say that the Black Plague killed off one-third of Europe's population during the second millennia AD. If only we had been so lucky and lost so comparatively few during that final battle. Chaos was much too soft of a word to describe the state of the human forces; hell is closer, but only slightly. Hundreds of millions of human warships, hundreds of billions of warriors, mercenaries, traders, and civilians had put themselves between the Death and our first and final stronghold—Earth, home. A living wall of metal and men were willing to die defending blue Earth from the Black Death, and die they did.

The Death were so numerous that they literally blocked the light of the sun; their weapons, however, replaced that light with a deadly version of their own. Humans fought hard, they fought long, but their planet was doomed. Where their fleets had shattered, they stood and died. When their shields fell, they did not fall back. When their guns were ripped from their ports, they used the only thing left—their lives and their ships. The Japanese called it "the divine wind" or "kamikaze"—the final sacrifice in defense of innocents, an ancient and instinctive response. It was the only thing that seemed to work against the Death, and so the remaining millions rammed themselves and their ships into the jaws of death itself.

The Battle of Sorrows lasted three hours, twenty-seven minutes, and sixteen seconds. Earth central command had been leveled in the wake of a devastating barrage, but not before one last order was broadcast to every last human ship, containing only two words: "Live. Run." And so they ran. Every surviving ship that had an operating Gravity Stream star drive locked onto the Cerberus as it left the system, blasting a swath through the Death with its triad of antimatter cannons, the most powerful weapons ever created by mankind. The Death tried to block their retreat, pouring volley after volley down the forward tubes of the Cerberus, only to receive the deadly bite returned from its cannons. But it wasn't enough. Only the smallest fraction of ships that had drawn the curtain at the Battle of Sorrow survived.

A refugee fleet cobbled together from many destroyed colonies had been hiding in the gravity of Jupiter; it was barely able to join the retreating shard mankind's military and enter the great exodus. They hadn't used any nav points. If they had, the Death would have been able to follow. They didn't need nav points, though. They wouldn't be returning. Earth was lost. And this dire flight was where Admiral Hancock found himself—staring into his mirror in a cold sweat, three months away from Earth, with no idea where he was or where he was going, dragging just over two and a half million refugees from his dead civilization. And they were running out of food fast.

1 >> Leadership

10/20/2453

Location: Unknown

Status: Bored to Hell and Back

Lieutenant Cormac Kincade sat in his bunk. He was bored. It seemed like he was always bored. He didn't usually have a problem with the classic military axiom, "Hurry up and wait," but this was different. Cormac had decided that losing his planet after the greatest battle ever fought by his race did one of two things to a man. It either made him depressed, dipping him into a despair from which few recovered (there had been a rash of suicides in the months following the Battle of Sorrows), or it could make a man angry, aggressive, willing to fight anything, anyone, and anywhere. Cormac was the latter. He hated being cramped, he hated rations, and right now he hated the metal walls that served as his prison, a living coffin in everything but name.

All I want, Cormac thought, *is some room, maybe some grass, some hard lemonade, and a hammock. But nooo, the Death hafta take my world and punt me across this dust bowl part of the galaxy, drifting with a million whoflunkers with no aim and nowhere to go. Come on, why couldn't the XOs just have sent us into that last world? It was only a colony from what the guys say!*

After his internal explosion of dissatisfaction, Cormac calmed himself. He would never let the men under his command know of his frustration. An officer didn't have the luxury of feelings, especially when there was a war to fight. *They just better not give up on this one,* he thought, looking at the little information he had been given about another system they had detected with a halfway decent planet. *I just can't stand the smell of this rotting ship anymore.*

The growing sound of a rhythmic *clunk-clack, clunk-clack* came down the hall, and a stiff uniformed IF captain stopped next to his bunk. *Great,* Cormac thought, *IF errand boys never bring good news.*

"On your feet, Lieutenant! You have been ordered to report to the Santa Monica. Your rank is now captain, and you are to whip the most rawhide group of trainees into something resembling the Fifty-Sixth. You are to report at 1200 hours for a full briefing." The officer snapped a packet of information into the shocked soldier's hands.

Cormac quickly recovered himself. Standing, he snapped a powerful salute. "Sir, yes, sir!" *Well, at least I won't be bored anymore,* he thought. *I guess this means the rumors about recruits from the civilian refugee fleet are true. They expect us to see some action. We already had over a hundred and fifty thousand troops that survived into the exile. If they are giving them officers, that must mean something is a-brewin'.* The soldier felt a huge weight fall from his shoulders that was immediately replaced by the older, more comfortable weight of real responsibility. Cormac arched his back, stretching and popping his muscles, and let out a deep laugh. "Finally!"

Cormac threw his few belongings in a sack and cleared the metal bunk. He stretched again, and as he twisted, there was more popping of muscles dormant for far too long. He headed down the hallway toward the ship's hangar.

After a short, windowless shuttle ride, Cormac Kincade found himself walking through a maze of corridors aboard the Santa Monica. He was in awe of the sheer number of refugees crammed into every nook and cranny of the ship. "And I thought that the barracks ship was cramped!" He finally found himself staring at a large, imposing double-reinforced door sporting an inscription: "Abandon all hope ye who enter here," he said aloud. "Cute," he harrumphed.

After a battery of eye scans, voiceprints, and finger impressions, the door opened, releasing the heavy smell of sweat and exertion. Inside he found a fully functional training center, recreated battle scenarios, obstacle courses, sparring rings, and a shooting range. Even so, Cormac had only one thought: *so...much...room!* He was dumbfounded that so much space could be spared for training. Before he could shake himself out of his stupor, a big man grabbed him by the shoulder. "Hey, buddy, you looking for someone?"

Cormac blinked, getting used to the near-sunlight brightness of the room. "Yes, where is Major Simmons? I was told to report for duty," he said in clear, carefully enunciated English. There were too many people from too many worlds in the fleet, and one had to speak clearly to ensure everyone would understand your accent.

"Speaking, and you're right on time. Your squad has been run through the gauntlet, but you really need to get them in shape if you expect them to survive a battle someday."

Cormac grunted. "Yes, sir," he said, but he did not move toward the huffing and panting group of near-civilians by a set of climbing ropes.

"Yes?" the major asked.

"No disrespect, sir, but what's the point?"

The short whipcord of a man took a long pull on a stim-stick device meant to clear the head and give energy through a convenient inhaler. They had proven rather addictive, and their use was widespread throughout the old allied militaries. "Why train soldiers when there's so few of us and no land to defend? Why fight to protect the lives of people with nothing left to live for?" Cormac grunted. The man didn't answer. Cormac was griping. He wasn't used to being higher ranked than a major, and he reminded himself that complaint goes up. He was now up, not down from the man next to him.

"Tell you what," the major finally said. "When you figure that out, be sure to let me know." He took another pull on the stim-stick. "Your platoon is currently on the climbing ropes." He hit some info into a data pad he carried. "The XOs know you're here now, so you better get to work." He saluted. "Congratulations on your promotion, sir." Cormac returned the salute and turned to the sweaty mass of men and women.

As Cormac approached the motley mass of people, he could tell that they had been given a decent basic training. He moved them to the sparring arena and found that, on the whole, they had been recruited from civilians with proficiency in hand-to-hand combat. He had them spar for a bit and found that they could handle themselves in everything from throws to full-out brawls.

"Atten-tion!" he snapped. *Hmm, a little sluggish, but decently ordered,* he thought. "I am your new commanding officer. You will do what I say when I say it. I don't need any half-brained loons in my outfit, so if I need to tell you how to do something, learn now, and learn it for good."

The rows of recruits standing in tight lines shouted in near unison, "Sir, yes, sir." The basic order-response of military training had remained the same for hundreds of years and showed no signs of changing.

"Now," he continued, "who here knows how to use a plasma rifle?" Every last individual stepped forward. *Good, they aren't slips,* he thought

"Okay, who knows how to use a battle shield?" Only two-thirds of the recruits took another step. *Okay, a little less enthusiastic on that one.* "Who knows how to use them together?" No one stepped up. *Okay, we've got some work to do.*

2 >> Blood

9/22/2444

Location: Tarsus Colony

James sat huddled in the closet with his hand clasped tightly over his sister's mouth. The large Harvester stalked through their family's apartment, the ground shuddering with every step, its grotesque claws digging deep into the floor. As it passed by the closet where James and his sister were hiding, Annah's writhing redoubled. He didn't want to hurt her, but if the beast saw her, it would kill them both. *I'm sorry, I'm sorry, I'm sorry*, he thought. *I won't let it hurt you.* The beast's terrible piercing eyes swiveled back and forth, searching the room; it could smell them. Fortunately for the children, however, it couldn't pinpoint where they were; the environmental circulation units were screwing with the direction of their scent. *Thank God for processed air*, he thought.

The beast turned to search the next room, not considering any hiding place that the massive creature itself could not enter. But before it could leave, Annah pulled James's hand from her face and shrieked.

Bursting from his grip, she raced across the lizard's path toward the door that had been ripped from its settings. "Annah! No!" was all that James could scream before the Harvester flicked its serrated tail directly into her path. In an almost annoyed fashion, it clotheslined her with deadly efficiency. Her body hit the floor with a sickening thud. Her head had been flung backward by the impact and now lay unseeing; her dead eyes gazing directly into the closet where James still hid, frozen in horror and terror.

James's anger boiled into a primal wrath. He tried to scream, but someone else was doing that for him. The duet of a piercing shriek and guttural roar from his parents filled the halls as they rushed toward the monster. His mother emptied cartridge after cartridge from her civilian-issued M229 while his father covered the beast with the acidic bite of the new Ironwood Plasma Repeater. The creature was forced into a wall by the harrowing barrage of weapon fire. James's parents were blind and berserk. They did not see that the creature's combined armor and thick frontal skin had absorbed most of the damage; they attacked repeatedly with heedless ferocity.

They emptied their last mags and switched to smaller weapons as they closed on the Harvester. When their weapons clicked empty and went silent, they rushed the beast with reckless abandon; his father drew twin curved knives and his mother her bowie. It was suicide. The beast was in a complete rage. It bellowed louder than James had thought possible and lashed out at his parents with lightning speed. Its first attack attempted to kill the pair in one broad sweep of its forward claws. His father swung wide, dragging his left hand across the alien's path, the blade leaving only a scour mark on the Harvester's claw.

His mother had avoided its retaliatory plasma blast in a limbo-like maneuver that put her lying on the floor. She stabbed her knife into the monster's leg. The blade punched deep between two scales, producing an earsplitting shriek as dark ooze spurted from the impact. The monster slashed its foot backward, carrying her into the air and across the room, slamming her into the far wall, shattering glass everywhere as it destroyed the pictures on the wall.

James was paralyzed with fear. He bellowed internally. Every fiber of his being demanded that he help his parents, but the dead white eyes of his sister held him transfixed. His father's last attack had placed the monster beside his sister's head, and he took advantage of the now exposed section of the Harvester's back. He used the blade in his left hand to hook onto the beast's armor and pull himself onto the small of its back where he began to repeatedly slam the second knife into the beast's neck.

It shrieked and thrashed around the room as it tried to dislodge James's father. His mother took advantage of the momentary opening and attacked its injured foot, but failed. The creature was completely insane with rage and pain. In a deceptively dexterous spin, it grabbed her in its fore-claw and squeezed. Her armored vest prevented the claw from cutting her, but her ribs cracked under the pressure. As her husband dug into the beast's neck, she hacked at the base of its claw with a frantic force and decreasing effect. The enormous pressure of the claw was snapping her ribs and she was shrieking. Eyes going wide, she coughed blood; the monster was crushing her organs. As crippling as the pain of death was, it couldn't touch the wrath of seeing her daughter killed. She flung her knife into the creature's face, the blade sinking deep into its eye. She shrieked one last defiant note. The sound ceased as she choked on her own blood. In that final sound her husband's roar joined her. James's father had been impaled by the creature's wicked tail, and his lifeless body was flung across the room and onto the little girl's head whose eyes had held James captive. The creature thrashed wildly around the room, clawing at the knife in its eye.

His father's now lifeless body obscured the unseeing eyes of his sister. In that moment the last strings of James's captivity snapped. He burst out of the closet, roaring as no human should. Heedlessly he sprang at the creature, which was still thrashing as it pulled his mother's knife from its eye. James slammed into the monster with every ounce of strength he had; its wounded leg buckled and it fell. It tried to grab James in its massive claw, but James grabbed a blocky crystal and metal data cube from the floor and jammed it into the creature's claw. The cube wedged itself into the joint at the base of the claw, sending a resounding crack throughout the room. The pressure and leverage from the beasts' own muscle against the device had separated its joint.

Writhing in pain, the creature slammed the claw into the wall, attempting to dislodge the mangled mass of metal and crystal, sending shards of the data cube and the wall in every direction. James followed the creature's path at full speed, the shards tearing into his skin as he seized the creature's now useless claw and leaped onto its back, following his father's example. The Harvester continued to thrash and buck, but James held onto the knife his father had left in its back. Slamming backward into the wall, it attempted to crush James between itself and the unforgiving surface. With blood streaming from his face and numerous wounds, James screamed as the creature pivoted away from the wall, recovered enough to use its deadly tail. As the serrated barb rushed toward his head, James slung himself into the air and off the creature's back. The tail slammed into the back of the creature's own neck, upon which James immediately landed. The barb had shorn the handle from his father's knife still lodged in the beast's neck. Using all his strength, James wrenched out the other blade from the creature's armor and slashed the joint connecting the barb to the creature's tail. The power of the blow combined with the wrenching force of the creature attempting to free the tail from its own flesh shattered the joint, separating the barb from the tail, and left the stump spraying its dark blood in a shower on the ceiling.

The beast's thrashes intensified. Its screeches evolved into one high-pitched ceaseless scream. Something popped and James's ears began to bleed. Clinging to the back of the creature with an insane tenacity, James plunged the remaining knife into the freely flowing hole in the creature's neck. His hand sank to the wrist. Without thinking, he clamped his hand on it and pulled with all his might. There was a wrenching, popping sound, and James's hand emerged from the pulped mass of red and black with a single vertebrae. The creature jerked once more and collapsed, falling silent and still in a single second. James stood on the fallen beast. He took the base of the tail barb and pulled it from the beast's neck. James stood there for a long second and stared at the vile implement. All his sorrow and rage seemed to flow into it as he watched the blood of his parents and sister drip onto the floor, where it mingled with the monster's juices.

There was a mass of noise at the door, and James turned to see a squad of EDF regulars enter the room. They stood in shock as they saw a boy no more than fifteen standing on the corpse of a Harvester, its tail barb in his hand. James saw them, but didn't *see* them. He took a step toward forward, and then another, and another, and with a scream charged.

"Kid! Stop! We are here to help!" He didn't hear them as he ran. He heard nothing. He felt nothing. "Break and back away, I've got this." The leader of the regulars allowed James to approach only to artfully sidestep him while drawing only six inches of an unusual blade to catch the barb. The big man flung James's improvised blade aside, spun, caught his legs from under him, and dropped him to the floor. "Sorry, kid, I know you're hurting." Before James could move again, the regular had slammed a field-medication delivery tube (FDT) into his neck, and James fell asleep.

9/24/2444

Location: Refugee Ship Huron

"Who do those psychologists think they are? They can't say whose fault it was! I was there, I let her go… I killed her just as much as that demon! I was too stupid, afraid. I will never let that happen again. I'll kill every last one of those monsters!" James continued muttering to himself, as he shuffled down the corridor of the refugee ship. He rounded a corner and entered a large dormitory with more than a hundred refugees from Tarsus. James wound his way down the maze of bunks, restrooms, and food dispensers to his bunk in a recessed corner next to a bathroom, all the while muttering about the pride and delusion of modern medicine and psychology. "Just because they say something, it doesn't make it right! Degrees don't make you a god."

A young girl sat in the bunk across from his. A large bandage covered half of her face. "Doesn't make what so?" she asked. Even though the girl was obviously only a little lucid from pain medication, she seemed genuinely interested. James did not answer. He strode over to his bunk, pulled a box out from underneath it, and began to rummage through it. The girl tried to look over the edge of his box from where she was sitting but jerked back from an obvious flash of pain. The blanket she had been under fell away; she was more bandaged than James had initially thought, and her wounds were far more excessive than James's. The damage was so grievous, it made him stop and stare despite himself.

"Why aren't you in the infirmary?" he asked.

"No more beds, and they said I wouldn't die."

"No kidding!" James wondered how that could be. She should already be dead, considering that half her chest and stomach was covered in bandages and the other half was sheathed in a thin metallic garment. The wrapper-like robe normally indicated the fresh addition of cybernetic augmentation or replacements. James wore the same shinning fabric down the length of his leg, part of his side, left shoulder, arm, and hand. Harvester neuro fluid was extremely corrosive and had left the area thoroughly infected. It was like having a dumpster of acidic rats and flies blended and dumped on him. His arm still had some of his original organic parts, but much of it had been replaced and fused with robotics.

The girl saw the shimmer of the sheath beneath James's shirt. "How did it happen?"

He responded curtly, "Harvester. Yours?"

The girl nodded her head in agreement. "Harvester. I tried to run, but it grabbed me and tried to crush me." She drew a hand across her lower chest to show him where it had grabbed her. "It would have succeeded if that EDF soldier hadn't stabbed it in the head with his sword. I've never seen a sword like that before."

James had only been half listening and responded with a halfhearted, "Hmmph." James rummaged through the box and took out his father's old knife handle, some titanium wire, a small contraption that the girl did not recognize, and a large curved piece of metal—or bone.

"What is that?" she asked.

James didn't respond. He just looked at her with cold, remembering eyes. Aggression seemed to curl upward from him, and as his eyes began to dilate. She realized what it was. "No! Why do you have one of those damned things? Get it away! Get it away!"

James sat there, with the massive Harvester tail barb in his lap, and stared at her. No, not *at* her—*through* her, to an unseen source of hate. The girl began to thrash. Her eyes rolled back in her head, and she fell backward onto her bed. A small rivulet of blood ran down her arm and began to drip onto the metal deck in cold, methodical beats.

9/25/2444

Location: Starship Huron

Jessica woke with a start, her arm burning in pain. She screamed. Panicked, she tried to get up, but her body wouldn't move. James was on the opposing bunk, in the same position he had been the night before, only he was rubbing something with an old piece of cloth. James got off his bunk and walked over to her, the barb hanging in his hand as if it were a cruel sword. He leaned over to her and looked directly in her eyes. "Does it hurt?" he asked.

Her eyes screamed the answer. She let out a cracked and weak "yes."

James nodded. "Good. Those idiots don't know how to install proper cybernetics; that, or they don't care. Your neural grafts weren't clamped to the proper level. Sometimes they do that to keep you from feeling pain immediately. It keeps us 'under control,' but it leaves long-term damage. If I hadn't tightened your connections, you would never have been able to feel anything in your artificial leg, and you would have lost control of all your body functions below your eyeballs. I've locked your systems so that you won't pull another stunt like you did last night. Considering the level of pain you should be feeling right now, can you control yourself?"

The girl choked, and a single tear rolled down the side of her immobile face. "Yes."

"Good." He hit a series of buttons on the side of her neck, and she slowly felt mobility returning to her limbs. He walked back to his bunk and sat down with the barb. Gingerly she pulled herself upright, every muscle burning with infection. "It burns!" she sobbed.

"I know. Your body doesn't know whether to accept or reject the augmentations. Mine burns too."

"I'm sorry about last night," she said in a meek voice.

"It would have happened whether I was here or not. The medical quacks set you up for it because they didn't want to deal with a patient feeling pain that drugs can't dull." Jessica clenched her eyes shut, trying to clear her head, and looked over at James. She could see sweat glistening on his forehead, and the skin around his augmentations was bright red and twitching. He was obviously in as much pain as she was. He also had bags under his eyes and was deeply hunched. It didn't look like he had slept at all. Even artificial as hers was, she had at least been asleep for some of the pain.

"Jessica," the girl stated.

James looked up. "What?"

"I'm Jessica," she said.

"I know," James replied. "Your name is on your arm along with all your medical information. At least they had the sense to put that on." James continued to polish the barb. Jessica could see that he had attached it to the long knife handle. It was one of those handles that your whole hand went through, like brass knuckles with a blade. The curve of the barb ran across the knuckles, hooked around the length of the arm, and then flared out from James's elbow near the bottom. It looked deadly, alien, evil, but James held it as if it were natural, almost essential to his existence.

"Why do you have that?" she asked.

"It killed my sister. It killed my family. Now it is mine." He took the rag and set it on the edge of the blade, then grabbed it on the bottom and pulled. The rag slid into two parts. He then took a tripled piece of the wire she had seen the night before and, while holding each end, slammed it down on the edge of the blade. It neatly cut the metal. "Hardest part of the beast," he said idly. "As hard as any metal we can find, it takes a diamond saw two hours to put a divot in it." Jessica shuddered.

Rubbing her eyes, she asked, "How long was I asleep?"

"Over fifteen hours."

"Have you slept?" she asked.

"No."

"Why not?"

James looked at her and then continued rubbing the weapon with the cloth.

"I lost my family too," Jessica consoled. Again, James barely looked at her. "You want revenge? So do I," she assured him.

10/10/2444

Location: Galion Colony and Forward Military Base

James and Jessica walked up to the massive shuttle marked MCO (military contracting organization), which was a rather unimaginative name for the colorful mercenary business. The military would not accept anyone under eighteen for combat roles; the war wasn't that bad yet. So the pair had signed onto a mercenary company. Jessica had been trained as a control coordinator, and James had gone straight for a line-of-fire position. He got double pay for direct hazard conditions, but that didn't matter to him. Only killing Harvesters mattered.

"Looks cramped," Jessica said hesitantly.

"Needs to fit lots of troops," James responded. They walked up the ramp and onto the ship. The manifest said that they would be patrolling for Harvester supply ships. *Good,* James thought. *We will be boarding them for tech; that means close combat.*

10/23/2444

Location: Harvester Forward Supply Lines

The flight of mercenary ships descended on the disabled Harvester feed ship. Its defensive cannons had been both blasted to dust by the humans' newly adapted plasma shell technology and ripped from their positions by gravity grapplers. James shivered with anticipation. Behind the thick blast-proof doors of the cockpit, Jessica sat at her station, poring over the statistics displayed on her screen. She had everything from the squad's helmet cameras to biostats on her console. She had so much information that she knew if one of them needed to pee.

"Number twenty-two! Rogers, I told you to tighten that breastplate. One hit and it will be ripped off!" she said in a matronly, matter-of-fact tone of voice.

"Yes, M-o-m," the mercenary responded.

Even though the soldiers wore similar armor, each held weapons of their choice. Most carried new plasma projectile-based weaponry, others stubbornly held to traditional bullets. *The fools*, thought James. He had a new plasma-based shotgun. It had twelve shots, all of which contained three ounces of the destructive substance, and would punch through two feet of armor. On his back he carried the barbed blade, what he considered to be the legacy of his family; today he would soak it in harvester blood again.

Every member of the unit was as young as James. The mercenary organization had nicknamed them the Children of Hell. Every member had reasons to hate the Harvesters with an unreal passion. Most carried a rage that can only come from the death of a loved one, and every last one of them was quivering at a chance for revenge. The organization had hesitated to put such a reckless unit into action, but the military had begun enlisting sixteen-year-olds, and the war needed soldiers. They had finally assigned the Children of Hell a combat mission.

Jessica's voice cracked into the ears of the unit. "Prepare for impact!" The craft jerked as it made contact with the alien ship. "Breach in five, four, three, two, one, breach!" The door to the bay swung outward. The smell of scorched metal filled the air as edges of the hall just outside the ship glowed red. The first boy out the door was thrown back, a gaping hole burning in his chest.

A Harvester stood outside the opening, holding a plasma cannon to its arms with its sheathed tentacles. The beast was immediately cut down by a salvo from the entire group. Covered by the rest of his squad, James propelled himself through the door. To his left he saw another Harvester pinned to the wall by a searing chunk of metal on its clawed arm. James walked up to it and uttered one word:

"Vengeance." In a powerful stroke, he opened the beast vertically with the barb. It had been so easy; the barb's strength and sharpness ignored the armor and thick skin that had proven so invincible just a year before. The creature was still alive, but it couldn't live long. It let out an unending, piercing scream, as James stared at its face in brutal satisfaction. Jessica shrieked in twisted glee as she watched the scene unfold on her screen and through James's eyes.

Three more Harvesters—a bull and two smaller females—charged into the room. They began the chopped screeches of angry Harvesters, and bellowing, they charged.

"James! What is happening? Your readouts are off the chart!"

James did not answer. His muscles almost burst with blood, and his eyes dilated beyond normal limits. Taking in everything around him, his nostrils flared, and he drank in every scent. James gripped his weapons with savagery and violence as his only thought, and attacked.

An hour later, James stood on the command deck of the Harvester ship, his body spent. He sat against a console. The remainder of the Children of Hell stood in the room, all two of them. James was covered in blood and wounds, and he was laughing. The other two were more terrified of him than any remaining Harvesters. The three were quickly joined by other squads completing their sweeps of the ship. It was over. Another victory for the forces of mankind, but James could not celebrate. He slipped into an exhausted unconsciousness.

9/29/2453

Location: Unknown

Status: Bored to Hell and Back

James sat staring at the wall in his small bunk aboard the Santa Monica. He thought of himself as the best cybernetics engineer in all of humanity. Unfortunately, after Earth fell, there was a good chance he was correct. He didn't know how many cybernetically altered humans were left: the only two he knew of were himself and Jessica. Born and festered by long years of discrimination and hatred, cybernetics, while used in lifesaving operations, was seen as disgusting and vile. James still felt a small amount of bitterness toward normal humans. After early mistakes and failures in the field that resulted in neuroticism and eventually homicidal insanity, humanity had branded cyborgs dangerously unstable.

A long string of hypocritical stigmas arose from popular hysteria over the accidents caused by a few inept scientists. James, Jessica, and anyone else unlucky enough to have a visible cybernetic component were labeled a cyverses. It was a not-so-subtle statement that "what is cybernetic is perverse." James didn't mind the label, but he hated the treatment he received from almost everyone he met. The men he survived with in the mercenary force, however, had seen the power his arm and leg had given him and had wisely refrained from mocking him. Instead, they feared him; not much better, but better nonetheless. But that wasn't a problem anymore. With Earth gone and the once great power of mankind utterly crushed, the only thing that mattered now was that he was human.

He did know one thing, though: he was bored. James had been waiting for a response from the fleet military; they were training recruits to keep people out of trouble. He had already fine-tuned every circuit on both his and Jessica's systems, and then had done it again just to eat up time. A light along a panel in his forearm began to blink. He mentally activated a series of commands, and an electronic crystal display snaked along the side of his face to his eye from the back of his shoulder. It was another transfer request from one of the "less spacious" ships in the fleet. Sighing, he disregarded it and wondered how any place could be more cramped than his own bunk.

Disabling his display and sitting back against the head of his bunk, James began to idly play with a few of the more "interesting" augmentations he had made to his arm. He slowly drifted into another haze of monotony and ejected a razor-sharp stiletto knife from the side of his forearm, caught it with the same hand, and slipped it back into place. The slow *ping-tick-click* echoed down the metallic halls of the ramshackle dormitory even though it was full of more humans than James thought could share a single ship, let alone a single room. As he continued his old practice-come-nervous tick, James became lost in thought, staring blankly at the equally blank wall.

He didn't know how long he had been sitting there, but he was roused from his thoughts when the sounds of his knife were joined by a fast approaching series of heavy footfalls. The view out of his cubby was blocked by a massive set of uniformed legs. "James A. Ursidae?"

James quickly scrambled out of his bunk and stood face-to-face with a middle-aged man in full military uniform. He was covered in muscle and scars and, from the look on his face, seriously bored with his assignment.

"Yeah?" James asked.

"Your offer to join the Interplanetary Marine Force has been accepted. As of this moment you are officially a member of the last remaining armed forces of humanity. Please follow me." The officer spun on his heels and barged down the narrow hallway without giving James a second glance. James quickly caught up with the soldier. He made several attempts to get the officer to tell him anything about his new job or even get the older man's name, but the man said nothing. The pair continued in silence for several more dormitories.

Over the course of several hours, James and the officer walked through the ship, picking up recruits. All the while, the recruitment officer said nothing more to any of the cadets than he had said to James. The recruits, however, talked incessantly.

Geez, these guys won't shut up! That's the thirteenth theory so far about what they are going to have us do. If this keeps up I am going to go insane. No wonder Mr. Scars never talks, James thought. They finally arrived at a massive set of reinforced doors, which opened to reveal an even more massive training ground. Having been stuck in spaces no wider than four by six feet, the area almost drove the group of youths wild with anticipation.

Silencing the recruits with a glare that could melt metal, the scarred officer took the group to a long structure on the far end of the grounds and left them with two gnarled-looking administrators. Clearly relieved that he no longer had to lead around a group of kids, the old officer quickly left the building, muttering something about losing a bet.

10/25/2453

Location: *Santa Monica*

"Come in, Cormac, I hear you've got some unorthodox ideas for your division."

"Yes, sir. I'd like permission to train my boys with the battle sword. I've been using it since basic, and I think it can be much more than a secondary and elective weapon. I used it almost as much as my rifle during the Harvester War. Killed fourteen of those murderers with it. It is my official opinion that a squad of men using a battle sword as their primary weapon would directly equate to battlefield superiority. They are perfectly suited for close-combat fighting, inside buildings, ships, and deep bush. This is, of course, in combination with normal tactical and combat instruction."

The officer stroked his short beard, which was barely more than long stubble. "Very well, Captain. I remember a few times mine came in handy. I was hoping you would do something extra with these kids; they showed an…unusual promise. They're virtually all mercenary veterans. That's kind of why I gave them to you instead of to the officer I had them slated for. That, and he went stir crazy and jumped out of an airlock. Good luck with the training, Captain Kincade. Dismissed." The officer turned back to his digital paperwork but stopped Cormac before he could leave. "Oh, and, Captain Kincade, don't get these boys killed."

Cormac smirked and snapped a salute. "Yes, sir."

That went way better than it should have, Kincade thought. *The military has been against the battle sword ever since it was developed. Maybe this is a perk to losing the top layer of brass.*

The next day Cormac activated his sword and stood in front of his division of three hundred men. A low hum accompanied by the smell of ionization filled the air. "This is a weapon of war. It died out from viable use in the early nineteenth century, nearly five hundred years ago. It was reborn twenty years ago in the form of the battle sword when it was discovered that certain plasmas could be held to the exterior of a unique blend of metals. The film is so thin that it almost cannot be seen. When deactivated it will dissipate within a second. However, do not activate the sword until I tell you to. Remember, when it's on, the sword will sear flesh and armor alike. It is the most dangerous combat weapon and, as such, the most volatile. Until now a soldier has had to petition his superiors and present several permits and expert certification before he would be allowed to carry a sword in addition to normal weaponry. Can anyone tell me why?" Cormac sheathed the sword and paced with his hands behind his back, looking like a combination sergeant-professor.

"No?" he continued. "It's because inept baboons kept killing themselves and each other with it. That means you people! Our goal for the next two weeks is simple—to get you all to a point where you don't kill yourself simply by holding it. Any questions?"

James stepped forward. "When do we get the swords?"

Cormac pulled him out of line and gave him a push toward the nearest exit. "Report to the infirmary, recruit!"

James did nothing but stand there with a startled expression on his face. "Uh…I'm not sick."

"No? There must be something wrong with you. Let me rephrase this in a way that you can understand. This…thing…can…kill…you!"

James remained standing, more confident. A twisted and slightly malevolent smile spread across his face. "I know," James responded, as he stepped back in line.

"Now if there aren't any other questions, everyone grab a stick, and we'll start with some basic handling." Cormac took a bokan out of a bin and tossed it to James. Although James was obstinate, Cormac was beginning to like the recruit. He wanted to make sure James lived long enough to put his energy to good use.

After a week and a half of intense training, the recruits were proficient enough to engage in heavy sparring and simulations. *Okay*, Cormac thought, *time to introduce the shield.* "Attention, trainees. I am going to shoot one of you," he declared. "What should you do?" James raised his hand. *This kid doesn't learn, but at least he has guts.*

"Kill you first!" James grinned his wolfish grin.

"Okay, James. How far away am I from you?"

James glanced at the dirt between him and Cormac. "Uh, twenty feet."

"Right. Now how fast can you attack?"

James's eyes brightened with understanding. "Uh, not fast enough."

Cormac flipped the kid the practice rifle and activated a battle shield, its blue energy pulsating between the interconnected framework.

"This is different from your normal battle shield; it's rounded and designed to withstand physical impact as well as energy. As you can see, the rigid nature of the frame, although allowing the shield itself to be used aggressively, prohibits more than one shape. While the rifleman will need to use theirs for cover, and in some cases entrenchment, you will use shields in a more tactical and direct manner. Observe." He leveled a thick, gloved finger at James. "James, try to shoot me," the man ordered.

James waited a beat, hesitating with the idea of shooting a superior officer, but decided it was a good idea when Cormac charged. The youth poured volley after volley at the large man, all of which the shield easily absorbed. Before anyone had time to think, Cormac had closed the distance and given James a good rap on the head with the practice sword.

"Remember," Cormac thundered, "the destructive potential of your sword will never compensate for the accuracy and distance of a rifle. Allow the ranks to lay down cover, advance quickly, dispatch your opponent even more quickly, and for goodness sake, don't let yourself get shot."

"Sir?" James probed, as he peeked around the corner into Kincaid's office.

"Let me guess," Cormac said, putting his data pad down and leaning back in his chair. "You got shot again, didn't you?"

Sucking in a guilty stream of air, James entered the room and sat down in the chair across from his commanding officer. "It was only a graze," he said, rotating his shoulder in an attempt to regain flexibility in the freshly healed tissue.

"So what's on your mind?" Cormac asked, passing James a cup of coffee from a dispenser built into the desk.

"It's about this training, sir."

"What? Not to your liking?" Cormac cocked an eyebrow. "If it weren't for your own sim-deaths, you'd have the highest kill ratio in the division."

"Ah, nah," James said, waving a hand dismissively. "I just feel like there's something missing, you know?"

"No," Cormac responded, "I don't, but I'm willing to listen."

James let out a pent-up breath and pulled a long piece of metal from a bag he had brought with him. "Reinforced strut bar," he said, tossing the object to Cormac as if it were a light baton. Cormac caught the bar, but the object didn't slow and his eyes went wide. It smacked his stomach, expelling a puff of air from him.

"What the…" Cormac wheezed, shoving the dense hunk of metal onto the table where it sank with absolute finality. "Okay," he said, taking a raspy breath to fill his lungs. "You've got a heavy piece of metal. Where's the point?"

"This," James said, picking up the bar with his cybernetic arm. The limb appeared identical to his natural arm, but the ease with which he picked up the metal betrayed its artificial nature. "This is the point." With grace from years of practice, James spun the bar around his hand, flipping it around and catching it from a toss into the air in an exercise he used to hone his precision in knife fighting.

"Vary impressive," Cormac said, having fully caught his breath. "But other than seeing your commanding officer with the wind knocked out of him, what are you getting at?"

James's face broke into a wide grin. He reached into his bag again and came up with a large segmented metal gauntlet covering his hand and a portion of his arm. Holding out the metal bar in his cybernetic arm, he gripped it in the now armored hand as well and neatly bent the bar in half.

"I'm impressed. But wouldn't that be a bit heavy for use in combat?"

"I'll get to that. First thing's first," James said, talking fast in his excitement at having impressed his mentor. "Here," he said, tossing Cormac a small plasma castor. "Shoot me in the hand."

"What? No!" the officer protested. "James, these aren't practice rounds." Kincade checked the cartridge to make sure. "It'll take a lot more than a trip to the infirmary to fix you up after a hit from one of these. Do you know what they called the convergence of metal, skin, and plasma?" James shook his head, forcing himself to remain serious and not interrupt the officer. "Sunny side up."

"But this isn't simple metal or basic armor. I've integrated multi-carbide interlocking polymers and posatronic neuro-synchronous reactant mesh into the base alloy while sheathing the entire thing in my own blend of wreath casing, the same stuff they use to make cannon-blast doors."

"I'm still not shooting you," Cormac said with a harrumph.

Exasperated, James sighed and tossed the bent metal bar onto the table, where it stuck with the finality of excessive weight. "I promise I won't be harmed."

Cormac mulled the decision for a minute before picking up the weapon and checking the magazine again. Sighing, he leveled and fired at James's outstretched hand.

Light exploded from James's arm, a concussion caused Cormac's ears to pop from the pressure wave, and the room went dark.

"Ha ha ha! Wasn't that great?" James shouted a second before the room's emergency lights came on to compensate for the destroyed light fixture above his head. An ugly scarring radiated out in a circle above James where the round had detonated.

"It bounced off!" Cormac shouted. In less than a second he was beside James, examining the gouge mark on the armor. "It freaking bounced off." The soldier was almost laughing.

"Well, not really," James hedged. "In reality the plasma and metal in the round were individually refracted in a repulse alloy beneath the protective casing. When that effect is combined with the hardened exterior alloy, it does give that impression though," he said with satisfaction. "The sub-dermal aspects were Jessica's idea. I…uh, had thought the armor would be enough and well." James rubbed the shoulder that had been hurting earlier. "Let's just say she was right."

"This is amazing, James. I can think of all sorts of uses for this material. Tanks, strike riders, even fighters could all use this. It's lighter and tougher than anything I've seen."

"Yeah, I, uh, hadn't thought of that," James said honestly.

Cormac cocked an eyebrow. He stepped back to view the hand, now dangling at James's side from the prolonged weight on his arm rather than the weapon blast. "Well, then what were you thinking?" he asked. "You couldn't seriously have been considering using that glove on the battlefield. You'd be useless after a few minutes from exhaustion. It must weigh sixty pounds!"

"Eighty, actually," James said.

"There you go." Cormac nodded as James slid the gauntlet off and put it back in the bag. "What did you really want to do with it? It's not really useful on its own."

28

"Exactly!" James shouted. He pulled a blueprint out and spread it on the table next to the metal bar. "It's just an example. Imagine encasing an entire soldier in such a material, cybernetically connected to its bearer and mechanically assisted. Such a soldier would be..." James trailed off as he became lost in months of thought with Jessica.

"Something new all together," Cormac finished for him. "James, my boy," he said, gripping the young man on the shoulder. "We have much to discuss."

5 >> Location

1/4/2454

Location: Unknown

System Status: Active Gravity Stream Travel

Lieutenant Johansson finished confirming his scans and was overjoyed with the result. "Sir, the scans read out. It looks like there is an M-class world, a habitable moon, and a habitable planetoid in the system! The central planet's gravity is only slightly higher than Earth norm, the moon in its orbit is rather chilly, and the one orbiting the third Gas Giant is rather hot, but it looks like they can all sustain human life."

For the first time in an eternity, relief flooded Admiral Hancock. "Good. Instruct all fleet commanders to implement a course deviation to intersect the system. What is our current ETA?"

The officer tapped a few panels before responding. "Four hours at our current speed." Hancock sat back in his chair and made a few notes on his console.

"We'll give a fleet-wide broadcast one hour before we enter the system. Before that I want a briefing with all ship captains, troop XOs, and the top five civilian representatives. We don't want anyone to get their hopes up. And, Lieutenant, let's not have this turn into a repeat of the X166D incident, shall we?"

"Yes, sir. I will inform all the military police to go to top alert. We won't allow any riots this time."

Hancock watched the three worlds in the ship's holo-display. "Pray that this system is not inhabited by the…what did they call themselves again?"

"I still can't pronounce it, sir."

The admiral leaned back in his chair and began to rub his temples next to a slightly receding hairline. "I don't think anyone can wait any longer. This exodus needs to end."

"Sir, it seems that there is a complex network of gravity wells in the system. We won't be able to enter orbit. The closest we can get without detailed readings is the third Gas Giant. They seem to be caused by the size and composition of the interior planets in respect to the star."

Hancock grunted. "Very well. It will give us more time to get the lay of the land and get out of town if this turns out to be another dead end."

Just then, a tall public relations officer came up flanked by two MPs. They saluted sharply, and the officer proceeded to give the admiral a detailed description of the preparations they had set for the fleet-wide broadcast. "It seems that one of the captains just couldn't keep his mouth shut. Word is spreading incredibly fast; everyone knows why we changed course and are decelerating."

"I see. Activate all security teams, lock down the fleet, and release the official information. We will not have any more riots, understood?"

"Sir, General Vienstine's teams aren't ready. I can't keep everyone cool without a military presence."

The admiral silently swore. "I was afraid of this. Every time we get close to anything with dirt and air, everyone loses their cool. This had damned well better be the last stop on this magic-carpet ride, or we are all going to go to hell in one big damned hand basket." Hancock punched some commands in his consul, giving the man more units to help in the effort. "Then get ready, Corporal! You've had two hours; that should be enough. Dismissed."

As the MP officer marched back to his station, angry and overwhelmed, Lieutenant Johansson came up for air from the sea of data and analysis streaming across his console. All the information from the fleet's sensors was being compiled and processed into meaningful data for the ship's holographic display showing strategic planetary placement and colonization prospects for system X145P.

"Sir, data confirms our previous estimates, but we have reason to believe that the planet is lightly inhabited, industrial, or early modern by our estimates. Also, planetary and orbital activity give us reason to believe that a major conflict is taking, or has recently taken, place. More intriguing, sir, is the disparity between energy signatures, especially in orbit. Our Xenotech experts believe that there are two entirely distinct races involved in this conflict, one native to the system, the other, invaders. Additionally, there is a large concentration of energy signatures from the second race in orbit: over three-hundred thousand distinct signatures from this range."

The admiral watched, confirming the information streaming across the holographic display in front of him. The central display was an elevated sphere in the center of the bridge with a series of command and control chairs orientated around it. Hancock stared at the data for several minutes before answering.

"Give me an activity report: aggression, combat, projected firepower of the involved parties." The officer tapped some commands into his computer, waiting for the machine's responses before he continued. "There also seems to be construction commencing around the planet. We have nothing to gauge their firepower or aggression on at this time. We aren't close enough, and there doesn't seem to be any major engagement occurring at the moment. The only activity is coming from a small pursuit occurring around the planetoid orbiting the Gas Giant.

"Three similar but more advanced signatures are closing in on a small craft, which is using primitive plasma-based propulsion. Its trajectory will take it to the habitable moon orbiting the Gas Giant just shy of gravity stream range. Based on the current velocities of both the pursuers and the pursued, the fleeing vessel will be overtaken before they can enter the planet's atmosphere. Given the disparity between the two technology levels, I seriously doubt that the smaller craft has any chance of survival."

The bridge waited in silence as the wheels spun in Hancock's head and a plan began to form. "Inform the PR corps that their job just got a lot harder. We can't approach potential landing sites at this time. Navigations, bring the fleet to the edge of the system and enter a holding pattern. Cease all open-band transmissions immediately and bring the fleet to a defensive alert. Commander Dawson, which destroyer is that surviving ambassador on?"

The personnel officer inserted the diplomat's name in his computer. "The Pila, sir."

"Dispatch her with three squads of Peregrine fighters and have them GS directly to that chase. Have them find out what is going on, but do not engage in combat unless otherwise provoked. We don't know what is going on, and we don't want to take any sides." Hancock paused. A slight smile formed on his face for the first time in months. "Yet."

The admiral's mind raced with possibilities and many uncertainties. *This makes things more complicated,* he thought. *But Lord willing, we just may be able to trade some firepower for a chunk of rock to call home.* "Also send the cruiser Legatus and two destroyers in silent mode to investigate the planet, and be sure to stay undetected."

"The Pila is away, sir," an officer stated.

"Good. Tell them to double-time it. We don't want that chase to end before we can find anything out. It's a small window of opportunity. And the fighters?"

"Docked and ready." Johansson paused for a second before continuing. "GS activation successful and message received. Revised ETA for the Pila strike group five minutes."

When the Pila deactivated its GS drive, the light trapped by the synthetic gravity-well was released, and a brilliant flash occurred. Their entry, however, was hidden from their targets by the solid mass of the planetoid's moon. Immediately after the squadron found themselves at sub-light-speed, the fifteen fighters retracted from their grapples on the exterior of the Pila and fired up their engines. They accelerated effortlessly into the emptiness of space. Sheathed in the glare of reflected light from the planet's ice rings, they began to sweep and scan the course of the pursuit they were investigating. It didn't take long. The primitive craft was screaming distress signals on every conceivable wavelength.

"Sir, are you getting that?" a rookie recruit shouted too loudly into his comm.

"Yeah, Joe. They seem scared, don't they?" Although the language was alien, the sensors caught a familiarity in the tone of their voices.

"Wish I could understand them." The first group of fighters adjusted their vectors to pass in front of the chase, while the others twisted back so they would cut around the engagement.

"Just be patient. It'll be a few minutes before the eggheads on the destroyer can get the computers to crack it." As the sensors calculated the distance, the clicks spun down, approaching zero on his display. Abram's comm crackled with information from the supporting destroyer.

"Commander Abram, this is the Pila. Hold position and see if you can get anything on the pursuers." Abram was already recording everything his sensors would give him.

"Copy, Pila. Abram, out." Abram didn't know if their transmissions could be caught by either of the approaching aliens. "Joe, take your wing back a click, and sit in our shadow. We can't be too cautious."

"Yes, sir...holy s—" Before the young pilot had a chance to finish his sentence, luminescent energy lashed out from three ships that were more than five times larger than the human fighters, bisecting his stationary craft. The fighter exploded as it decompressed into the blackness of space.

"Abram to all craft, engage! Engage! Unidentified craft are hostile! Pila, are you getting this?"

As engines roared to life, the Pila responded, "Yes, we will arrive in forty seconds. Weapons hot!" As the fighters broke away from each other in a talon-strike formation, Abram could see the primitive retreating ship begin to list at an awkward angle. They had been hit as well. "All craft, this is Abram. Primitive ship still classified as neutral, engage pursuers only."

A heartbeat of silence gripped the squadron as they threw their craft into attack mode; then it got ugly. The three unknown craft approached well above normal combat speed. "F3, veer off. They are coming too fast!" His warning was too late. The oblong ship tore through the fighter in a shocking ram maneuver.

"Damn, they're rammers, all craft-evasive action!" As he issued the command, the flight of fighters blossomed outward in a sweeping arch using their inertia to swivel their crafts. They layered the flight path of the ram ship with glowing plasma shells. It would have taken only a fraction of the unleashed firepower to destroy the offending craft.

The alien attacker ruptured under the first volley and vaporized under the second. "Don't forget about his friends, people!" The other two craft closed on the remaining thirteen fighters as the Pila arrived. Its heavy cannons, flak, and Gatling turrets filled the assault vessels with deadly firepower. The destruction of the two ships was almost completely hidden by the shear mass of weaponry leveled against them.

The backwash from the combat exchange rocked the craft that the aliens were pursuing, and its engines went silent as they overloaded. It sat dead in space. *Better for them*, Abram thought, *than simply dead.*

"Commander Abram, this is the Pila. Grapple that runaway ship and get it under control. Let's see what these people have to say for themselves."

"Understood, Pila." Commander Abram had a bad taste in his mouth. "This had better be worth it. I lost two good men today."

1/4/2454 Location: Unknown

System Status: High Orbit—Unknown World

The cruiser Legatus and its two destroyer escorts had begun its deep scan of the second planet. The results confirmed most of the fleets' previous estimates. The planet had undergone massive warfare very recently, but the technological disparity between the two races had been far greater than previously assumed. "Captain, I am reading a squad of five ships heading this way. They have not postured for attack and are running continuous active scans; I believe they are a routine patrol, Ma'am."

A'ssia nodded. Her medium-length black hair was tied tightly in a braid behind her head. She clasped her hands tightly behind her back as she weighed the unfolding information. "Understood. Go dark and keep that moon between us. If they haven't noticed our arrival, their sensors shouldn't pick us up through that rock."

The situation reminded Captain A'ssia Harrington all too much of fighting in the Harvester War. Back then, however, she had been the one with inferior technology. *Those ships are moving too fast, damn it! The men have been getting lazy, too little activity these last months. I was afraid of this.* "Double time it, Ensign. At this rate they're going to see us."

"Yes, ma'am...ma'am! The Alecto has stopped! She has ceased running dark and is powering all offensive and defensive weaponry."

A'ssia stopped pacing and pointed at the communications officer. "Open channel!"

"Channel open," the officer confirmed.

"Captain Johnson! What do you think you are doing? You're in violation of direct orders!"

"Sorry, sir!" the captain of the smaller craft apologized. "They've seen us. Figured there's no point in hidin'. Stay hidden and we'll take care of 'em. I don't see why they need to know there's more of us."

A'ssia activated a display that showed a revised analysis of the aliens' sensor capacities and quickly examined it. "Affirmative. We will send you fighter support. Ensign, continue running dark, but bring us and the Clotho to battle stations, and launch all fighters. Helm, take us to the minimum safe distance and keep us hidden."

With preparations underway, A'ssia turned back to the communication link with the Alecto. "Johnson, see if you can get them to talk. No need for hostilities here."

"No offense, Captain, but it don't seem like talking's what they've got in mind for us." As he finished his sentence, the alien ships opened fire. Their energy streams made contact with the Alecto's shields in a brilliant array of red and blue.

"Captain Johnson!"

"Yes, comm?"

"We are receiving a transmission from the enemy ship. It's garbled by shield interference but still readable."

"Respond in kind. Send a generalized peace broadcast. Maybe their translation computers are better than ours." As the Alecto began broadcasting, the alien warships opened their batteries with a second volley. "Sir, their attack has not slowed, and they appear to be sending a signal planet side." Captain Johnson glanced at the information flowing across his display. "Record and send for analysis as well."

The alien vessels continued their attack with invigorated force as they quickly approached the human warship. "Sir, shields are weakening both forward and starboard. No signs of a cease-fire by the enemy," the officer shouted, as the sounds of impacts echoed through the ship.

"Very well, open fire!" the captain commanded. As the swarm of lightweight gunboats closed on the Alecto, the human destroyer's large plasma cannons burst to life, forcing the enemy craft into the path of its more accurate flank and high yield Gatling turrets. When two craft fell victim to the deadly crossfire, the aliens turned blistering away from the destroyers, each at an oblique angle to the craft. Twisting from their speeding arches, they converged on the ship's aft in an attempt to attack the Alecto's more exposed engines, safely away from its large side cannons.

"They learn fast. Efficient little cretins." The ship shuddered with a wrenching motion as it temporarily lost internal gravity systems. "Sir, engines hit," the officer reported. "Thrusters one through three are going critical."

The captain activated several fail-safes on his console while shouting orders. "Cut power to the primary engines. Let's see how well those auxiliary thrusters work." Before the officer could execute the captain's order, the ship rocked again. This time the internal gravity died completely.

"Sir, GS drive's been hit. Communications array hit. Gatling and flak group on the aft section are destroyed!"

Flicking his attention to the holographic display, the captain shouted a string of orders. "Helm, initiate battle roll. Weapons, begin spiral burst. Ops, send out a distress beacon. Where are those fighters?"

"Ninety seconds out, sir."

Too much time. This is getting ugly, really fast, he thought.

The gunships continued to pound the destroyer and skillfully avoided the line of fire from its large cannons. Even so, they couldn't avoid the flak and Gatling turrets as they lashed back at the attacking ships with deadly precision. But there were simply too many of them. For every ship the Alecto removed from space, another filled the gap. More came by the minute.

"Sir, the attackers have reinforcements. Streams of gunships coming from the planet. If we don't do something soon, this is going to turn into a conflict that we can't win!"

"Cease spiral! Use maneuvering thrusters to angle cannons toward the planet, and fire a close-proximity burst. Direct our momentum away from the source of those ships. Weapons, initiate a sweep of our flight path using all remaining Gatling and flak ports."

As the ship was torn from its rotation, several crafts tried to enter her wake in an effort to take out its cannons and open up her side. The cannons that had been firing in rotation now fell silent as the maneuver was executed. In a concussion of fire, the Alecto fired all her side cannons in a single concentrated burst, but there was no escape from the wall of burning plasma as the shells tore through everything in their path. Three large ships where obliterated by the blast, which created a screen of debris between the Alecto and her adversaries. The force of the explosion propelled the ship into a sideways glide away from the battle. The growing distance allowed her to lay a path of shells in her wake, forcing the attackers to regroup before they could press the assault.

The aliens didn't take long to reform. The swarm was continuously growing, pressing hard on the Alecto's path, keeping their ships spread out along the outer edges of her flight path to avoid her cannons. "Rout all shield projectors to port. Keep them between us and that swarm!"

It was just in time. The swarm regained firing range and began blanketing the side of the Alecto in their luminescent barrage. The ship's shields began to wear thin, and streams of energy intermittently broke through the barrier and carved ugly swaths of destruction on her outer hull. One of the cannons took a direct hit and buckled under the heat and strain. As the pursuers prepared another wave of attack, the space around the Alecto streaked with a network of the glowing plasma. The fighter detachment from the Legatus arrived, blasting streams of vengeful fire into the alien craft. Even though the twenty small fighter craft were severely outnumbered, they had superior maneuverability and firepower to their advantage. The aliens who had outmaneuvered the Alecto found themselves outmaneuvered by the magnificent agility of the Peregrine squadrons.

The alien forces, however, disregarded their losses. As more and more craft entered the battle, their advantage grew. Again the balance of power shifted to the attacking aliens. A ship twice as large as the Alecto entered the battle, rising from the planet like a corrupt creature of the abyss. "Captain Johnson to Peregrine wing. Fall back and create a screen beside the Alecto. It's suicide out there!" As the fighters peeled off from their entanglement, the enemy fire grazed several of them; one spun out of control, rupturing as they raced back to the destroyer.

"Status report!" Johnson called.

"Half the small turrets are down, cannons three and five are down, shields fore and aft burned out, and communications are short-range only. GS out."

The captain slammed the chair's arm in frustration. "Roll the ship to give them the starboard side. Use enhanced yield shells. Fire!"

Again the Alecto rolled, and her cannons blazed into the depths of the enemy fleet. Several of the gunships exploded, and the larger craft took the remaining seven shells. The large juggernaut's shields burst into brilliant colors as they buckled under the strain. But it wasn't enough: the juggernaut and its swarms of gunships continued its charge toward the Alecto.

The sounds of destruction and chaos reigned aboard the Alecto's bridge. Squealing, the communications system sparked to life. "Alecto, this is the Legatus. Fall back and concentrate on long-range cover for the Clotho." The huge cruiser cast a long shadow on the Alecto as it passed over her, settling itself between the damaged ship and the hostile fleet.

The Legatus's single antimatter cannon leveled blast after blast at the enemies' capital ship while its cannons and guns proceeded to swat the smaller craft from its path. As the Legatus bore down on the greatest concentration of the enemy fleet, the Clotho spiraled in the wake of the Alecto. It blasted anything moving toward the limping ship with concentrated bursts of its guns. The shimmer of alien craft that had been so overwhelming before broke like a pane of glass under the hammering guns of the Legatus. It blew ship after ship out of the sky. With the sounding of its huge forward cannon, the large alien craft cracked and shattered, sending fiery shrapnel throughout the surrounding space and into the swarms of smaller craft, clawing them from the sky.

Aboard the Legatus, Captain A'ssia followed the conflict with the cold calculation of a seasoned commander.

"They have broken, Captain, and are in full retreat!" an ops officer shouted.

A'ssia confirmed the report with another glance at the central holo. "Good," she affirmed. "Pull back and get the Alecto under tow, and send a courier ahead to inform the fleet of the encounter. Set a course for the nearest point where we can activate GS." The large cruiser pulled itself back from the engagement, its shields hardly scalded, and positioned itself alongside the Alecto to grapple it with a web of magnetic wires. "All craft, this is Captain Harrington. Return to formation and move out."

7 >> Expectations

1/4/2454 Location: Unknown

System Status: Fleet Preparing for System Entry

The Pila flashed into existence alongside the Cerberus; the remaining thirteen fighters dislodged from their grapple points and returned to the adjacent carrier. "Pila, this is the Cerberus. You are ordered to transfer the diplomat Davison along with all data pertaining to the alien communications. It looks like you brought some friends. Care to explain?"Admiral Hancock tapped the arm of his chair in a nervous tick as he listened.

The Pila responded, "Affirmative, is Admiral Hancock there? He'll to want to hear this. The ship was transporting an exiled prince from the central planet deeper in the system. He and his entourage have requested asylum, or their version of it. Those ships were sent to eliminate him as a political factor." The communications officer recorded the information and glanced at the admiral before continuing.

"Thank you, Pila. Please extend our offer to come aboard. They can enter the Cerberus's main bay. We will transmit the docking protocols."

It took several hours for the docking crew to guide the shuttle into the massive craft. The gap in languages and lack of comparable technological concepts made the relatively simple task unusually difficult. But not nearly as difficult as it had been to discover even the basic rudiments of Harvester communication in what seemed like an eternity ago. "Dang, she looks more like a huge metal bowl with an engine on it than a spacecraft, don't she?" a deckhand commented.

"Sure does. Don't look now, but here come the bigwigs. Time to make ourselves scarce." The two techs quickly moved down the hull toward the flight crew living quarters.

Hancock made a clicking noise and got the attention of everyone in the bay. "Okay, men, we don't want to scare them. They didn't have visual communications in their ship, so we do not know what they look like, and they don't know what we look like. Refrain from any sort of reaction; their culture will be vastly different. Do not react to anything unless I say so. Is that clear?"

A chorus of, "Yes, sir!" filled the bay.

A small man with glasses and a look too serious for his own face turned to the admiral and asked, "Are you sure all this is necessary? You brought an awful lot of soldiers for a first contact of this nature."

"Davison, you are aware that the first race encountered by humanity considered us a culinary delicacy, the second was happy to eradicate us, and the third ran us out of a system with perfectly good uncolonized worlds just for the heck of it." Hancock paused and took a deep breath. "No, I don't think we can be too careful."

The diplomat stammered, "Um, of course, sir. Good point."

Hancock turned and continued preparations for first contact. "One last redundancy check on the translation computers. Ops, you sure they can breathe our atmosphere?"

"Yes, sir. I am reading an Earth-norm oxygen-nitrogen environment inside, same temperature as out here and all." The admiral seemed to relax. It was a false impression for the sake of those under his command, but it helped the men around him prepare for contact.

"Good," he nodded. "Signal them to open the hatch. Let's see what our guests are."

With a hiss of equalizing pressure, the hatch slowly pulled itself from the side of the craft. It was so expertly melded with the ship's hull that the grooves were almost invisible until it began to move. A diminutive figure, looking much like a human but with no hair and understated features, cautiously walked out of the craft.

"Astounding. Even the pigmentation of his skin is similar to the human epidermis!" a scientist commented beside the admiral as he furiously tapped buttons on a mobile analysis station.

The human diplomat, Davison, stepped forward slowly and calmly and efficiently stated, "Welcome aboard the human battleship Cerberus. I am the resident diplomat, and this is Admiral Hancock. We are prepared to offer temporary sanctuary in exchange for information about what is transpiring in this system."

The alien blinked and shrank back slightly, shock showing on his face as the computer began to repeat the diplomat's statements in the alien's own language. He then began to speak in a smooth, cantered language. "I am Vilnir, chief administrative aid to Crowned Prince Tinek. I am relieved to see that you are not hostile. How is it that you look like Illani?" As the computer translated his inquiry, he pushed a button on his shoulder, and a taller alien surrounded by four guards exited the craft.

"We do not know," Hancock replied. "You are the first species that we have encountered that shares even a bipedal nature with us." Vilnir made a gesture with his shoulder that Hancock assumed was similar to a nod.

The central individual then strode directly up to the admiral. "You are the leader?" he asked.

"Yes," Hancock responded in an even tone.

"I am Prince Tinek. I have been exiled from my planet by a vile invader that has massacred my people, destroyed our cities, exterminated my family, and killed my father, the regent. I request sanctuary."

A spark of understanding and a grand plan began to form from the fractured elements of hopes in Hancock's mind. "Then we have something in common. I grant you sanctuary, and we have much to discuss."

At this, the guards surrounding the prince and the admiral's soldiers relaxed. The prince's men, however, didn't look like they were in any shape to defend him from a fruit fly, let alone twenty elite soldiers. "Davison, show the prince and his men to the diplomatic quarters, and find out if we have anything they can eat. They look hungry."

"Yes, sir," the energetic young officer replied.

"Davison will take care of your accommodations. If there is anything you need from your craft, my men will retrieve it for you. We would greatly appreciate the opportunity to interview your men for information on the current situation in this system. After you have rested, please join us for dinner."

The prince seemed to understand, demonstrating, at least basically, a similarity of culture that surprised both himself and the admiral. The concept that species originating on entirely separate worlds would have not only similar appearances but comparable enough cultures to understand a formal diplomatic dinner was simply…not possible. Yet there it was, standing in the bay next to an artful, yet primitive vehicle.

"Thank you, Admiral Hancock. I look forward to it," Tinek responded. At that, the small group of tired aliens followed Davison down the hulls toward the ship's transportation hub.

Later that evening, Tinek sat discussing their predicament with Vilnir. "I still don't understand why you are so ready to trust them, Your Excellency," Vilnir said. "We do not know anything about them." The small man looked down with a sour expression before continuing. "Much less their motivations."

Tinek finished washing his face in the room's ornate sink. "I know, Vilnir, but we don't have much choice. If we had denied their ship's invitation, they could have done to us what they did to the Tarin'Tal hunters. Besides, what could we have done from that little hunk of rock with little more than a hydroponics bay? These people have power and warships! If we can get them to help us, we may be able to take back Lintalla."

Vilnir's face curled in a deep, sickened distrust. "Do you honestly believe these strangers will help us? And why would they not keep what they conquer? We have no army and nothing to match these mighty warships. Remember how the Tarin'Tal swept our forces aside? How do we know that these people could even triumph?"

Prince Tinek stood up, anger evident, as his skin flushed. "Because we have no alternative. Like you said, our armies are lost, my father is dead, and I am in exile, but we will not abandon our people and run! If these people will help us, I say we let them! Even if they take control afterward, at least our overlords will walk on two legs like us, unlike those horrible beasts. I doubt there could be a worse ruler for our people than the Tarin'Tal."

Vilnir's discontent faded slightly as the reality sank in. "Quite right, sir. I was only attempting to be a voice of caution."

Tinek put a hand on his assistant's shoulder. "I understand, Vilnir, but we need to work with what we have, and what we have right now is a strange fleet of ships larger than anything we have ever seen." Tinek opened his arms wide to illustrate the point. "That fleet has allowed us onboard, not taken us prisoner. They have given us clean rooms, food, rest, and even sanctuary. This is more than we could have ever hoped for."

Vilnir nodded. "True. Shall I have the men cooperate with their intelligence gatherers?"

"Yes. Based on their actions so far, I doubt they would torture us for information, and I don't want to risk offense. Their culture may consider withheld data aggressive. Have the men give these humans a complete history of the Tarin'Tal invasion and all our tactical information on their ships."

Vilnir made his way to the door. "Yes, Excellency."

Several hours later, Tinek and Vilnir entered the fleet admiral's meeting room, which doubled as a dining room on unique occasions. "I am surprised, Prince, that you did not bring your guards. Do you trust us this much already?" By now the computer had achieved a conversational rate of translation, putting its words almost on top of the admiral's statement.

"Not at all, good Admiral. I just decided that they needed rest, and Vilnir here could provide more protection than the four of them combined." The admiral himself had not brought any guards. The only other people in the room were the admiral's second-in-command, A'ssia (the commander of the fleet's secondary task force) and a civilian representative from the cobbled-together exiled government. After a hearty meal enjoyed by both races, the two leaders began to talk business.

Tinek described his civilization before the arrival of the Tarin'Tal as a middle modern society with the technological development found on Earth during the 2020s. His species called itself the Illani, and their planet Lintalla. Their civilization advanced more slowly than others and remained at various periods of development for much longer than mankind. Tinek described a methodical and artistic civilization that thrived on the perfection of each individual's endeavor; they took their time on what they did, sacrificing speed for the beauty of the act.

Recently, they had even begun to build research stations on the habitable moon and planetoid in the system. But before they could truly build a space-borne civilization, the Tarin'Tal had arrived. The Illani culture had been without war for the past two hundred and fifty years, and the two major powers on the planet seemed relatively content with their borders.

The other country was less content. Tinek's great-grandfather's superior armies and nuclear capabilities had kept them at bay. After fifty years this pacifism became norm on Lintalla, neither nation holding much of a military to oppose the Tarin'Tal invasion, which had gained full control of the planet in less than a week of conflict. The Illani weapons had been primitive metal-based projectiles that did little to the invaders; their only effectiveness was against the hostile aliens' ground troops, but with pinpoint air superiority, the resistance had been quickly crushed.

The invasion began shortly after a Tarin'Tal envoy had arrived and offered the Illani membership into their empire as a subjugated race. The Illani, of course, said no. When the refusal reached the Tarin'Tal, an invasion fleet, which had been waiting just outside of the system, moved in. The Illani civilization fell in one great battle. After listening to an in-depth depiction of the fall of Lintalla, Hancock described the events that led to the human exile, covering the Battle of Fallen Earth and their entry into the Illani's system.

"You name your battles? As if they were a living thing or a crafted object?" Tinek asked after Hancock had finished.

"Yes, we name them not only because they are to be remembered, but they irreparably change the lives of many people. It honors those who fought and died."

Tinek contemplated that for a short moment. "That does make sense. In this light, I name the fall of Lintalla the Illani Battle of Sorrows." He sat for a second, thinking. "Our struggle bears a similarity to the origin of the plight of your people."

The two talked for many hours, discussing everything from the remarkably similar cultures of the two people, to the military and political traditions of human and Illani civilizations.

When their conversation began to wind down, Tinek asked Vilnir to leave. At first the prince's aid adamantly refused, but at length, he agreed. The few other humans who had been in the room had been called away earlier to deal with some unrest about the fleet's inactivity. In this new silence, Tinek presented an idea that would change both races permanently.

"Admiral, your people need a home, my people need a savior. You have the power to drive the vile Tarin'Tal from our world—a world that both our beleaguered races would benefit from rebuilding. I, as the crown regent of Lintalla, hereby do swear that if the human exiles drive the vile ones from our home, then that home will truly be ours together. I offer free settlement on our planet and system, and I offer a sharing in government to you and your race. If you will save my people, our races can be a single people."

Admiral Hancock's face broadened into a massive smile. "I couldn't ask for a better offer. If I had the power, I would accept your proposal outright, but there are several major problems we must discuss. Our culture has a history of oppressive government, and they will not be willing to live under an alien ruler. If, somehow, we can create a government that would suit both our races, then yes, we will drive the invaders from your world, and it can become our new home."

Tinek's excitement rose as possibilities rushed through his mind. "Let's hear what you have in mind, Admiral."

Royal Guardsman Nin Serbel was very uneasy; he sat with Tinek's three remaining guards in a large white room filled with instruments of healing, or at least that is what he hoped they were. "Ral-Serbel, why are they treating us like this? All this medical treatment, and they haven't even asked us any questions. I had expected they would interrogate us first."

Nin shot the younger guardsman a hard glare. "Stop thinking like the Tarin'Tal, boy. We don't know who or what these creatures are. Tinek said to cooperate, so do so." A small woman in a white dress with a red cross on her chest and back came up to the group of Illani. Although she was much shorter than the majority of the humans Nin had seen—only four feet, nine inches—she was at eye level with the muscular guardsman.

"Mr. Nin Serbel, will you and your men follow me, please? We would like to conduct one last scan of your basic physiology. We need to compare our compiled data to the genetic profiles that we've gathered so far." The group of Illani shuffled toward a series of tubes and beds. Nin didn't like it; it reminded him too much of a morgue.

All his men had patches on their skin of some sort of healing jelly the humans used to speed tissue regeneration. Fortunately, the substance worked remarkably well on his species, even though it had been designed for human use. The injuries his team had sustained during the final retreat had been left to fester for the duration of their flight from the Tarin'Tal; they had been pursued across half the continent and then the breadth of the system. Nin had started with two thousand men to guard the regent's son, but the power of such a huge number had been tissue paper against the destructive force of the Tarin'Tal Communal Purification Force.

After the initial resistance had been crushed, they had sent swarms of those red-painted warriors after the remaining royals. Nin shuddered as he remembered the brutality of those beasts, their massive heat cannons and hideous curved blades. His last memory of his home planet was of a fellow guardsmen being slaughtered by Tarin'Tal. Heat cannons burned men alive; many unlucky soldiers lived long enough to feel every nerve in their body cry out in pain as they were cooked to their core. Those not incinerated by waves of heat were rewarded with a quick, yet brutal, death by the Tarin'Tal's six-foot hooked blades carried. The primitive nature of the blades meant nothing when combined with the massive strength and leverage the Tarin'Tal could deliver. The resulting combination of weapons was the most horrific battle zone Nin had ever imagined. The sights, smells, and sounds of the carnage still burned his senses. He remembered all too well the smell of burnt Illani flesh, the voiding associated with death, the screams of men being cloven by swords or burning in agony, and the sight of his fellow soldiers falling before the hideous beasts. To those gnarled, massive, blood-soaked beasts whose only aim was the death of the last member of the royal family, his soldiers were nothing more than a nuisance.

Although the battle took place only two days ago, the guardsman doubted he would ever receive a full night of sleep again. They had been chased every second until the humans arrived, and the strain clearly showed. The last batch of stimulants he'd taken was beginning to wear off, and he was barely able to regain his feet after he stepped off the scanner's bed assembly.

"I'm sorry, sir. We just needed to finish the tests so we can adjust our equipment to your physiology. Some men from Military Intelligence are waiting outside with some questions for you, but I am sure they can wait 'til you've had some sleep." Nin responded to the nurse with a half smile. It seemed strange to him that she understood his body language, but he was too tired to care. Five minutes later, he was in a soft bed, where he fell immediately into sleep—a restless sleep, but sleep nonetheless.

When Nin woke up, he couldn't tell how long he had been asleep, but it felt like a mere fifteen minutes. On the other three beds, he counted the men under his command.

Hearing movement, Vilnir came in from Prince Tinek's adjoining compartment. "Ah, I see you are awake. Are you rested, Nin?" Vilnir stood in the entrance.

"How long was I asleep?" the scared guard asked.

"The guards at the door said that you came back at 1500 ship time; it is now 1000 the following day. Their time keeping is pretty much the same as our own."

"I have been asleep for nineteen hours? It feels like I just went down!" Nin said in disbelief, rubbing his face to get the circulation flowing.

"Yes, I would imagine. I have briefed the human intelligence men on everything I know about the Tarin'Tal. Tinek has them headed to Sh'in to begin harvesting the local herbivores. These humans—" Vilnir pronounced the word carefully in English "—are very short on food. It seems they expect to engage the Tarin'Tal soon. Our new allies would like to debrief you and your men for a more strategic assessment on the strengths and weaknesses of the invader's forces. They would also like you to report to their tactical assessment and strategic command center to provide insight on some battle scenarios."

Nin's eyebrows rose. "Are they planning a war?" he asked, surprise and hope in his eyes.

"Nin," Vilner said with excitement, "things have changed while you were asleep."

Nin could not believe what he was hearing; his face flushed with hope and the ramifications of what he was hearing. "Wait! Did you say allies?"

1/4/2454

Location: Sh'in (Planetoid Orbiting a Gas Giant)

The destroyers Madrid and Eidolon flanked the Explorator and her frigate escorts as they traveled through GS. Following the three ships was a small fleet of pre-exile private craft, all renovated for military and colonization purposes. Some of the older craft, however, didn't need any more than a call sign, having been drafted from the bountiful ranks of mercenaries active long before the first war. Back then, mercenaries had found plenty of employment accompanying the spread of humanity into space. When Eidolon signaled the task force, the whole colonization fleet dropped out of GS in a synchronized formation; the flashes of the escaping light from their gravity wells temporarily illuminated the ice rings around the planetoid. The symmetry of the fleet's exit from FTL prevented each craft's gravity drive from backwashing the others. The unavoidable sliding caused by gravity engine wake, however, was insignificant, and the few listing ships quickly pulled themselves back into rank.

Every ship immediately separated and attended to its assigned tasks. Each destroyer traced asymmetrical paths into orbit around the planetoid, preparing to deploy sensor buoys. The fighters, which had been latched onto the sides of the two destroyers, began peeling off, dragging the individual buoys to their predetermined positions around the planet. The combat mules, former mercenary and civilian craft, began lazily drawing themselves up in a loose escort around the colony ship Explorator. A group of the Mule's noncombat counterparts clustered themselves in geosynchronous orbit above the Explorator's targeted landing location, gathering and transmitting topographical information on the area surrounding the small Illani outpost. A mule with one of Tinek's guards onboard began its descent toward the planet to inform the scientists of the situation. The Illani on the planet were in for a surprise.

"Captain Sergey, the envoy has reached the planet, and they have relayed a suitable landing location." Idly confirming his officer's report, the captain sat further back in his chair.

"Very good. Prepare to land the ship. Set all stations and platforms for permanent deployment." The ship lumbered toward the planet's atmosphere, rolling its massive belly toward the hazy blue sky. Slowly, the craft unceremoniously entered the atmosphere. The fire associated with atmospheric entry was less severe than normal; the size of the planet didn't allow for a thick upper atmosphere, but it was bountiful enough for life. "She has a good, strong atmosphere, sir," the man at a science station stated. Everyone on the colony ship was beside themselves with joy at the prospect of walking on land, actual dirt.

"Good. Please continue to confirm our orbital readings during descent."

Twenty minutes later, the Madrid was rounding the opposite side of the planet. "Sir, I've got a contact. I don't think we could have detected it further than 100,000 clicks."

The captain seemed to wake from a haze of boredom. "Begin a thorough sensor analysis."

Alarms blared a second later. "Holy hell! Sir, we've got contacts! Lots of them. My screen is on fire!"

The captain's attention snapped to his holographic display, glowing with the positions of unidentified ships. "Hail them! Continue the deep scan, elaborate, and relay all related information to the fleet! Battle stations!" The wave of yellow dots in the display turned a menacing red.

"Sir, they are opening fire!"

A swarm of gunships assailed the Madrid, pouring their streams of kinetic fire toward her unprotected side. The ship's shield flicked into existence a second too late, and large sections of the ship glowed hot with freshly scorched ravines. All but one of the cannon ports had been hit, several of them had been scorched shut, and one had been breached, the atmospheric decompression throwing its crew into space. The heavily oxygenated atmosphere from the port burned brightly as it left the ship until the safety shutters slammed into place, sealing off the port from the rest of the ship. "Sir, we've lost pressure in gun ports two through five!"

"Automatic emergency measures?" the captain asked, sweat forming quickly from the sudden stress and heat.

"Active!"

"Spin the ship and return fire!" The ship spun into the firestorm, its shields glowing brightly under the strain of constant barrage. As her rotation brought the ship's port side to bear on the Tarin'Tal warships, the Madrid's cannons opened fire, the plasma-filled rounds detonating in the heart of the enemy cloud. Even though twelve ships were wrenched from existence, it seemed to make little difference against the vast numbers of attacking Tarin'Tal.

"Sir, they are jamming our signal. We can't get a message to the Explorator or the Eidolon!" The captain turned as the images of both himself and the alien ships on his display begin to contort as the jamming increased.

"Set course to the Explorator's projected location, maximum burn!" The massive engines on the back of the Madrid roared to life, pivoting her around sharply. The Madrid accelerated quickly, but the Tarin'Tal were already traveling at a far superior velocity. The gunships continued to hammer at the rear of the Madrid, wearing her shields thin.

"Sir! The rear shield generators are about the blow!" The ship shuttered with a series of metallic blows as the port and rear shield generators began to buckle.

"Redirect the forward shields to port, interlace them with the foremost emitters from the top and bottom." Outside, the barrage continued. "Done. Shields at forty percent of optimum."

The destroyer reached its top velocity just as the foremost ships in the swarm reached her. "Sir, they are firing magnetic grapples! It appears they intend to board us."

"Fallen Earth," the captain muttered behind clenched teeth before barking, "Time to entry?"

"One minute, twenty seconds."

The captain tried to force clarity back into his mind. "Reduce speed. Charge the acceleration matrix and emergency thrusters!" With the excess drag and reduced engine output, the Tarin'Tal pilots began to pull the ship into the heart of their cluster. They ceased firing and continued attaching their magnetic grappling lines, entwining the Madrid in a spider web of cords and Tarin'Tal craft. "Status of the fighter wing?"

"Waiting for orders, sir."

"Tell them to attack the cloud around us at full bore. Disregard friendly fire cautions! Fire the emergency burn, bring the engines to full, and activate a full-scale battle roll! All cannons, fire! All Gatlings and flak, fire!" The ship lurched forward, spinning and lashing out with all its weapons. The centrifugal force and acceleration of the destroyer slammed the mass of ships connected to her with line into each other as she spun. The Peregrine fighters screamed into the disorganized swarm, each pouring an unceasing stream of fire into the enemy mass. The space around the destroyer erupted into pure fire and shrapnel, causing a chain reaction of explosions and debris that tore apart their close-flying counterparts.

The Madrid emerged from the explosion, fire pouring from numerous hull breaches, its shields sparking as they attempted to reactivate. Its exterior surface was almost unrecognizable. "All secondary hands to escape shuttles. Commander, prepare the trireme!" The officer inserted an ancient-style key into a terminal and typed a code.

"Trireme ready," the ship's first officer declared.

"Target the vessel at the heart of that swarm, and engage the trireme device," the captain ordered as he pointed to a large smear in the holo-display. A few seconds later, the remaining shuttles peeled off from the Madrid. The doomed ship flipped along its vertical axis and fired its engines in a prolonged burn. As the captain watched the proximity reader tick down, he gave one final order to his men.

"Shuttles, initiate immediate emergency landing. Peregrine squad, retreat to the Eidolon!" The Madrid continued to accelerate, pushing its engines beyond their max. A series of long, barbed spikes extended from the front of the ship as it approached the Tarin'Tal juggernaut. The captain stared at his forward screen as it flared brightly from incoming fire; the Tarin'Tal had realized what he was attempting to do. "You beasts won't take this land from us!" he declared defiantly.

The destroyer slammed into the larger vessel, buckling both ships' hulls and expelling the two remaining humans through a shattered port. The captain survived long enough in the sparse cloud of escaped gasses to watch the trireme activate. In a flash, a massive self-destruct antimatter bomb simultaneously detonated with every last warhead the Madrid carried. The explosion blanketed the entire Tarin'Tal swarm in its envelope of destruction. In the space of two seconds, the miniature fleet had been erased from reality.

The five remaining Peregrines weaved through the oncoming wreckage at full speed, desperately rushing away from the ever-increasing number of Tarin'Tal swarms evading both weapons fire and shrapnel. "Captain! One of the swarms is closing on the escape pods..." The man's face grew sickened. "They just took one down!"

"No, Jack, continue to the Eidolon. Set a continuous broadcast of what happened."

"Anyone who wants to help those shuttles, follow me. Volunteers only!" Amid Jack's vehement protests, the other four fighters veered sharply toward the shuttles, their accelerators burning as they forced every last ounce of speed from their craft. "No questions, Jack. This is an order. Good-bye."

Cursing the Tarin'Tal, Jack angrily slammed his accelerator and rocketed toward the vulnerable colony fleet. Although severely damaged, his craft was still faster than anything the Tarin'Tal could field. The distance between him and the pursuers began to grow.

"Battle-net sensors are detecting at least two hundred and fifty gunships and a juggernaut in the cloud, sir," one of the squadsmen stated.

"Status on the shuttles?"

"One down, one damaged and about to be overcome, three in midrange, and five approaching the atmosphere."

"Dave, Pete! Intercept and defend the midrange pods. Rob and I will hit the center and buy you some time!" Punching their engines again, the two fighters screamed into the center of the alien cloud. "Switch to fragmentation rounds. Let's show these crawlers some pain!"

Both fighters released a stream of shells into the mass of alien ships before them. Their rounds shattered into thousands of individual shards, ripping holes through the gunships and venting their air, fuel, and weaponry alike. As they hit the exterior of the cloud, a series of missiles impacted their shields and Rob's craft disintegrated. Captain Bartholomew's craft lost its wing and one of its two Gatling cannons. The force of the impacts sent him spinning without control. The fighter pilot's mouth was too full of blood to speak. *Ha ha ha! You guys like heat? Okay!* With a flick of a blood-covered finger, he switched to incendiary rounds and fired. The vented oxygen in the swarm ignited, charring more than a dozen gunships. In a wave of return fire, the fighter shattered and detonated in a final concussion of flame.

The last two fighters sped toward the wounded shuttle. As they approached the limping craft, it burst into a cloud of flame, burnt from the inside out by the Tarin'Tal's brutal kinetic heat weaponry.

"Ah, hell no! Roast those monsters!" The two craft unleashed a torrent of plasma rounds on the craft that had destroyed the shuttle. It never had a chance to dodge before the glowing rounds it ripped apart.

"The shuttles have hit atmo. Let's follow them down!" the lead fighter broadcast. As the Tarin'Tal cloud swarmed through the debris of the former shuttle, the two fighters slashed into the planet's atmosphere following the retreating shuttles to the planet's surface. "Damn! Their jam still works through atmo!"

"Set course for the outpost and relay to the shuttles. Flank them and follow at their maximum speed."

Jack's engines were about to buckle as he sped toward the colony fleet, but the missile continued to gain on him. He had used the last of his chaff on three guided projectiles the Tarin'Tal swarm had sent after his faster vessel. Both missile and fighter screamed toward the human task force, skimming the atmosphere faster than it seemed possible to the young pilot. The computer clicked down the time to communications breakthrough. "Eighteen, seventeen, sixteen, fifteen, fourteen, thirteen..." Unfortunately for Jack, the missile continued closing at the same velocity. "Twelve, eleven, ten, nine...zero." Clicking over the remaining numbers, the computer interrupted itself. "We have communications with the Eidolon." The missile exploded behind Jack's fighter as a flight of seven Peregrine buzzed his tail.

"This is the Eidolon. We have detected antimatter activity. Report!"

"Thanks, Eidolon, we have a problem!"

"Admiral, a large mule has dropped out of GS. They are blaring a distress signal and a recorded video on all frequencies. The colony ship and its escorts have been attacked! The Madrid and most of her fighters have been destroyed, and the Eidolon is badly damaged and being forced back. Mules are dropping like flies."

Another officer interrupted before the communications officer could continue. "Sir, sensors report GS activation fleet wide! They are jumping without orders!"

"No!" the admiral exclaimed, as he stood and watched the image of the fleet powering up on his holo-display. "Activate the GS, contact everything without a level five merc shield or better, and order them to stand down. Order the Leviathan and two destroyers of your discretion to remain behind and guard the civilians. All combat ships are to array themselves behind us and the Princeps. Place the Legatus between us, and set up a shield screen."

The navigation officer interrupted again. "All ships have warmed both GS and weapons, the fleet is ready to engage hot!" The admiral surveyed his fleet for a moment.

"Enter grav-stream!"

"Forty seconds to the combat zone!" someone shouted.

"Hancock, to all ships. Prepare for full-scale battle."

"All ships show green on shields and hot weapons," the weapons officer confirmed.

"Hancock, to all ships. The Tarin'Tal are attempting to deny us both food and a beachhead in this system. They have slain our brothers and sisters, and they have launched a brutal ground assault on our colonists. The have already brutalized our Illani allies. Show them no mercy; purge them from the planet! Burn them from the sky! They have no natural respect for anything. Make them respect us. The evils of the Harvesters and Death shall not happen here, not to us, not to the Illani. Go! Drag them from existence so that we may continue ours!" Though it was inaudible though space, Hancock could swear he felt a million voices call out in challenge.

"GS exit in five, four, three, two, one...contact!"

Hancock's eyes went wide as the sheer scale of the attack was shown. "All ships, open fire!"

The fleet dropped out of GS directly beside the Eidolon. Its fore and port shields buckled in a wave of fire. The few remaining human fighters attempted to defend seventy or so mules from vastly overwhelming forces. That deadly imbalance, however, ceased to exist. "Sir, we have twelve swarms of over five hundred gunboats, over thirty juggernauts, and two spire ships."

Hancock was infinitely grateful for the tactical information Tinek and his men had given him. "Launch all Peregrines! Have half of them, three destroyers, and the Legatus attack the swarms. Have the mercs, combat mules, and a quarter of the fighters cover our assault on the capital ships. Hold all remaining fighters for discretionary deployment on the exterior of the Princeps, and have her cover our wake until further orders. All destroyers are to pick targets of opportunity and engage!"

For a second, the human fleet's assault flowed though space like the spirit of death itself. Their volleys tore through the forward ranks of the Tarin'Tal as if they were dry grass before a flame. Recoiling from the initial shock, the Tarin'Tal wasted no time in reforming; their gunship clouds raced toward the spire ships with their juggernauts close behind. Every last human ship pursued the Tarin'Tal at maximum speed, pouring volley after unrelenting volley into the retreating adversary with a brutal vengeance.

"Okay, people, the easy part is over. Signal the ships to reform the line in preparation for capital engagement!" As the Tarin'Tal ships entered the protective range of their spires, the human fleet began to veer off and reform along their newly assigned positions on the battlefield. Those too slow were caught in lashing tongues of fire from several spire ships.

"Sir! I am reading over a thousand more gunships and twenty more juggernauts. They are detaching from the spires!"

"Engage the interlocking shield screen. All ships, prepare for capital line engagement!"

The fleet drew themselves up behind the massive shields of the Cerberus, Princeps, and the Legatus, each one of them focusing all capable shields forward. The destroyers turned sideways to present their broadsides, and the smaller craft prepared their respective cannons. Morphing from its vengeful frenzy, the human fleet transformed to a rigid line, prepared to engage the larger Tarin'Tal fleet.

The Tarin'Tal swarmed about each other in lustful anticipation of battle. Hancock watched the teaming mass of alien warships but didn't wait for them to make the first move. "All craft. Forward assault. Fire at will!" The human fleet surged forward in concert with each other. The Tarin'Tal fleet began to blast the human starships with a continuous barrage, which harmlessly splashed along the forward shields of the three capital ships, shimmering in a dazzling light show and washing away from the fleet.

"All craft, as one: fire!" The blast was intense, appearing like a miniature nova as it crossed the gap between fleets. It tore through the inferior shields of the Tarin'Tal and burned deep into their ranks. The faster fire from the light strike human ships slashed paths for the heavy artillery and devastating antimatter weaponry.

The effect on the alien's resolve to fight, however, was far less successful.

"Sir, the Tarin'Tal ships are charging at an extremely high velocity; they will be too close for capital line in ten seconds." Analyzing the information and his resources in less than a second, Hancock switched his tactics to compensate.

"At zero point, all ships return to previous assigned targets!" As the two fleets crashed together, the human line dissolved into numerous engagements. Ships slammed into each other as excess space in the crowded skies quickly disappeared. The more heavily armored and shielded human ships consistently won these sumo contests against almost all their nemesis. The one exception was the aliens' strange rammers, which assaulted the agile Peregrines in swarms. Filled with vengeance, human mules attacked the ships with their gravity grapplers. As the Tarin'Tal passed by, they were snared and crushed between the small craft's gravity manipulators.

A juggernaut broke through the outer lines and attempted to assault the less shielded side of the Princeps, only to be carved apart by armor-piercing rounds from the flights of Peregrines waiting along her sides. At a word from the admiral, the reserve fighters entered the battle, creating an undulating wave of unexpected and devastating force. Unable to withstand the bombardment of the Cerberus's heavy cannons, one of the huge spire ships cracked along its length and erupted into flame. The component modules of the ship were breaking up or descending toward the planet under barely controlled trajectories.

The first spire ship broke apart, and the second turned to run, as the large juggernauts tried to create a screen between it and the massive antimatter cannons of the human ships. They failed. The combined firepower of the human capital ships ripped the screen of juggernauts to shreds and punched holes through which the Cerberus and Legatus could pour salvos of antimatter weapons upon the now defenseless spire ship. As the shields of the second spire ship began to buckle, it separated all of its constituent parts in a desperate attempt to save its crew and devote them to the conflict on the ground. The large human cannons couldn't hit all the pieces, and the lighter craft were still too far away to engage them before they could land.

"Send the reserve Peregrines and frigates after those segments along with three destroyers. Engage the remainder of the fleet. Send four squads of Peregrines to disable one of those juggernauts, and have the mules bring her into the Princeps."

With the removal of the spire ships, the battle ended almost as suddenly as it had begun. Many of the gunships attempted to ram the Cerberus and Princeps, hoping futilely that they could take the massive ships with them.

Every last juggernaut fought to the end. None of them, however, could inflict much damage upon the superior human fleet. None of the defeated fleet asked for quarter, which was convenient, because not a single human soldier was willing to give it. Even after the battle was over and the last Tarin'Tal warship had been eliminated, vast numbers of warships cruised through space looking for one last target. The victory had been both complete and decisive.

That couldn't have gone better, thought Admiral Hancock. *The fleet obeyed orders. I couldn't ask for a more decisive victory.* "Hancock to fleet, congratulations on your victory!"

With a signal to the comm officer, the whole fleet was placed on an open channel with each other. More than five hundred thousand humans chorused, "Victory! Honor! Victory!"

With a nod, the commanding officer switched the communication back to one way. "Now prepare your ships for planetary bombardment and support. All troops prepare to land! It is time to claim our first piece of solid ground. On men! To victory! And the survival of our race!"

Again the commander switched to fleet-wide, and the sound resounded with an additional five hundred thousand troops: "Victory! Honor! Victory!"

Cormac stood in the assault ship, his back to the door. He addressed his division, all three hundred of them. "We have been chosen to lead this assault on the Tarin'Tal. Their continued existence here prohibits ours. They stand between us and the very sustenance and lives of our people. They have assaulted the civilians aboard the Explorator, and they wish to slaughter us like the Harvesters did. Like the Death! But they shall fail! This land is now ours! Drive them from it!"

The roar from the division vibrated the metal walls of the transport, only cut off by the bone-shattering crunch of the craft slamming into the ground.

The transport's door hammered into the ground, and the armored division was exposed to the hot winds of the planet. The valley swarmed with Tarin'Tal, tearing their way over shanty, cobbled-together defensive positions surrounding the Explorator. The closest Tarin'Tal paused to look at the humans in surprise, as both sides stood motionless for a bloodless second.

Somewhere in the ranks someone activated his sword and slammed it into his shield, then another, and another. Within a second, the entire division was hammering their shields and chanting the division's slogan in unison: "Necamus!" We kill. Faster and faster they chanted, leading to one prolonged yell of wrath. Wrath for fallen family and friends, wrath for their lost home world, wrath at the

Harvesters, wrath at the Death, and wrath at this new enemy who was trying to murder the last of their kind and deny them a new home.

Their cries resonated with their shields, reverberating across the valley in a shockwave of sound. Following the challenge of their own voices, the new division charged, slamming into the first line of Tarin'Tal who were still clinging to their ursine ears on the side of their heads, reeling in agony. The humans cut them down before they had a chance to lift their massive blades or thermal weapons. At first the Tarin'Tal line disintegrated under the swarm of the human assailants; their size advantage yielded them nothing against the number and ferocity with which the humans attacked. The human warriors' cybernetically enhanced armor allowed them to spring over and through the Tarin'Tal's first counterattack to assault directly their exposed necks and faces while dodging the six-legged monsters with expert precision. The humans' swords burned their way through armor and flesh alike, leaving the stench of ionization and charred flesh in their wake.

The initial shock wore off within a few thin seconds, leaving the tide of battle to numbers, strength, and firepower—all of which favored the Tarin'Tal, as they reformed and swarmed the new human line.

Having lost the element of shock, the human line slowed as the Tarin'Tal began using their massive kinetic weapons and numerical superiority to get their soldiers within range of close combat. The aliens' powerful hind legs allowed them to close an astonishing distance with extraordinary power, matching the humans' cybernetically assisted assault head-on.

The carnage was devastating. Both sides refused to falter against blasts of plasma and heat that cooked and vaporized both man and alien in devastating numbers. Both sides closed to close-range combat, seeking to find cover from more powerful long-range weapons in the melee of physical combat.

Cormac, leading his men at the point of the charge, hurdled a Tarin'Tal as it fell. Using its tumbling body to change the trajectory of his leap, he impacted another beast, splashing blood as he planted his blade in the center of its chest. He tore up and out in one strike, drawing a single agonized death roar from the creature before it died. The beast nearly clamped its merciless jaws on Cormac's legs in a death strike, but James removed the beast's face with a clean downward strike.

Before the Tarin'Tal's body met the dirt, James had found his next target. The youth's face was a mask of rage and twisted glee as he carried the momentum of his last strike into another mechanically assisted vault, hurdling into the midst of a pack of the creatures. James's helmet had been partially ripped open, allowing Cormac a sliver of a glimpse of the young warrior's face before he disappeared again. James's pupils were dilated, and his mouth hung open in a vicious smile, as he sailed through the air. He set loose a massive bellow as he dropped out of sight behind the charging beasts.

Cormac did not have a chance to see what happened before another Tarin'Tal attempted to behead him. He sidestepped the curved metal blade and followed it up to the exposed side of the beast and planted his sword beneath its arm. Cormac tore the blade loose again, drawing his bladed shield in a parallel arch through a lower section of the beast, spilling its organs on his metal boots. It clamped its clawed hind foot on Cormac's boot as it died in its own waste. Cormac wrenched his foot free, tearing the flesh of the creature in a gruesome arch across his field of vision.

In his periphery, Cormac saw a soldier take a massive blow from one of the aliens. The man's armor was crushed in, and his breastplate protruded from what had once been his back. The creature turned its attention to another of Cormac's men, but before it could strike, Cormac slashed his shield across the back of its left back leg, pulling it from its reared position and onto the ground in a painful, spasming mass.

The creature spun and tried to backslash Cormac with a massive claw. Cormac allowed it to impact his shield, burning the creature's hand in a spurt of smoke. Both man and beast were thrown off balance, reeling from the concussive force. Even with its head slashed and its leg bleeding, the beast reared and launched itself at Cormac. Countering the attack, Cormac propelled himself into the air, holding his shield above him and his sword behind. The two warriors closed at an impossibly rapid pace. The Tarin'Tal brought his massive sword down toward the man, its point aimed at Cormac's head. The human adjusted the angle of his shield to deflect the blow back toward the beast. At the second of impact, he brought his own sword around in a blurring horizontal arch, neatly slicing the creature halfway through its body. Both combatants sailed past each other. The beast landed and thrashed like a chopped fish, no longer the brutal and intelligent creature it had been.

The other warriors of the Fifty-sixth continued to fight fierce battles of their own with the veteran beasts of the Tarin'Tal army, both reeking unimaginable carnage upon the other. It had turned, almost entirely, into a close-combat battle, both sides wielding swords and shields, interspacing each with blasts from their weapons. Huge and thick, the Tarin'Tal armor necessitated the use of the heaviest of projectiles or the burning bite of the plasma swords to damage the creatures beneath. When the battle began, more than fifty human assault ships dropped thousands of human regulars and marines into the battle. Those with heavier armor saw much more success than those lacking shields or close-range plasma weaponry. It seemed not to matter how many died on both sides; there were simply too many combatants. At length, even the best troops began to fall due to exhaustion and the shear amount of power leveled against them as the battle wore on. But there were always fresh troops from the rear.

As the Tarin'Tal began to push the human regulars back, they redoubled their efforts against the Fifty-sixth, the armored division positioning itself between the alien horde and the Explorator. To punch through the new lines, the aliens brought heavy mounted versions of the kinetic weapons, which burned swaths of ground to cinders in seconds. The humans responded in kind with heavy artillery of their own, their large turrets blasting tunnels of destruction through the ranks of the beasts. The battle grew steadily fiercer, its roar only shattered by the crescendo of a mind-numbing blast that shocked the entire field into gazing up at the sky as it began raining chunks of cylindrical metal and spewing fire. The field devolved from a chaotic battle to uncontrolled mayhem as the downed ships began ramming the surface. The disarray of the Tarin'Tal worsened as the descending Peregrine fighters poured streams of riveting fire on their ships and debris.

The impact of the ships threw men and beasts into the air as they carved ugly craters in the field. The Peregrines continued to blanket the sea of Tarin'Tal with incendiary and fragmentation rounds, tearing them apart before they could regain their orientation and reorganize. Most of the humans pursued the retreating aliens, but the Fifty-sixth took full advantage of their new equipment and slaughtered the Tarin'Tal in full retreat.

They had nowhere to run; the valley was almost entirely enclosed by cliffs. Seeing their imminent doom, the remaining Tarin'Tal fled to the cluster of fallen ships. Pulling survivors from them, they prepared to make their final stand. En masse, the regular human forces began to arrive, surrounding the surviving aliens with leveled weapons and locked shields. A loud speaker demanded in the alien's own language that they surrender, to which a large Tarin'Tal bellowed a challenge. Their challenge was answered by a single blast from a destroyer in orbit, which vaporized the entire circle in a flash of burning plasma. The battle was over.

A wave of chanting surged over the field: "Victory! Honor! Victory!"

9 >> Understanding

1/5/2454

Location: Sh'in (Planetoid Orbiting a Gas Giant)

Admiral Hancock sat in his office, watching streams of statistics pour across his screen. "Ten small civilian mules destroyed, fifty-three severely damaged; two large civilian mules destroyed, seven severely damaged; seventy-nine Peregrine fighters destroyed, two hundred and ninety-four severely damaged; three frigates destroyed, four severely damaged; one destroyer destroyed, three severely damaged; light damage incurred on the Legatus; light damage to the beta hull on the Princeps; light burn incurred to the Cerberus's forward shield emitters." As specifics and repair requirements scrolled across his screen, the admiral tapped a button on his console, connecting him directly to the communications center of the Cerberus.

"Signal the Leviathan and have her bring the remainder of the fleet to Sh'in. Inform the MIC station to prepare for permanent deployment and to begin fleet repair activities. Have the Princeps hook up with her to refit all damaged craft and begin production of defense and sensor network buoys."

"Yes, sir," the voice on the other end confirmed. With another series of signals, the admiral connected to the limited science department aboard the Cerberus, which contained almost all the remaining scientists at humanity's disposal. "How is the progress coming on their cloaking technology?"

Hancock heard a rustling of equipment before the scientist responded. "It's fascinating, sir! It seems to rely on some sort of shearing technology and is somehow connected with their heat manipulation technology as an adaptive shielding. It hides them from our gravity sensors while leaving themselves vulnerable to solid mass penetration weaponry."

"Do we have a way to counter it?" he asked.

"If we could have a copy of the technology for study, we could possibly modify our sensors to detect any abnormalities generated. The result of their shielding is a complete lack of visibility, including to the naked eye, unless there is an energy buildup within the sphere of protection. This, of course, would explain why their shields didn't hide them from our sensors during the battle."

"I will take that as a no."

The scientist began to stutter as he responded. "Our apologies, sir, but without a physical copy of their technology, we have no way to identify its weakness."

"Keep trying."

"Yes, sir."

Admiral Hancock turned off his communicator and turned his attention to the soft glow of the ship's shields outside his window. A cloud of debris scrabbled against the ship's static defenses. A small mule quickly followed the debris and scooped a large, twisted metal tube away from the ship. The remains were obviously from the enemy fleet; the light red tent of the metal streaked with white was consistent throughout their ships. The mule swerved in and out of the human fleet, winding its way to a space-borne junkyard to deposit the wreck for analysis. The humans hoped the answer to the alien shield riddle was somewhere in the tangled mass of destruction that remained of the alien fleet.

The retribution against the aliens for attacking the exploration task force had been utter destruction. Every last ship from the Tarin'Tal task force had been burned from the skies. Unfortunately for the refugee fleet, that very violence had left little enemy technology for them to analyze, let alone determine anything about the constitution of the alien forces. A few ships had tried to follow the admiral's orders and capture a juggernaut, but it had self-destructed once the aliens determined they had no hope of escape.

The Exile Empire

Hancock wearily rose from his desk and treaded down the halls with the lucid determination of a man who had been up for far too long and still had a disturbing volume of work remaining. The endless corridor of uniform metal doors would have confused most men, but the admiral didn't even need to consult the numbers above each door to find his room. He considered sleeping, but instead he took some stimulants, showered, and wound his way back to the command deck. "Status on the remaining Tarin'Tal ground troops?" he asked with more energy in his voice than he actually had.

"We have tracked a significant number to a mountain range seventy clicks east of the Explorator's location. They didn't get close enough to the battle to take part, and they escaped extermination. Exposed remnants are being eliminated by orbital strikes and Peregrine sorties."

Hancock inwardly grunted in satisfaction. "Numbers?" he prompted.

"Current estimates place them at about nine hundred and fifty thousand troops and over sixty thousand assorted crew from downed craft."

"Firepower?"

The officer tapped a few panels and spoke quietly into an earpiece. After waiting a moment and acknowledging the person on the other end, he turned back to the admiral. "Sorry, sir, we don't have estimates on their weapons or defensive capabilities. All we know is that twenty large ships and over eighty smaller craft all made landfall in that vicinity and there is heavy activity."

"Assign the twelfth fighter wing to scout the area and support the frigates Orthoseterni, Chaerilida, Brotheini, Neochatina, Megacormini, Vaejovidae, Diplocentridae, Hadurinae, Bothiruridae, Lispominae, Nebini, Urodacine, Iuridae, and the Hormurinae. Assign each fighter a squad of fighters and bombard the area in rotation. Keep them holed up or burned up."

The officer grunted. "Understood, sir."

1/5/2454

Location: The Surface of Sh'in, Fifty-sixth Lander

Jessica sat glued to the monitors at her control station even though her shift was over. It had been more than four hours. She had been up for over a day, but she couldn't sleep. She couldn't even look away from the screens. An itch clawed at her cheek, and she scratched with an impatient annoyance. Her hand came away with a powdering of salt that covered her face from tears dried after several hours of negligence. James's suit had stopped broadcasting information just as the battle had ended. There had been no fluctuation, no sign of injury; it had just stopped. She had waited for it to reactivate. *Maybe it was a glitch*, she thought, but no signal ever returned. She scanned a stream of wounded and deceased statistics scrolling across her screen, none of which was James. She had hacked into every military computer and camera on the ground using her cybernetics in unorthodox ways that James had taught her. She had even got a large group of men from the unit to look for him over the charred battlefield. Seven of the nine remaining soldiers in James's squad had immediately volunteered to look for him even though they were exhausted and wounded. The others had tried to join the search, but the doctors sedated them before they could aggravate their wounds.

Jessica knew there was something about James that made people follow him, but the men were growing tired and she was growing impatient. Dead or not, every desire demanded she find him. Her thoughts were interrupted by the voice of Rick, one of James's men and personal friends. "We haven't found him anywhere around where the Fifty-sixth was fighting, and our scans won't pick up anything from his suit if its power is off."

Jessica shrieked in frustration. "Look for the largest stack of bodies. He will be near that!" she hissed, venom dripping from her voice.

Again, Rick's voice came through the device in her cybernetic ear, distorted by both his damaged communicator and his fatigue. "Look, Jessica, the only way we will be able to find him is by going through every corpse the Fifty-sixth lost. I know it's morbid, but they have been pulling guys out of their suits all day. Somehow they are acting as stasis chambers when the guys are really hurt. We would do better to let the recovery teams handle this."

"No, no," Jessica choked. "No! We need to find him, we have to find him!"

The young soldier at the other end of the com-link couldn't see the pain on Jessica's face, but he could feel it. "I'm coming out there. I've linked all the communications systems directly into my neuro-center. I'll know if anyone found him, and I can still look for him myself."

With speed from grief and anger, Jessica tore down the halls of the command and control segment of the troop ship. It had been moved to a cluster of temporary structures on the surface to help with triage and ground control. During the battle, the ship had literally landed in the field, providing a close, hard-to-jam communications and control center as well as an artillery platform.

Just outside the main ramp, a large shuttle waited for its passengers to unload. It was busy ferrying medics and field engineers to the surface from the orbiting fleet. Halfway through the encampment, Jessica was met by Rick and Sam, another of James's men. They were out of breath, and their suits were twisted and charred from the battle. Both were in obvious pain, though neither would ever admit it.

"If you're gonna come out, you could have at least have waited for us!" Rick chided. "Follow me, I'll show you where we lost contact."

Before they could reach the battlefield, however, Jessica was pulled to the ground by a massive spasm stemming from her neck and traveling down her cybernetic leg. "It's him!" she said, elated. "I can feel him, I know where he is!"

Dragging herself up, she hit a series of panels on her leg, putting it back under her control. As her body equalized with the new electronic strain, Rick could see a light electric field forming around her neck.

"Fallen Earth," he spat. "Did she rewire her nervous system? How the hell is she alive? I can't imagine how much that hurts."

Giving Rick a quick thanks, Jessica bounded off toward the stinking landscape, muttering a vaguely intelligible statement about adjusting the warning settings in her neuro-link before she was out of hearing distance. Her cybernetic legs carried her faster than their armor could carry the two men.

Rick and Sam found themselves alone in the crowd of emergency personnel rushing past them from the now empty transport. A quickly dissipating trail of dust showed the path Jessica had taken.

Turning to his friend, Sam asked if they should follow her. "She could get hurt out there; there's still weapons and shrapnel everywhere."

The larger soldier laughed. "That girl could take our whole squad out if we stood between her and James! Do you really think a few charred corpses are going to be a problem?"

The other man responded with an amused, "Touché."

"Besides," Rick continued, "did you see how fast she can move? Her cybernetics are as good as the boss's. I doubt a full-grown Harvester could take her down."

The smaller soldier chewed on that for a second. "Probably," Sam replied. "But right now, I just want to eat and hit the sack." Without any further delay, the remainder of the division made their way to a wide-open mess hall that had been set up near one of the large medical constructs.

James woke with searing pain pulsing through his lungs; he couldn't move. He tried to look around, but he couldn't see. He tried to speak, but his voice seemed muffled in his own mouth. It took a moment for him to comprehend his situation. Slowly he realized that he was still in his battle armor, still on the battlefield, and he hurt all over.

His suit was out of power. It was burned and caked in sand, blood, and the bodily juices of his fallen alien foes. Normally a soldier would be helplessly trapped in such a situation, forced to wait for rescue, or his own armor would become his coffin.

Reaching out through his cybernetics, James pulled on the connection between his synthetic arm and the cybernetic routs within the armor. He pushed a small current through his suit to crack its seals and climbed out toward air and freedom. Fresh oxygen flooded his lungs as he sat on his battered suit. His only breath had been flowing from reserve pressure alone, and it had been very stale.

As he surveyed the desolate battlefield, James began to recall the final moments of the conflict. He had lost control. It had been just like the time he had boarded the Harvester ship, and just as then, he had lost consciousness as the battle ended. He remembered disemboweling a large Tarin'Tal before it could kill a group of unarmored and unprotected men from another division. He remembered launching himself aside as a line of soldiers formed a phalanx and blasted wave after wave of plasma into the ranks of Tarin'Tal, burning them to pieces in a scour of plasma, flame, and death. He remembered the Tarin'Tal counterstrike crushing that line from both the side and above. He remembered attacking and slaughtering the aliens as they killed the last of that unlucky division. He remembered the air strikes, the shocking turn of momentum as the battle shifted, and the crippling loss of energy as the battle ended. The light was blinding as the retreating Tarin'Tal were blasted from orbit. Somehow, he also remembered his sister's face before she died. And then he didn't remember anymore.

As the memories faded, he realized that his blinding headache was fading as well, and his eyes finally began to do what they were told. James sat for several more minutes, taking in the aftermath of the battle. Insects were already buzzing around the dead, leaving him with the impression that opportunistic pests could be found universally throughout the galaxy.

With a little more alertness and energy, James began to move. Surveying his own body for damage, he was surprised to find that although his body looked like it had been mauled, he felt very little pain from wounds that should have paralyzed him in agony. The most worrisome problem, however, was rows of thick, dark inflammation radiating from his cybernetics.

Pulling himself to his feet, James was surprised that only a slight limp slowed him as he walked toward a row of emergency structures that had been erected more than a mile away. He had expected it to be worse. The ground cracked and shattered as James walked; it was charred from the bizarre weapons of the Tarin'Tal and blistered by the plasma used by human forces. The resulting effect on the planet's soil was a brittle, baked clay-like substance, jagged and broken. Anything organic had turned to dusty ash, puffing up and dissipating when disturbed. His foot brushed a particularly large clump of ash, and he wondered why he wasn't disturbed by the thought that it could be one of the hundreds of thousands of bodies strewn and smoldering throughout the landscape.

Where the ground had not been turned to brittle clay, it had become a swampy mess of human and alien innards, an ugly soup that the dead earth refused to soak up. It stank worse than anything James had ever experienced, even in the Harvester War.

By the rate of decay and the fact that the landscape was devoid of the most seriously wounded human soldiers, James figured he had been unconscious for several hours. There were still many thousands of men sitting or laying throughout the battlefield, some unhurt but in too much shock to move. Others sat nursing small wounds, patching cuts, bruises, and other minor injuries. Still more lay with larger wounds, either dead or wishing they were.

Several hundred yards from the encampment, James came upon a young soldier sitting by an extremely large Tarin'Tal. The dead creature was covered in deep gashes, and a large knife was protruding from its eye, sunk so deep that only its handle was showing. The gashes and scorch marks all over the side of its body were mostly facing the boy, and its insides had begun to seep out of the cracked flesh.

James walked up to the boy, who had several major cuts and injuries, and decided that he belonged in a medical construct, not sitting next to his rotting kill on a battlefield. While clearly alive, the boy was in severe shock. He wasn't moving, and his breath was short and irregular. James put a hand on the boy's shoulder, startling him, and bringing him only slightly back to reality.

"Come on, we should get those cuts looked at. When I left mine like that, they got infected and this happened." James held up his hand and wiggled his fingers. The synthetic skin had been pulled away in some parts, and the cybernetic nature of the limb was clearly present.

The boy said nothing, turning instead to look at his own arm, which was still gripping his rifle. Seeing that the boy wasn't planning on moving, James sat down beside him on the blackened earth that cracked beneath him.

"Is this your kill?" James asked rhetorically.

The boy looked at James with glazed eyes and gave him a small nod. After a few more moments, the boy spoke. "It killed my captain, my whole squad, and it was coming for me. I didn't want to die. It killed Steven. He was like my brother, and it killed him. It picked him up and…and it tore him in two. So I killed it. It got me with one of those blasts, but I killed it."

James felt a degree of kinship with the soldier, understanding both his desperation and rage. He knew from personal experience that the boy needed more than medical help at this point. First, he needed some water and sedatives. Putting a hand on the boy's shoulder, he offered his synthetic hand. "Come on, let's get you something to drink. Go ahead and put the gun down. It won't work anymore anyway."

Again, the boy turned to James with a haunted expression. "I can't," the boy growled bitterly.

Surprising himself and responding with patience, James reassured the boy. "Sure you can, just let go."

Giving James the same look again, the boy insisted. "No, I can't." The boy's face twisted in pure agony as he lifted his arm; his rifle did not leave his grip. The skin along the length of his arm began to crack and slide in a horrid display of melted skin, muscle, and fat, all partially dried. The pain grew too intense, and he dropped his hand back to the ground, sucking a massive breath in and holding it. He kept his sanity by staring at the sky in a massive unvoiced scream.

The bond James felt with the boy deepened as the memory of losing his own limbs swept back to him. Looking at his own hand instead of the boy's, James offered him something that he hadn't shared with another since he had met Jessica. He hadn't even had the opportunity since the Harvester War. "It's okay," he said in a calming voice. "You can take it off. I'll make you a new one."

The Exile Empire

In one smooth motion, James picked the boy up under his shoulders. Ignoring his own pain, which was growing with every second as his body started to understand its damaged state, he carried the boy toward the encampment.

Seeing the metal hand and fingers holding him up, the boy realized for the first time that his "good Samaritan" had a completely cybernetic arm. Looking at his benefactor's arm and then his own, he tried to talk. "I…I wo—" Giving up on speech longer than a single syllable, he simply stated, "Thanks," and passed out.

James sat on a medical bed. The boy he had dragged in from the battlefield was in the intensive care unit separated from him only by a cloth partition. A nurse had just finished sealing a large gash on James's leg that he hadn't even realized was there. But he certainly felt it now, and the pain was almost unbearable. He reached down to rub the itching-burning sensation that the sealant gel was causing on the surrounding muscle and skin but received a quick slap from the nurse as she read some information off of the scanner that hung above the bed.

"You need to leave it alone or it won't heal properly. We still aren't sure what sort of infectious diseases are to be found on this world, and we can't take any chances. Is that clear?" The woman's tone was authoritative and final, leaving James no choice but to solemnly assent to the woman's advice.

In a flurry of movement involving sanitation equipment and skin sealant, the nurse patched James's remaining wounds, leaving him in a mass of sealant gel, bandages, and anti-inflammatory medications. To James's utter bewilderment, he hurt more after treatment than before. As the nurse turned to leave the room, she told him to stay. "You have a nasty tear in the primary ligaments of your leg, and the muscles in the area have torn themselves. Thankfully it looks like the internal bleeding is minimal. A surgeon can take care of you later today when they finish with the critical cases. Until then, you are confined to this bed. I will be back periodically to check on you." Mortified that he would be stuck in a medical construct, James nodded solemnly.

A series of loud shouts and a crash pulled the nurse from the room, leaving James to sit alone in the noise of the triage center. His solitude didn't last long. A moment after the nurse left, Jessica barged into the room, shaking off the nurse and two huge guards as little more than nuisances. She froze when she saw James; then she darted across the small room, grabbing him with desperation, barely believing he was actually there. She didn't say anything; she simply hugged him, sobbing uncontrollably. Finally, she told him, "I couldn't find you. Why couldn't I find you? Don't ever do that to me again! I thought you were dead. Why couldn't I find you?" Before she could continue, she was overcome by a series of uncontrollable sobs. James couldn't think of anything to console her; he simply hugged her back. They sat there for a long time, reassuring each other that they were both safe.

When Jessica finally calmed herself down, she sat down next to James's bed. His aches and pains had caught up with him, and he almost lost the ability to move. His leg had swollen to a third larger than normal, and his other limbs felt like they were going to fall off. He was beginning to realize why he had been confined to bed. The two began to talk, Jessica still gripping James's undamaged cybernetic hand in a continual yet unconscious reassurance that he was there. The pair dealt with problems, both personal and practical, in a similar manner, examining everything as if it were a faulty circuit or a broken motor.

Their conversation didn't last long. They were too exhausted to communicate coherently for more than a few minutes. Their conversation became slower and less important until they stopped talking all together. Turning to look at her, a new pain in his neck making it difficult, James saw that she had fallen asleep still clutching his cybernetic hand. *Good idea*, he thought. Carefully lying down, being sure not to drop her hand, he fell asleep as well.

In the next room, the doctors continued to operate on the young soldier James had brought in. His chest was wide open, and more than a dozen machines were connected to his frail body. A doctor used a large cutting implement, based on the same matter shearing technology as military ships and soldier shields, to remove the boy's arm in one clean stroke. It had been burned to the bone. A number of his less vital organs were being replaced with light cybernetics. They did not, however, have anything more than a rudimentary cybernetic arm. The complexity of a limb that functioned as well as an original was still beyond the capabilities of a field medical construct, and no one in the fleet had anything better. As stigmatized as cybernetics were, doctors feared that advanced medical cybernetic technology, as a viable medical practice, had died with Earth.

The operation continued for several hours. When it was finished, the boy had been reduced to a mummy of bandages. Even with advanced tissue regeneration technology, the boy would take several days to recover. When he did wake up, he was disoriented and confused. The memory centers of his brain had been hurt by prolonged blood loss. Strangely enough, he remembered his conversation with

James after the battle as clear as day, and while he did remember his life before the battle, it was patchy, faded, and somehow foreign. When he was able to write again, he put in a transfer to the Fifty-sixth. To his extreme disappointment, he learned that there was already a long waiting list for the now famous unit. Soldiers, both those involved in the battle and those shown combat footage, volunteered in droves to use the new technology themselves. Frontline or not, they had taken a hundredth the casualties of any other unit and delivered several fold that ratio in damage to the enemy.

1/8/2454

Location: Sh'in (Planetoid Orbiting a Gas Giant)

James sat in the new barracks, reviewing applications for his squad. Cormac had begun allowing each squad commander to pick their own replacements from the mass of applicants. It seemed to yield the most skilled and fit warriors for each team. As James scrolled through the profiles, complete with recent action statistics, one caught his eye: a twenty-year-old soldier who was the sole survivor of his division—the hardest hit in the fleet. He had killed two Tarin'Tal in the recent engagement. The most any other single unarmored man had killed was one. He had experience with advanced robotics and posatronic applications. Even more surprisingly, the soldier had used every military credit to his name in an attempt to flag his profile for the position. The only "negative" James saw in the profile was the fact that the man had recently been re-designated as a "cyborg" with limited use of his right arm. Even though the stigma of cyverse had faded since the loss of Earth, it would hurt his chances of finding a division willing to accept him.

When James pulled up the man's picture, he wasn't surprised to learn it was the same soldier he had pulled off the battlefield. He still remembered promising to make him a new arm. *Well, now I know your name*, James thought. *Thomas Hilben, welcome to the team.* With a tap, he accepted the man's transfer application. He turned his terminal off. Thomas was the last addition his squad needed to replace the men lost in battle. He now had time for other pursuits.

Spinning in his chair, he faced Jessica, who was working on a new cybernetic trinket and humming to herself. With a satisfied smile, he picked up a box of parts he had requisitioned from the Princeps during a supply run. "Now let's see how our new design works," he said. The pair began working on a fresh cybernetic arm.

11 >> Orchestration

1/7/2454

Location: Sh'in

Karen sat impatiently as her shuttle began its descent toward the desert planet's surface. Even though the battle had been over for an entire day, the debris from the battle continued to fall, dotting the sky scape with specks of fire. The shuttle in which she rode was of a unique design, the only one of its class left among the vast human fleet. Based off an old style prospector's craft, used at the dawn of man's true space age when gravity stream drives were completed, the craft was perfectly suited for airborne analysis of construction and cleanup operations on both small and large scales. It had a large bulbous forward compartment with sensors displaying a broad spectrum of detailed geographic data, providing her with an almost panoramic view of the land below and the ability to amplify and analyze any section of the map with a constant stream of details.

The middle-aged woman had more experience with construction and operations than anyone in the fleet. Before the Harvester War, she had been the central operations officer of one of the largest development firms in the colonies, making a fortune easily capable of putting all the titans of industry from previous centuries to shame. With the onset of war, Karen had offered her unstoppable intellect to the combined human forces. She had been called one of the most constructively deadly individuals in the history of mankind because of how she had revolutionized the arms industry.

She was, in fact, the lead designer and chief engineer on the massive Echelon station, out of which the Cerberus project as well as the MIC project had been based. The implementation of the MICs, or military industrial complex, was one of the primary methods through which humanity succeeded in analyzing, developing, and quickly and successfully incorporating designs based on Harvester tech into their fleet. Once deployed, a MIC could support an entire fleet with everything from structural components and equipment to fresh fighters and small craft. The stations supported a fully functional medical complex capable of almost limitless expansion, provided the station's resources were dedicated to that purpose alone. The station's greatest weakness was its single deployment nature: once established, a station could never again enter gravity stream. In order for the heavy-duty machinery inside the craft to function, the station had to be locked down to prohibit a reversal of the process. In short, when the station was deployed, it became a permanent satellite station—unmovable, save for several small maneuvering thrusters.

Karen still couldn't figure out how Commander Nielson had got his MIC to enter GS, let alone the level of speed and time it had endured before being tethered to the Princeps, allowing the massive vessel's engines to take the burden. As she subconsciously considered the physics involved between two structures moving in concert at faster-than-light speeds, she saw a flash and a mass of movement on the edge of her screen. The two behemoths had arrived. The last MIC in existence was about to take up its second permanent home—above a desert alien planet several months from Earth at maximum GS, among a region of space swarming a hostile alien horde. She was only able to gaze at the ships for a second before her screens blanked and the pilot informed her that their shuttle was entering the atmospheric burn zone. The turbulence only lasted a second, and the pilot seemed pleased. Her screens quickly restarted, and her topographical maps became much more detailed.

The devastation on the planet below had been minimal by the standards of the Harvester War. It was probably due to the lack of planetary structures; it had been a field battle. Like the ancient wars at the dawn of the gun, the remaining carnage of man and beast clearly showed the path the struggle had taken. It ended with a massive crater in the far corner of the valley. The mile-wide hole still billowed smoke as the ground continued to release parched carbon. Even though the surviving human forces and the refugees of the downed colony ship had been working tirelessly to clear the bodies from the field and burn them before rot could take hold and spread disease, the field was still littered with corpses. Not surprisingly, the heaviest concentration of alien corpses surrounded a group of heavily armored drop ships from the Fifty-sixth; some had begun calling them the Immortals.

Karen resumed her analysis of the carnage and the mangled colony ship. Her craft continued its path over the valley before landing in the center of a row of freshly erected military constructs, most of which were being used as triage facilities for those wounded in the battle. The flow of men needing immediate care ebbed, however, and more and more of the structures changed to an organizational nature. A few temporary barracks had even been erected. The survey skiff smoothly swiveled itself between a hospital construct and the regional command post. After a few moments, Karen could hear the engines shut off and the rear-loading ramp extend. Ducking through the banks of sensors and equipment in the craft's rear, she was met by a young officer who, by the relatively intact state of his uniform, had clearly not been a participant in the recent battle with the Tarin'Tal.

A strong wind had been blowing through the valley, and most of the smoke and the foul odor of cooked flesh had been blown away. The strong scent of rich dirt remained. The ground, parched as it was, lay covered in a thin layer of the local equivalent of grass. Intermixed with the ground covering were numerous stalky plants, their stems and bases resembling that of corn but covered with bunches of what looked like grainy clusters of nuts. "Sand nuts," the officer said, jerking Karen from her thoughts.

"Pardon?" she asked.

"The guys have been calling them sand nuts. Don't eat them. Some of the numbskulls tried 'em before they could be sent to the labs." His face curved in a barely restrained mask of devious humor. "They still haven't come back from the latrines."

Karen worried about the men and the dangers of eating unknown plants. "They did get checked by a doctor, didn't they?"

Laughing, the officer reassured her. "Oh, yes. They ran straight to the emergency tent when their insides decided they wanted to be on the outside. The doc took one scan and found that, in its natural state, the plant is a powerfully harsh laxative. Said that as long as they drink a whole lot of water tonight, they should be just fine. A little hungry and flushed out, but fine."

Reassured, Karen made an entry in her mental journal. *Unless I am really stopped up, don't eat the plants!* Their conversation came to an abrupt halt as they entered the command tent.

The young officer saluted the guard inside.

The other man returned the salute. "Thank you. You have been reassigned to the field." The soldier's face instantly soured, reminding Karen of a man who'd been sentenced to a life of latrine duty. Of course, she couldn't blame him; he had just been told that he would be spending the next few days burning the dead bodies of humans and aliens.

As her escort left the tent amid a string of almost inaudible curses, a tall man with the worn features of a career military man walked up to her and introduced himself as Sergeant Nathanial Taft. "Mrs. Emerson, please follow me. We have a full briefing prepared."

Thus far Karen had been told only that she had been tasked with the construction of a planetary base and preliminary sustenance attention along with the initial management of all planetary activities. *Geez! Why can't these people speak English? What's so hard about saying that they need me to build a base, get some food, and keep things in order?* she thought. "What have you got for me?" she asked, as they began winding down a series of halls filled with communications equipment. The older man began to explain the situation.

"As you know, the fleet is suffering from an extreme food shortage. Regent Tinek has informed us that this planet is rich in large herbivorous life that easily fulfills the nutritional needs of his people. Analysis of the creatures has determined that they are safe for human consumption. Your first priority is to establish a complex to gather these creatures, initially for immediate slaughter, but also for a medium- and long-term domestication program."

Taft led Karen to the center of a small room full of displays and computers. Once the pair had positioned themselves in a circle on the floor, Sergeant Taft commanded the computer to display the current mission objectives.

Responding to his words, the room darkened, the door closed, and the banks, displays, and consoles came to life. A sphere around the pair shimmered and solidified to create a dome of holographic projection displaying a three-hundred-sixty-degree view with more information than anyone could quickly absorb. Sergeant Taft explained the setup.

"We designed this interphase from your lab from the Cerberus project. Here is a pair of holo-tactile gloves; the display should respond the same as your old lab. We have all your preferred settings on file." A surprised note of satisfaction escaped Karen as she slipped on the perfectly fitting gray gloves. The second she snapped the strap shut on her gloves, the program began running through an automated system check, ending with a choice between an additional manual check or the initiation of a detailed mission analysis. With a flick of her wrist, the system began cycling through topographical information, land-based assets, orbital assets, personnel, and all other resources that could possibly be used in the effort to provide food to the starving fleet as quickly as possible.

For several hours the computer continued displaying available assets. Karen remained in the center of the room, examining a dynamic map of the planet that displayed its weather patterns, topography, animal and plant life, and every piece of information Karen would need. Sergeant Taft remained present, monitoring the flow of information and ensuring that everything displayed on her screens was the most current and accurate.

Finally, the flow of information ceased, leaving Karen alone in the dark. She took a long pause. After centering herself, she began to orchestrate the information on her screens, arraying the constructs that had formed themselves in her mind in brilliant harmony. Each resource was placed in alignment with the others to create an optimum efficiency that not even a computer could manage. This was not a resource operation to Karen, nor was it a job. It was not even a means to sustain her race. It was an art form, a way to express the flow of man and machine to produce new, interesting, and beautiful things. To her, creating supply chains and bringing order from chaos was as harmonious as the greatest piece of music and more beautiful than the finest piece of art.

Karen became completely engrossed in her designs. Her hands interacted with the holograms, allowing her to seamlessly meld her mind and medium, providing a conduit through which her thoughts and ordered creations could flow into the database. The volume of data and speed of such a task would drive most people insane, but somehow Karen was able to sustain and comprehend the flow of information with a grace that was as natural to her as breathing. Chaos flowed in, and order flowed out as her fingers danced along the edge of the holographic dome. She pulled schematics, labor statistics, and resource availabilities into existence, changing them at will until a finished product began to take space. More than ten hours later, Karen placed the finishing touches on the final piece of the puzzle: the designs for a new skimmer. With a wave of her hand, the display receded from existence, the lights came back, and the door opened.

Karen slumped into a chair in the corner, utterly exhausted. "Coffee?" Sergeant Taft asked.

"Yes!" Karen said in relief. Taft tapped a series of buttons on his console, and a robotic office assistant entered the room, providing a large steaming cup of thick black liquid. It wasn't true coffee. That luxury had run out after only a month in space. This "coffee" was a chemical concoction designed to provide the body with amino acids, caffeine, adrenaline, and a vitamin complement yielding an unparalleled boost of energy. It tasted like a combination of motor oil and bovine fecal matter, but it helped though. It helped a lot.

"I assume that it's finished, ma'am?"

"For now." She nodded.

"Shall we start sending the orders?"

"No, just authorize my system. I have preprogrammed everything I need to begin the project. Other than construction, however, I need forty system operators to screen problems. Everything important must be forwarded to my communications relay."

Sergeant Taft pressed a series of keys and informed the computer that Karen's programmed commands had complete military authorization. Throughout the entire human fleet, thousands of commanders received simultaneous orders. The fleet, which had been licking its wounds since the battle, blossomed into action. Most of the human craft had been repaired and rested; they were ready, and they were hungry. The MIC had finished deploying, the Princeps was actively transferring raw materials to the station, and mules were busy dragging debris from the previous battle into the smelting plant on the exterior of the MIC.

The Exile Empire

A swarm of atmospheric-capable crafts descended on the planet, using everything from high-intensity lasers to mono-directional shields as they carved foundations for new structures. Troop ships landed personnel with engineering and construction experience, and the engineers, robotic fabricators, and colonists from the Explorator buzzed through construction zones, rearranging prefabricated structures into various forms to produce the much needed food.

With Taft providing support, Karen exhaustedly made her way back to the survey vessel. In moments, they were stationary above the largest construction site, directing some of the bigger operations that were too complicated for the computer to orchestrate. The margin of error and human involvement produced far too many unknown factors for it to handle. Having taken advantage of individual expertise and efficient accountability structures, Karen had, for at least the time being, successfully directed the entirety of mankind toward a singular goal.

Sergeant Taft put a hand on Karen's shoulder. "Karen, you need to rest. You have been working for twenty hours straight."

She shrugged his hand off with a sound of exasperation. "No, I don't. I'm fine."

"No, you're not," he protested. "If you don't rest, I will be required to relieve you of command. Your judgment may become impaired through extreme exhaustion."

"There is nothing wrong with my judgment!" she snapped.

"I did not say that there is," he replied calmly. "Just that you need rest. I will wake you if there is a major problem."

Karen seemed to relax, realizing her physical state was interfering with her work. She hated that. "Maybe for a few hours." Karen made her way to the cot in the rear of the survey craft and barely lay down before falling into an exhausted sleep.

When Karen awoke, she felt as if she had slept for a few hours, but the clock said that it was morning of the next day, more than fourteen hours later. It was midday on the moon, and work had progressed without cessation throughout the local night and excessively long morning. As Karen entered the forward compartment of the craft, Taft handed her a cup of "coffee" and a piece of meat.

"The first fruits, ma'am," he greeted her cheerfully.

The coffee was as expected; the meat, however, was surprisingly good. It had the gamey nature of elk or deer but tasted earthy and mild like a bean. It wasn't the best thing she had ever tasted, but compared to the preserved nutrients the fleet had been surviving on for the past few months, it was heaven. After a few minutes, Karen felt more alert and returned to the project at hand. "Status?" she asked.

"The mobile operations are performing as expected. They have already produced enough meat to supply half the fleet with a solid meal. The foundation and initial frameworks for nine hundred structures has been laid, and the MIC has begun to turn out the first of the modified skimmers, which has greatly increased the rate at which the camps are turning out meat."

For the first time since the exile, Karen smiled. "Good. And the agricultural facility?"

"Operational. Ma'am, are you sure about this instant privatization? Wouldn't it be more efficient to retain control of the supply lines at least until the crisis has been averted?"

Karen huffed. "The desire for profit doesn't slow in an emergency, Nate…is it okay if I call you Nate?"

"Yes, ma'am." The soldier nodded.

"Good. With the implementation of a planet-wide credit system, the administrators can take the construction costs as loans from the fleet. Workers can take similar loans for their personal equipment, creating incentives to produce as quickly as possible. The faster they pay them off, the faster they start earning real money for the first time in years. With week-long loan terms and instant foreclosure penalties, there is every incentive for the best workers in the best jobs to produce the greatest amount of product in the shortest time. It may not be pretty, but it will fix the problem. Additionally, after the crisis has been averted, we'll have a fully functional agricultural industry separate from communal control and all the problems that it has historically created. This is the reason they hired me, Nate. They didn't want a repeat of the Celestas or Orion incidents."

Karen and Nate sat in silence, watching a symphony of man and machine as the infant industry rose from the dusty land in concert with Karen's masterful plan.

The redesigned prefabricated structures were developed as fast as a child's sand castle. But instead of the brittle fragility commonly associated with haste, these structures could withstand the gale-force sandstorms of the moon's desert seasons. The roofs sloped gently and lay low to the ground, protecting the recessed structure below. Large doors pivoted inward reminiscent of old Earth barns, exposing ramps to the naturally cool workspaces below. The large grounds surrounding each structure were provided with water to facilitate either grazing land or agricultural produce.

All four colony ships were working around the clock to bring Earth's old staples back into existence, using their stasis chambers, cloning labs, and genetic libraries. The structures were arranged independent of each other, taking into account future growth and the domestication of the large indigenous herbivores, which some of the men gathering them had already dubbed "abes."

Karen took a moment to read the report a low-ranking officer had found time to write describing how the name had come about. The first people to catch some of the beasts had said they looked like alien buffalo. In almost no time, the name had been shortened to AB as an abbreviation. When workers saw this abbreviation, they started calling them abes, pronouncing the two letters as one word. Since then, the name had stuck. Turning back to her real work, Karen noted, with satisfaction, that the colony ship's reanimation of earth staples, such as wheat and corn, continued on schedule.

Already Karen had received a plethora of entrepreneurial requests, almost all of which she had authorized. As it turned out, if the grains from the "sand nuts" were lightly toasted, the plant lost its laxative quality, and its nutrients were open to be exploited and consumed. Unfortunately, it had a bland taste similar to sand. *Well, at least we don't need to change the name*, she thought.

"Karen," Taft interrupted. "I have a request for a hops farm. Apparently one of the mercenary vessels had three whole seed shipments in storage when the exile began."

"Let me see," she said, swiveling her chair to view the communication.

"Actually, they would like to talk to you if you're willing."

"Uh…okay, I'll bite. Put them on." As she swiveled back to the main station, the display of the land below was replaced with the bridge of a rather large mercenary transport craft.

"I'm sorry, gentlemen. While I admire your spirit, we don't have the resources to spare on beer."

A short man with a large belly, white hair, and a fading red beard moved forward to fill most of her screen. "Ah am well aware o' that, ma'am, but we don't need any o' the fleet's stuff. Our lunker don't wanna run no more, and our seeds were modified for just such a climate as this little spot we found up north. We could just use wha' we've got. The fleet assignment cannot use our equipment for production, said its incompatible or whatnot. Me boys are bored outa their skulls, and it would do wonders for the fleet's morale jus ta know that someone, somewhere, is workin' on brewin' real beer. The military boys already took everything useful for fighting from our ship to overhaul those, eh, battle mules is what they're callen 'em. Our engines are burnt to ah crisp so we can't GS no more. We got the stuff for et. We were chartered to supply the materials for three breweries. What dya say, ma'am? Give a lad and his boys a chance?"

Taft leaned over with a fairly desirous look in his eyes. "I don't see what it would hurt, ma'am," he said eagerly. "The fleet would lose nothing more than a few idle hands." Before he could say anything more, a priority alert cut him off and interrupted the communication signal. The mercenary captain was displaced, and his image slid to the left. The space was filled with Admiral Hancock's sulking features. "Emerson, I think you should do what he says; the fleet could use the morale boost."

A slightly annoyed look came over Karen's face, followed by a refreshing smile. "I was already going to authorize it, Admiral," Karen quipped, as she stood and put her hands on her hips. "It's a no-brainer. Captain…um—"

"Torry, ma'am," the freighter captain prompted, a hopeful look in his eyes.

"Captain Torry, you have full authorization. Any unclaimed or plotted land you can plant or build on will count as your loan, with a matching endowment depending on how good your beer tastes."

"Thank 'e kindly, ma'am! We won't disappoint!" The sounds of celebration erupted behind the pseudo-Irish captain as the communication shut off.

"And you, Admiral, we need to talk about you eavesdropping on my conversations."

A broad smile spread across the man's face. "Oh, I wasn't eavesdropping, Emerson. The word *beer* came to me through space and time, and I couldn't resist." Karen and the admiral had a good chuckle, and the communication cut off. *Okay,* Karen thought. *In the last twenty-four hours, I've set up an agricultural industry composed of abe ranching, lax farming, and hops. And I've found out that the admiral has a soft spot for the dark and frothy stuff. All in all, not a bad day. Not bad at all.*

1/7/2454

Location: Orbit above Sh'in

Commander Casey Nielson sat in the makeshift bridge of the now mobile MIC base, wondering how he was going to get his craft's engines to work again. It was a miracle that he'd been able to make his station GS capable before the Death had arrived. He was the only commander who had successfully brought an MIC to GS after being deployed. It had taken the engines from more than three hundred frigates, but his crew had been able to cobble together enough power to crawl their way out of the Sol System ahead of the Death onslaught. His standing orders were to keep his craft moving. Even with its supporting tethers to the Princeps, his craft would tear violently into normal space if it couldn't maintain at least a quarter of the thrust necessary for GS.

While the base's massive fusion/fission and antimatter reactors produced more than enough energy, the problems came in distributing the power and keeping the engines operational. Before the exile, they'd had enough time to fabricate the immense power lines it had taken to run the huge engines. They had even removed some of the structural components required for the construction of anything at least frigate-sized and attached them to the exterior of the base to prevent violent destabilization in GS. It wasn't pretty, but they had done it. The cobbled-together propulsion system for the MIC had worked. Unfortunately, the cables, which had not been designed for such intense and consistent use, had finally given out. This made his task of keeping the MIC mobile problematic. Casey would need to deploy the craft to fabricate the conduits, but deployment would permanently prevent the MIC's mobility. He had barely got the thing moving the first time. There was no way he could do it a second.

Nielson was pondering several unconventional methods of keeping the craft mobile when his communication terminal began to go wild. "Sir, we are receiving orders to deploy."

Casey looked up, more in annoyance than anything. "Please remind the admiral that such an act will invalidate our previous directive. We will no longer be able to keep or retain mobility once we have been deployed." The officer listened a second more before continuing.

"They understand, sir. We are to proceed with deployment. We have also received orders to activate the light craft production bays, the smelting bay, and the recycling bay. They said to be prepared for exotic alloys."

"They aren't going to have us use that stinking wreckage, are they?" Casey asked in disgust.

After listening to the line for another second, the tech's nose wrinkled in disgust. "It appears so, sir."

"I barely kept this station alive, and they want me to pollute it with unknown alien garbage?"

"Sir?" the officer said, slightly shocked at his superior's outburst.

"I know, I know. Bring us into a geosynchronous orbit above the Explorator and begin the deployment. Watch for any unusual activity in the port rotational platforms. Inform work crews twenty-two through eighty to begin separation and reintegration of the main factory components. Send their desired schematics to my office. Jack, Sarah, Julie, join me in my office. Well..." Casey mumbled, as he began to walk off, "at least I don't need to get her moving again."

The bridge exploded in activity as the station's commander and his three chief engineers headed toward the main design room. Displays, blueprints, and readouts blanketed every surface, but Nielson still insisted on calling it his office. Outside, the station unfolded from the diamond shape it had been locked into during the voyage. A contingent of true worker bees, not mules, began to stream out of the craft's exposed ports, heading toward the cobbled engines and stored production equipment. The engines were easily separated from the MIC. As the cables to the Princeps were removed, the massive station was left to the mercy of its orbit and the planetoid's gravity. The ship's segments continued unfolding until a multi-tiered, circular base took shape. As the ship began locking itself down into the station, Nielson and his engineers were hard at work bringing the designs to life. Although the plans for the ship they had been tasked to build were preliminary, the group easily discerned the skiff's intended functions. It was an elongated low-altitude skimmer designed for short bursts of speed, and it was equipped with robotic arms to capture the abes on the planet below.

The crew had every necessary component except for the materials required for the fabrication of the craft's hull. The craft was an extremely simple design, containing only two large hatches, rear and below, and a decently sized segmented cargo bay. The bottom hatch contained a series of robotic tentacles, agile enough to snag the animals as they passed by, while strong enough to haul their weight neatly into the craft. The only additional measure necessary was a method of delivering sedatives to the animals to keep them under control. One of the tentacles could serve this purpose in addition to its normal tasks. *Ha ha ha*, Casey thought to himself, *they want me to make a cowboy skimmer!* Liking the name as it came to him, Nielson walked up to the display and wrote "cowboy skimmer" in the title slot.

That got a good chuckle from his staff, but they still had a major problem: the material for the chassis of the craft. Nielson remembered the three hundred half-built frigates rusting in the belly of the station. The same incomplete frigates he had torn the engines from to achieve grav stream. *Perhaps those rust buckets haven't outlived their usefulness.* "Whooo, boy! Those are going to make some u-g-l-y skimmers!" he whooped. "Julie, pull up the schematics on the frigate hulks down in the bays." With a quickness that meant she shared his thoughts, the hulks appeared on the room's large screen.

"Computer, analyze and apply necessary segments on the equivocal segments of the specified chassis. Align and present." After a second, the large crystalline display shifted and contorted to portray an ugly blocky craft with disproportionate doors and panels. "All right, people! This is going to take some work."

After several hours and two office droids full of coffee, Nielson and his team stood back, looked at their finished designs, and took a deep breath. "Here it goes. Hit it, Jack!"

Jack activated the prototype production bay. It was much faster than the production floor, but it lacked integrity that long-term manufacturing demanded. It was fast, easy to change, and amazing to watch. With the precision of machines and the artistic talent of the bay's human operators, it spun and rotated as it received suspended frigate chassis welding, meshing, and wiring until a finished skimmer sat on the bay floor no more than a half hour later.

"Sir…it's hideous!" Jack said in disgust.

Sarah and Julie began to play along and seemingly in concert blurted out, "Oh, the humanity! It's an abomination! What have we done? We simply must kill it and take it out of its misery."

Casey Nielson rolled his eyes in exasperation. "Oh, come on, you guys, it's not that bad. Not our most beautiful creation, but it will fly and snag those beasts off the plains just fine." Casey walked over to the craft and began testing its systems. After fussing for a few minutes, a sound of unadulterated frustration came out of him. "Signal the Princeps for a large transport, and prepare my mobile lab and communications post. We are going for a ride."

Within an hour, Casey was driving his new creation down the transport's long ramp and onto the unending plains of Sh'in, ready to find and fix design flaws in a trial-by-fire field test. His team had already set up his observation and design posts and had a string of sensors arrayed along a long path. Without waiting, Casey gunned the engines. The craft lurched forward along the string of sensors accelerating from zero to seventy in just under two seconds. That's when the problems started. The craft began to list dangerously to the side and lose altitude, causing it to slide awkwardly through the air. Its acceleration ceased, and the skiff slammed into the ground at a dangerous speed, far too fast for the craft's limited inertial stabilizers to compensate.

Casey was flung against the forward window that he had built to save time and limited sensor equipment. The craft's weight was the only thing preventing it from cartwheeling down the field as it dug a trough in the dusty earth. With its forward left extensions gouging the land, the skimmer slid to a halt, leaving a long, ugly scar in the land.

Furious, Casey climbed from the craft, bleeding from his forehead and muttering to himself. "Did you get that?" he yelled.

His team rushed over to him, concerned for both their commander and their creation. "Are you all right, sir?"

Casey ignored the question. "Did you get that?"

On the verge of tears, Julie pulled a pad from her belt and looked over a few numbers. "Yes, I got everything, every sensor's angle…Casey, you almost died!"

"No, I didn't. Now show me the pad!" Snatching the pad from the young woman's quivering hands, he muttered about power relays, sensor imbalances, and posatronic interference. "Jack, check for damage! Sarah, check the robotic arms. I think their posatronic relays are interfering with the sensors and stabilization systems. *Thank God, we didn't use a conventional navigation display or this design would have been shot, and I would've been dead.* Julie, stop crying and call the medics. I don't want to bleed on the equipment."

He stomped off toward the equipment banks as a swarm of mechanics and medics descended on the scene. Casey's head only required a quick patch; the cut hadn't made it past his skin. If he had fractured his skull, the master engineer would have been out for at least a day, and he had neither the time nor patience for such a delay.

As he walked over to his equipment, Casey batted away medical personnel who tried to scan his eyes and head to check for additional damage. Eventually he gave up and let them scan him just so they would leave him alone. After the techs were satisfied that there wouldn't be any lasting damage, they melted into the background, allowing the young officer to work.

Scanning the wealth of data caught by the sensors during the crash, Casey was able to determine which of the craft's systems had failed. His initial assessment of robotic interference had proven correct: there just wasn't a way to reconcile the level of posatronics necessary for a fully automated grappling system with the high intensity sensors and operational equipment the craft required for atmospheric speed and agility. On the verge of utter failure, Casey got out his metaphorical shears and removed everything not entirely necessary from the skimmer.

Casey removed more than half of the intelligence from the robotic arms and left only enough to grab the abe, relegating the target placement and speed compensation to human operators. He cut out almost all the craft's sensors other than the landing and targeting scanners for the arm operator. Within another hour and a half, he and his team had ripped out the majority of the craft's high-level technology, leaving nothing but a highly mobile abe-snatching machine. The result did not look anything like the craft Karen had initially requested, but it did everything that they needed. The craft would take a six-person crew instead of two, but it would get the job done.

Once again climbing into the craft as his own test pilot, Casey slammed on the accelerator, now controlled by him instead of a computer. Without a hitch, the ugly craft slid across the landscape, effortlessly gliding wherever he directed it. He hit the accelerator all the way. Responding to his command, the new craft rocketed forward, screaming across the dusty landscape at 100, 200, 400, 600, 800, 1000, 1500—the craft accelerated exponentially until it reached just under 23,000 miles per hour. Casey became engrossed in the thrill of the speed and tried to push until the craft's engines were maxed out. It blistered across the landscape, tearing up a long stretch of the native prairie with the pressure wave caused by its velocity. When the craft began to exude, wrenching and twisting sounds under the strains of its speed while passing through a proto sandstorm, Casey eased the throttle down, coming back below the sound barrier. He swiveled back toward the test site, racing back at a more sedated speed

"All right, boys, let's put her to work at what we made her for!" He slammed the speed down as they approached a herd of abes, swiveling the craft to float above the beasts as they began to stampede. With a signal, the operator grabbed an abe as effortlessly as a man scooping a puppy from the floor and placed it in one of the built-in pens. It was unhappy but sedated and unharmed. As Casey watched the herd below and listened to the celebratory *whoop* from the engineer in the back compartment, he couldn't help but sing the old Earth tune, "Get along little doggy. It's your misfortune and none of my own!" Smiling from ear to ear, he hit his communications console. "Jack! Get on the horn and send up the plans. Get the factory humming. We got ourselves a cowboy!"

13 >> Scale

1/10/2454

Location: Orbit above Sh'in

Captain Cormac Kincade sat in one of the gunners' seats as the frigate slowly rose from the encampment. It had taken several days, but his men were finally patched and settled in one of the new barracks on the planetoid. Cormac was impressed and pleased with his men's performance. They had maintained better than a one-to-one ratio of losses with the alien forces. Every other force in the fleet had lost four or five to one against the huge beasts. Maybe it was the new tactics they had employed. Maybe it had been the new armor—it had certainly helped—or maybe he just had a good lot of men. Cormac hoped that it was all three. At least his men could rest now. They certainly deserved it. Some of them looked like they could sleep for a week, especially James and his unusually cliquish squads, who exerted themselves at an inhuman level.

James had taken down twenty-three of those monsters himself, which was surprisingly close to his own twenty-six. The boy's three squads had seen some of the most intense fighting of the battle and had lost only six out of thirty men. He was vicious on the battlefield but somehow maintained order and coordination among his men, leaving Cormac with only one conclusion: the kid had some serious potential. James reminded Cormac of himself; that is, if he had been an angry Irish-German kid who had lost his family.

The frigate he was riding had been pressed into service as a temporary cargo hauler. Such a huge volume of men, machine, and supplies were moving up and down from the planetoid-moon that they had run out of the plentiful cargo haulers and were resorting to military vessels. Cormac had even heard rumors concerning the possibility of the fleet landing a second colony ship farther to the north. Most of the civilians in the fleet were fed up with wandering space in cramped ships, and this vast desert prairie had started to look like a slice of heaven. There were even rumors about severe unrest aboard the Sacagawea, the most populous ship in the fleet.

As the frigate exited the last of the planet's atmosphere, Cormac watched hundreds of ships flowing up and down from the planet to the starships. The majority of them entered and exited the massive bays of the Princeps and the MIC. Both the ship and station had proven invaluable to the construction efforts on the planet. The benefits had been tangible to his men, not useless information. His division had got a full dinner of meat stew—with real meat—and they had slept in newly erected barracks.

His men's greatest problem was a lack of proficient cybernetic engineers for their armor. They had all been taking lessons from James, but of all the boy's qualities, "technical instructor" was not one of them. Although the suits had protected his men, they took an incredible beating, and most of the heavy-duty equipment required for maintenance was still in transit from the Santa Monica.

It was amazing. The entire ship was being dismantled in space and trucked to the planet to construct the new city. It would be several more days before they could reassemble the training bay into a much larger base on the moon's surface. While he wasn't complaining, it would have been nice to have his unit operational as soon as possible. If there was one thing Captain Kincade hated, it was letting his men sit around at less-than-optimal combat readiness. It made him feel foolishly exposed, like mooning a cobra.

He spent several more moments watching the parade of vessels until his own craft reached the main hangar aboard the Cerberus. The battleship's ability to house, supply, and maintain fighter and light craft contingents was minuscule compared to the Princeps, but its hangar was still an impressive feat of human engineering. Once aboard, Cormac wound his way through the crowded flight deck, full of off-duty personnel embarking on leave to the planetoid below. The city was still little more than a shantytown for a hastily created agrarian industry, but they already had a bazaar, food, and the most important thing to humanity in its current situation—room to spare. It didn't matter who they were, whether they served aboard the Cerberus or sat playing poker on one of the rusty refugee hulks—the one thing everyone wanted was legroom.

The battleship was so large that it had its own internal transportation network, a form of frictionless rail that glided smoothly between levels and sections of the craft. Stepping aboard and informing the navigations console of his desired destination, the system quickly confirmed his identity. The advanced systems simultaneously scanned his retinas, fingerprints, even his genetic profile in a fraction of a heartbeat. The transit symbol blinked green, and the pod sped toward the command deck with mechanical efficiency. Even at the impressive speed at which the pod traveled, the journey still took ten minutes.

The doors opened to a hub similar to the one he had left, only this one had four heavily armored security guards. With more than a little satisfaction, he noticed that they had begun using a few pieces of equipment pioneered and promoted by his unit.

One of the guards stepped forward and held a thin pen-like device in front of him. The device scanned Cormac in more detail, but it flashed green in the same manner. Cormac pondered the long-term effects of those scanners, which he assumed couldn't be healthy, as the silent guard motioned for him to follow. They proceeded down a wide corridor. After passing between several more security guards and checkpoints, he was scanned twice more. Receiving a very sour look from an obviously disgruntled secretary, Cormac found himself in the entryway to the bridge.

The doors were reinforced, and contained more than six interlocking layers. They were designed to withstand an internal battle for control of the ship, and Captain Kincade believed they could do just that. The bridge itself was a massive circle with three tiers, all open to each other in the center where a dozen chairs sat. Each chair had more communications equipment than Cormac had ever seen on a piece of furniture, and they looked highly uncomfortable. They were clustered around a central holographic projector, which could present a flat image, a single three-dimensional image, or a dynamic battle map to each chair.

A large older gentleman sat in the biggest chair facing the bow of the ship. He stood and quickly made his way over to Cormac. "Colonel Kincade! Congratulations on your victory!" the admiral almost shouted, as he handed the shocked soldier an insignia doubling his rank and greatly magnifying his responsibility.

"What you did with those men worked, and we need you to do it again. Follow me." The admiral led Cormac back down the length of the bridge to the holographic display. "Please take a seat, Colonel."

Settling into one of the excessively wired monstrosities, the admiral initiated a sequence of commands on his chair, and the projector sprang to life.

Flowing with the liquid grace of water, the screen formed itself into a recording from the land battle. "As you can see, Colonel, this footage is from the Fourteenth, which was engaged in some of the heaviest fighting, besides your unit." The screen showed a grotesque spectacle, more of a wholesale slaughter than a battle. "They overran the entire unit and burnt all three drop ships in under fifteen minutes. Only twenty men survived, all severely wounded, and nineteen died of their wounds within twenty-four hours. One man out of three hundred, Colonel! We simply cannot afford losses like that."

The scene ended when one of the Tarin'Tal warriors blasted the camera with one of their heat weapons. "And this is the Eighteenth." The screen showed a similar rout. "The Eleventh, the Twentieth, and the Seventy-seventh were all eradicated within minutes of contact with the enemy. Your division was the only one to maintain favorable odds with the Tarin'Tal warriors, and our statistics have shown that your armor can take up to seven hits and continue functioning. The only thing that kept our forces from utter annihilation before air support arrived was their shields. We need you to train more divisions in your techniques and armor. The MIC has already begun a line of suits similar to the Fifty-sixth's. I believe your boy, James, helped them with the designs. The commander is quite impressed with the young lad. He seemed quite disappointed that he couldn't convince him to work on the MIC."

Cormac felt a surge of almost fatherly pride at the boy's abilities. "Yes, sir. Lieutenant Ursidae is one of the most brilliant men I have had under my command; battle is an art form to him." The admiral nodded in agreement, emphasizing the point with a light grunt.

"Well, I'm sure you can find ways to exploit that brilliance with him under your command, Colonel."

"Indeed I will, sir."

"Good. I have placed the First, Second, and Third directly under your command. You are to do to them exactly what you have done for the Fifty-sixth. The Fifty-sixth will also remain under your command, so feel free to move personnel at will. You can train your men from the new planetary base, which will also be under your jurisdiction. Lieutenant Colonel McAlister and Lieutenant Colonel Johnson will help you with any organization, personnel, and equipment you require. Any questions, Colonel?"

"None, sir," Cormac said, snapping a salute. "How soon do you need them ready?"

"ASAP, Colonel. I understand the difficulty in training new troops, but these aren't green recruits. They are our most hardened divisions with the highest density of technological know-how. I have given you the largest brain and brawn available to humanity. Please don't waste it."

"No, sir," Cormac said, shaking his head solemnly.

"Excellent. Dismissed, Colonel, and good luck."

With that, Cormac spun and headed out the way he had come. Three months ago, he had been a lieutenant, and now he was a colonel. *At least the fleet doesn't lack career opportunities,* he thought with a smirk, expressed only by a crease at the edge of his mouth. The responsibility he had just been handed weighed heavily on him. Cormac was uncertain; the only direct instruction he had ever given before the Fifty-sixth was small-group martial arts and tactical training, and now he was expected to train an entire military arm. He didn't know if he wanted the responsibility. He was a fighter, a one-on-one guy, but this…this was just too big.

His head was swimming with the enormity of the events and the options he had to consider when training new men. His mind was so full of confusion, concern, and possibilities that he barely noticed he had reached the hangar where the frigate waited to take him back to the surface. He didn't even see the other two officers climb into the craft until they had been seated. A strong female voice roused him from his thoughts.

"Sir, your insignia." Cormac looked at his hand where he still held the silver eagle for the rank of colonel and quickly placed it on his collar. The woman who had spoken was a tall, early middle-aged woman with dark red hair and a very athletic build. "Lieutenant Colonel McAlister, sir. Equipment and Operations. This is Lieutenant Colonel Johnson, head of Supply and Personnel."

The other man in the craft greeted him with a short, "Sir."

The woman handed Cormac a data pad. "This is a list of all available resources for the construction of the new armor, along with all base facilities to be completed within the week. I also have a full list of weaponry and posatronic assistance systems available for the command. The fleet, however, is far short of the systems required for onboard assistants. The MIC is capable of fabricating them, but we will need to wait for additional materials from the surface before production can commence. Karen Emerson has been apprised of the situation and is in the process of establishing a resource operation for the required materials."

Cormac looked at the pad, obviously relieved to find he had competent personnel running the nuts and bolts of the base. "Our job is to take care of everything not directly related to the training of your men, sir. The admiral believes this will allow you to get the units operational as quickly as possible."

"Good." Cormac was quickly starting to believe that he might be able to accomplish the task he had been given. If all he had to do was train and work with his men, he just might be able to get them ready in time for some real deployment.

The three sat in silence through the remainder of the flight. McAlister watched the landscape below. Johnson worked diligently on his data pad, orchestrating supplies and materials for McAlister and Colonel Kincade. To digest the enormity of his assignment, Cormac began breaking it down into tasks and routines, through which he would be able to train the masses of men efficiently and quickly. The speed and agility of the frigate brought them to the new base faster than any transport in the fleet could have. Many of the large structures throughout the base were still under construction. To his satisfaction, Cormac saw that the training field had been assembled; it had been the only task he had left to his men for the day. James had motivated the men to complete the project by midday with the promise of unplanned leave for the afternoon and an evening in the fledgling city. It had worked well.

The base was abuzz with activity by the construction crews from MIC. The Princeps's and the Explorator's colonists were building a huge hospital that would provide medical services for the new city. Mounds of sandy dirt with a light red tint appeared throughout the camp. Several mules attempted to spread the piles across the grounds, although without much success.

The trio left the craft, and it again lifted off to return to the Cerberus. The odor of turned dirt was strong in the air. It wasn't unpleasant; in fact, it reminded Cormac of Earth. Lieutenant Colonel McAlister demonstrated a similar sentiment by taking several deep breaths in obvious pleasure. It was her first time on solid ground in months. Slowly stretching, Cormac turned and led the two junior officers to the recently erected command structure.

Other than the bustle of construction crews, relatively few people remained on the base. A few soldiers milled around the barracks and the mess hall, but the majority of the men were enjoying some time stretching their legs off base. Even though it was dusk, they still had until morning before they would be back on duty for training.

The planetoid's unusual orbit around its Gas Giant, and the giant's own orbit around the star, produced unique seasons and weather. The combination of the two light and heat sources and the moon's rotational speed produced a length and quality of day much different from most planets. During the growing season, a hemisphere on the planet would enjoy a nine-hour night followed by an eleven-hour dawn, during which the land was bathed in the soft glow of the Gas Giant; then the planet's star would rise, increasing the temperature dramatically for seven hours before night returned. A partial eclipse by the giant prevented the planetoid from overheating in the light of both planet and star. The hemispheres experiencing the desert season, however, were exposed to an intensified dawn as the star's warmth was reflected to the moon along with the planet's own natural heat. During the growing season, temperatures varied between sixty and one hundred degrees during the day. In the desert season it was an oddity for the temperature to drop below eighty, and it was common to reach more than one hundred and twenty degrees. The nights, however, were consistently cold, often dropping below freezing.

Karen's foresight in recessing the buildings' lower levels below the ground reduced the need for temperature regulation equipment. While they were still necessary to make the buildings comfortable, the minimalist recessed structures were definitely livable. The dozens of buildings half sunk into the ground, dotting the landscape created an interesting sight. Cormac thought that it looked like a town built on quicksand.

Cool, refreshing air greeted the three officers when they entered the main command structure. The structure's main levels were already filled with the Fifty-sixth's equipment, and McAlister had scheduled the remaining divisions to move in during the next several days. James sat at one of the main consoles with a large pile of raw cybernetic components and a half-finished arm. "Hey, chief!" James shouted.

"Chief?" Cormac repeated in mock annoyance.

The lad played along. "Chief, sir!" He threw in a salute to cement the feigned reverence. Not comprehending the situation and uncomfortable with the colloquial relationship between the differently ranked officers, Lieutenant Colonel Johnson shuffled off to one of the subterranean levels where his equipment was actively being deposited.

Lieutenant Colonel McAlister, unlike her associate, seemed to take a liking to the young man as he came over to introduce himself. "Good evening, Colonel…?" he said, seeing her insignia but not a name tag.

"McAlister. It's a pleasure to meet you, Lieutenant Ursidae. You have an impressive file."

"Thank you, ma'am, although I can't say the same. It seems that you have an advantage in this situation."

The woman smirked. "Indeed I do; that's my job. Your ingenuity and innovation in cybernetics has been noticed at the highest levels of command." In an unusually good mood, James colored in response to the compliment as he returned to the pile of machinery.

"Thanks, that's what I do." As James settled back down in the oversized chair with his horde of cybernetics, Cormac decided it was time for serious business.

"Don't sit down, lieutenant. We have some business to attend to."

Confused, James put the arm down again and returned to his feet. "Sir?"

Cormac forced himself to keep a straight face. "Please explain to me why my base is empty of soldiers!"

James began to stutter, suddenly second guessing his actions. Quickly correcting himself and planting his feet in a regimented manner, James looked straight into Cormac's eyes and replied, "Sir, I deemed it would be excellent motivation for the men to be allowed leave for the remainder of the day once the arenas had been completed. Furthermore, after the cramped status of their previous living quarters and the mental and physical exhaustion of the battle, it seemed necessary for the men to have some decent leave, sir." Remaining in a rigid, at-ease stance, James waited for a response.

Cormac allowed a tense moment to pass before responding, "That is exactly the kind of cockamamy idea that I would expect from a division commander, not a lieutenant. Your insignia, please!" Shocked, James removed the barred pin from his collar and handed it to the larger man, who promptly threw it behind him.

"You are hereby removed of your rank as lieutenant. You have been placed in command of the Fifty-sixth mobile marine division and given the rank of captain. Your duties will begin at 0600 tomorrow morning. Is that understood?"

James was floored. "Sir, yes, sir!" James said, finally allowing his grin to break through, as Cormac gave James his own old pin.

"Now why don't you go celebrate with that girl from Ops who's always hanging around?" With a whoop, James dashed from the room, excitement exuding from every pore as he ran across the compound toward the forming city.

A moment later, Cormac and McAlister were alone in the silent control room. "So, want to go over my data with some of that sorry excuse for coffee?" Cormac suggested.

"Sounds good," she said. "Maybe they'll start growing some decent beans soon."

Cormac chuckled. "By the way, you never told me your first name," he pointed out.

"No, I haven't." Leaving him to hang, she left the hall for one of the holographic conference rooms in the back.

1/20/2454

Location: Orbit above Sh'in

Admiral Hancock sat in his command chair watching the holo image of a Tarin'Tal juggernaut as it slowly rotated on both its vertical and horizontal axes. The fleet's most recent scientific data was gathered both during the battle and from the debris afterward. Unfortunately, that data hadn't changed for the past seven hours. The combined science teams from both the Cerberus and the Princeps had hit a massive snag in the conundrum of the Tarin'Tal's cloaking shield. Despite the obviously more advanced technology of the human fleet, the Tarin'Tal around Sh'in hadn't been detected until they attacked.

With a command of "Replay," the image morphed into a distant image of the ship, which began moving when it was hit by a long string of plasma rounds from a squad of fighters. The ship's shields moved in a pulsating rhythm, attempting to slough off the assaulting energy and matter rather than absorb and redirect like human technology. The alien shields were far inferior to those used by the human fleet. Their technology seemed so antiquated that the admiral could actually see waves of material successfully diverted by the device. The wash of particles and energy that rained down on the ship through those shields, however, was testament to the frailty of their systems. It made no sense that their shields behaved so much like early versions of mankind's own, while at the same time effectively cloaking the vessel when there was no major activity within the shield's sphere of protection.

"Replay shield footage one," the admiral requested. The image morphed into another shape, but this time it was of a blank screen. A swarm of gunships appeared at the front of the screen, with several others wavering into existence behind them. Stranger still was the faint outline of a spire ship behind them— twisted and contorted by a cloak that failed to keep the structure hidden. The same ripple effect had been seen when the shield fought the plasma shells emanating from the points at which the gunships were leaving the large craft's protection. The destroyer had only got a few seconds of video before the dome erupted into color as they deflected Tarin'Tal weapons.

Without solid data, the computer could only display probabilities. It told him that the cloak seemed to work on the same principle as their shields, shifting the ship's gravity and light instead of matter and energy. The fleet's scientists had surmised that it was entirely possible that the cloak was nothing more than a fortunate byproduct of alien shield systems. It didn't really matter; all that Admiral Hancock cared about was the fact that he could not detect any of the enemy's forces unless they were expending high levels of energy or traveling in extremely large groups. Even then, they could only detect them by a special distortion as the light bypassing them was deflected, leaving an empty spot in space and a faint echo of its true gravity.

Pounding the arm of his chair in frustration, Hancock activated his communication consul and called for the commander of the Legatus. The view in his display shifted itself into a flat image portraying the features of A'ssia Harrington. "Yes, admiral?"

"Captain, we've hit a snag with the Tarin'Tal's cloaking system. We need a functional craft for our scientists to analyze and dissect."

"Understood. What are your orders?" she asked.

Tapping a command into his computer, Hancock sent a stream of data to the Legatus. "I need you and your task force to locate and capture one of their larger crafts. A juggernaut would be excellent, but anything with one of their cloak-shield systems will suffice. You have complete autonomy on this mission until you drag one of those alien trash heaps back here. What is the status of your task force?"

"The Pila and Clotho are fully operational. The Alecto is in the process of being rearmed, but its repairs are complete."

The admiral brought up a display confirming her statements, then pulled several flights of frigates onto his screen. "I will deploy two flights of frigates to assist, and the MIC has supplied you with six tugs they can attach to the fighter ports on the destroyers. Signal the Princeps to supply you with a full complement of fighters. You will also need assault troops, at least three divisions. The troop ship Toronto will accompany you on your mission. Feel free to pick the divisions."

Signaling one of her officers, A'ssia acknowledged the information before continuing. "Thank you, sir. The Tenth, Thirteenth, and Fifty-sixth should do."

The admiral hesitantly agreed. "The Fifty-sixth has undergone a change of command recently, but I will speak to Colonel Kincade."

Captain Harrington glanced down from her screen as a stream of authorizations flowed across her data pad. "Thank you, sir. My ships will be ready to depart within the hour. We'll move out as soon as the Toronto has been loaded and secured."

"Excellent. Godspeed, Captain."

"Thank you, sir." The admiral closed the link with a single tap to his consoles. The image of the Legatus's captain faded and was replaced with that of the enemy ship coming out of cloak. *If they can't catch one of those cretins soon, we are going to have some serious problems.*

James had finished running his division through its morning exercises; more than three hundred men stood on the sandy arena, dripping sweat and holding their swords in identical positions. "At ease, gentlemen! Dismissed! Go get some food." James was still having a hard time believing that he was in command of his own division. His men respected him, the food was good, and he had even got Jessica's Ops team transferred to his lead squad. Life was good.

As James walked toward the mess hall, Jessica left the command structure to meet him. She grabbed his arm as they walked and began to talk. "They are getting even better, aren't they?"

James smiled, knowing that at least a part of the improvement had come from their combined technology and training. "Yes, they are, but they still need a lot of work."

"They always will. Not everyone can be a berserker like you."

"Cormac doesn't go berserk, and he got more kills than I did."

"He was lucky."

James looked toward the training yards—still full of men Cormac was training. "No, he's just that good."

Jessica heard more than a hint of jealousy and bitterness in his voice.

Just as they were about to enter the barracks/mess hall complex, James's communicator began flashing red, accompanied by a repetitive chirping sound. "I need to take this. It's a priority signal."

Jessica entered the complex alone as James stepped behind a large pile of rubble from the building's foundation and hit a series of buttons on his cybernetic arm. His communications device snaked up toward his ear and eye, giving him the equivalent use of a holographic communications terminal. "Ursidae here."

"This is Captain Harrington. Congratulations on your promotion, Captain."

"Thank you, Captain," he replied. "But I doubt you used an encoded red level hail to give me a hallmark greeting."

The friendly grin on the vessel commander's face faded. "Correct, captain. I have been tasked with the capture of a Tarin'Tal shield device, and I need the division with the greatest punch. That would be yours, Captain. I know that you have just taken command and probably want to take time to settle into your position, but this is a top priority mission. Colonel Kincade has assured me that you would be up to the challenge. Due to the extreme risk associated with this mission, I am only asking for volunteers."

James was visibly shaking. He realized he was giving the Legatus's captain the wrong impression, so he burst out laughing.

"Thank you, Captain! I will let my men know immediately. We will be ready for your transports in fifteen minutes. Oh, and Captain, thanks for letting us in on the fun!"

Captain Harrington couldn't hide her satisfaction with James's enthusiasm. "Excellent! The transport will be waiting."

James deactivated his communicator and ran into the mess hall, calling for his men to gear up.

Five minutes later, all thirty squads of the Fifty-sixth, including their controllers, stood outside their barracks with full packs loaded for bear, or more specifically, Tarin'Tal. "Anyone who wants to go hunting, step forward!" Virtually the entire division advanced with a massive stomping sound. Three men from two separate squads, however, stood where they were. Looking at the stationary men with an expression that could melt metal, James asked, "Tired?"

After several excruciatingly uneasy seconds, the largest of the men ventured a response. "Sir, we just had a battle. Why can't they send one of the divisions that hasn't fought yet on this miss—"

Halfway through his statement, the tall man was cut short. He hung in the air suspended by James's mechanical fist. As a thin trickle of blood leaked from the man's mouth, disappearing onto the dusty ground, James growled, "You've answered your own question, coward."

James dropped him unceremoniously to the ground, tearing off the man's division patch with the same motion, and then turned to walk away. "You don't belong here," he said, his tone dripping in spite. Taking the cue from their commander, the more aggressive members of the division ripped the patches off the other two men, and they threw all three out of the squad.

As James reached the loading ramp, he turned to the division once more and flashed them a huge smile. "What are we, boys?"

As one, the division shouted, "We are the hunters!" The sound vibrated the entire platform on which they stood. James smiled again as he looked at Jessica, who was struggling not to squeal with glee. "Thought so," he said in a low, satisfied voice.

The exchange had strengthened the group's identity. There was a low murmur of anticipation as the mass of men began moving into the now landed transport. James had only one thought going through his mind as he strapped in next to Jessica: *this day just keeps getting better. At this rate, we will meet them by early afternoon.*

His happiness intensified as he looked at the eagerness his men radiated. A swell of pride hit James in a sudden wave of realization: they had never been excited to fight under Cormac. They were loyal and fierce but had never wanted, never desired, to fight. He watched the conversations between his men as they settled in. They were anxious, aggressive, and behaved more like a pack of hungry wolves. *My pack, I like that. My pack of hunters, let's go to war.*

Captain A'ssia watched as the three divisions' transports docked with the large troop ship. Her miniature fleet sped down the length of the Cerberus and off toward their predetermined jump point. The small frigates activated their light gravity stream devices in a ring around the Legatus to take advantage of the large ship's wake. The piggyback system would allow the smaller vessels to keep up with the more powerful crafts at they pushed themselves to a higher rate of travel. In one fluid motion, the space directly in front of the Legatus buckled under its own artificially enhanced weight, blurring the surrounding light into itself as the fleet prepared to jump. The resulting phenomenon looked like a series of blackened tears or fissures in space. The ships entered.

The gravity well was thrust forward as their source; the ships projecting them propelled forward at almost unimaginable speeds. The blackness dissipated instantly as the immense gravity no longer trapped the local light. "Sensors are reading all the frigates in assigned patterns. We are also receiving the beacons of all destroyers and support craft."

A confirming voice came from the station across from the Ops officer. "We have green from all stations across the fleet. Synchronizing streams and waiting for further orders."

Captain Harrington got up from her chair and inserted a crystal block in the navigation officer's station. "The Cerberus has detected a large distortion near the large planetary moon the Illani call Sa'ber. It is currently believed that the Tarin'Tal are constructing a supply depot there; it will be our first target."

The officer adjusted the fleet's course before responding. "Understood, Captain. Relaying orders to the fleet...they have confirmed. We are engaging in a synchronized course change. Current ETA, five minutes."

The group of ships exited gravity stream simultaneously, using an immaculate level of precision provided by a high level of interdependency between their navigational computers. As the ships decelerated from their GS exit, a stream of fighters left the Legatus and attached themselves to the exterior of the destroyers on all the smaller ship's ports not currently in use by tugs. Another stream of fighters left the Legatus and began fanning through the immediate space.

Aboard the Legatus, Captain Harrington sat with her eyes closed, listening to reports streaming from stations aboard her ship. "No signs of an enemy presence yet," she said. "The moon is devoid of any energy signatures. All activity is currently centered closer to the planet. I am detecting over fifty signatures on the magnitude of the spire ships we engaged over Sh'in. And something...something that is off the scale—" The reporting officer was cut short by a young man at navigation.

"Sir! I am detecting a large-scale gravitational disturbance. The gravity well is in close proximity with the planet...and is moving."

A'ssia examined the crude outline shown in her display. "Is it a ship? A station? What is it?" The officer didn't look up from her display, which was pouring out information as fast as the ship's sensors could gather it.

"I don't know. It shares some similarities to a GS system, but it's relatively stationary, and it's disturbing the gravity networks throughout the system. I am detecting massive tidal forces on the planet. It must be hell down there."

"Launch a low-profile probe. Find out what it is."

The bridge continued to buzz with activity as each station received reports from both the Legatus and the fleet. Before the probe could transmit anything useful, a series of warning beacons activated. "Sir, we have detected a patrol. I don't see how they can miss us."

"Let's do this just like last time." Captain A'ssia remembered the alien's previous response and was willing to bet that the Tarin'Tal fleet would exhibit the same behavior again. "Send the frigates ahead. Make sure the enemy gets a signal out, but don't let them know you are doing it. Launch all fighters and have them run dark with the destroyers and frigates in our wake. Prepare the assault troops and inform the division captains." A'ssia turned her chair back to the science division's officers. "Change of plans. Send every probe we have at that piece of junk. You better be able to tell me what the hell it is before this is over."

One by one, the small human fleet fell behind the massive warship, disengaging the majority of their power in an effort to reduce their visibility to the alien ships. The ruse was effective. The slow hum of the Legatus's engines combined with her immense silhouette blocked the fleet from detection. The last of the human ships entered the shadow of the cruiser, and the fleet sat silent, waiting. After five excruciatingly long minutes, the frigates engaged the flight of alien gunships. There were only fifteen of them, but they were pissed. As the frigates began an arching sweep around the offending craft, they picked up a stream of communications between the attackers and the alien fleet.

"They know we're here, Captain!"

A'ssia watched a holographic representation of the miniature battle on her display. "Excellent. You've set the bait. Now reel them in, lieutenant."

The frigate's commander flicked her a quick salute. "Yes, sir. Will do." The replicas on her screen peeled away from the group of gunships and made a beeline toward the fleet. She could see the two groups of fighters waiting for orders on the edge of her holographic sensor display. Even though they were visible on the Legatus's sensors, the gunships had not seen the Legatus yet.

The frigates' agility allowed them to avoid the majority of the energy blasts leveled at them from the alien craft. What little offensive energy that actually impacted the frigates' shields was easily absorbed. Reacting in well-organized concert, the frigates crossed each other's paths and hit their afterburners, leaving an expanding ring of fire and quickly dissipating smoke in their wake. The Tarin'Tal were thrown into confusion, but a moment later, they began pursuing the two ships. The chase began screaming through space, approaching the human fleet at breakneck speed. Within a second, the Tarin'Tal saw the mighty cruiser, but by then it was far too late. With one round from its massive antimatter cannon, the Legatus vaporized all but three of the two frigates' pursuers. Spinning on their horizontal axis, the two frigates pummeled their remaining pursuers, ripping them apart before they could recover from the blinding blast.

"Sir! We have contacts! Lots of contacts! Holy hell! I am reading three spire-ship-sized signatures. Seven juggernauts have left the protection of enemy cloak shields and...uh...sir! The sensors can't identify the number of gunships." The sensor operator was beginning to sweat as he watched his displays.

The warship's captain retuned her gaze to her holo-screen. "Fleet status?" she asked.

"As of yet, undetected."

"Fighter squadrons?"

"Undetected."

"Good. Inform all commanders to prepare for imminent battle." A'ssia tapped a panel on her chair's armrest, cycling through images of the ships prepared for battle.

"Green signals from across the fleet. We are ready!"

The Tarin'Tal were forming an assault fleet at an unsettling rate. Already, a mass of ships had arrayed themselves in a wedge and were accelerating toward the Legatus at a vicious rate. "Sir, a large group of ships are approaching. ETA two minutes and thirty seconds. The majority of the enemy force appears to be farther to the other side of the planet. We are still within the gravity well of the planet, which will prevent them from using their faster-than-light drives. They will be here in one hour and thirteen minutes."

A'ssia nodded. "We should be long gone by then. Open fire!"

The Legatus unleashed its antimatter cannon on the approaching fleet, ripping gaping swaths through the front ranks of approaching ships with each concussive detonation. Even with their losses, the alien ships attacked with vicious ferocity. The front ranks locked onto the Legatus, blanketing her in fire. The ship's powerful shields dispersed the enemies' attacks, its cannons returning the attacks with lethal intensity. Captain Harrington hit a panel on the surface of the display in front of her, opening communications with the entire fleet.

"All craft, attack, fire at will. Inform the Toronto to prepare her assault; we will disable one of the lead juggernauts."

The communications officer echoed the command to the waiting warships. "Fleet signals green," he confirmed.

The fleet waiting behind the Legatus powered up and accelerated. They violently smashed into the surprised alien ships as they made their own path down the length of the massive cruiser. The humans were ready; the humans were vengeful; the humans had the element of surprise; and the humans had cut the alien ships to ribbons. The assault was so overwhelming and so destructive that not a single Tarin'Tal ship from that first wave survived. Debris and flames from the Tarin'Tal craft spilled out into the surrounding space, blanketing the human fleet. Shrapnel spilled off human shields without harming them, and the human forces emerged from the shattered first wave like a flight of angry dragons about to feast on a field of the dead and damned.

Despite their earlier courage, the remaining Tarin'Tal fleet hesitated. Their charge faltered as they were confronted with the wall of human warcraft. Their hesitancy, however, dissolved as they realized that their engines were far inferior and retreat would be their doom. The Tarin'Tal forces began to behave like a wounded animal; diving toward the human fleet, they swarmed the Legatus's main cannon, pouring all their entire fleet's power at the single point on the massive ship.

"Pivot!" commanded Captain Harrington. "Get our side to them before they break the forward grid. All cannons cover the forward generators!" As the ship began swinging in an arc, her side battery unleashed a fusillade of cannon fire. The resulting detonations deposited a mesh of electromagnetically charged particles between the advancing aliens and the human warship.

"Full barrage, fill that field with live rounds!" A'ssia watched her display as the newly formed cloud expanded to meet the new debris field, and both were filled by rounds from the Legatus and her escorts. "Pull the fleet back. Form a battle line behind the cloud."

Instead of blindly charging through the cloud to attack directly as before, the Tarin'Tal fleet surged upward and over the swirling cloud of shimmering blue, probing it the entire way with licks of fire from their cannons. A'ssia watched the unusual display on her monitors with critical intent. "Signal the fighters! All craft, concentrate on their center. I want that spire ship removed from my sky!"

The Exile Empire

The fleet again phased forward, spewing round after round at the first of the forms that came into its line-of-sight. As the seconds ticked by, the two capital ships continued to pummel each other, blurring the space between into a brutal plane of destruction. The Tarin'Tal spire ship quickly began to show the stress of the combat, its shields sparking and sputtering under the powerful barrage from the Legatus's antimatter cannon and lighter batteries. Just as the alien craft began to lose its shields in a blister of arching energy, the remainder of the human fleet attacked. The fighters, which had until now been waiting on the edge of the battle, drilled paths of destruction with their Gatling cannons. A riveting crack pulsed the engagement, throwing debris across the battle as the bottom segments of the spire ship exploded, their reactors rupturing. With one final volley, antimatter and plasma tore into the spire ship and out the other side, leaving nothing but charred chunks of twisted metal hurling away from the battle.

As one of their mother ships was torn from existence, a line of juggernauts surrounded by hundreds of gunships burst through the firestorm to bear down on the weakened Legatus. "Now is our chance, gentlemen!" A'ssia said into the communications link. "Each squad, take one juggernaut. Quicksand rounds…fire!" Winding their way around their own engagements, every ship in the fleet with an IC cannon fired on the approaching Tarin'Tal reinforcements. Instead of the green burn of plasma, however, a brilliant array of blues and golds filled the sky around the enemy ships. Four of the juggernauts and their escorts were engulfed in the shroud, their engines choking as the electromagnetic mesh overloaded them. The entrapment field had spread over half the area surrounding the human fleet, creating a curtain of imminent doom for any ship foolish enough to enter its dead zone.

The humans, however, had come prepared; their tugs and drop ships were hardened against the fields. Their fighters and warships, on the other hand, could not be so protected without sacrificing virtually all their critical functions. With a coordinated grace that contrasted sharply with their ugly forms, the tugs and troopships broke away from their hiding spots under the Legatus and sped toward the disabled crafts. "They are ignoring the fighters, frigates, and destroyers and are heading toward the troops. They know what we're up to."

A'ssia watched the screen as the human craft sped toward the blue-engulfed Tarin'Tal juggernauts. The human craft were on the other side of the enemy fleet in a failed attempt to draw their attention away from the boarding divisions.

"Bloody hell! Engines full! Get us between those juggernauts and our ships! All batteries alternate between armor piercing and full plasma rounds. Tell the fleet to cover our ass. This is going to hurt." The engines of the Legatus burst to life, allowing the warship to bridge the distance between the juggernauts and herself almost instantly. As the ship ground to a halt between the disabled juggernauts and those still very much alive, she tore a path through the insidious blue mesh. Reacting to the field, the Legatus's shields on the side now touching the quicksand fell with the arching electricity of overloading conduits. Her engines died in a cough of expelled gasses and antimatter residue, as they futilely attempted to reengage and push the ship forward.

"Starboard shields, weapons, and sensors are down. We have lost control of the engines. We are dead in the water!" The image of the Legatus on the captain's monitor flared red on the sections of the ship that had been disabled.

"The enemy fleet?" she asked.

"Highly active, but we are entirely blocking their path to the disabled vessels. The vertical and forward alternate paths to the targets are blocked by EM clouds, and the fleet is covering the remainder," the tactical officer said.

"Any remaining quicksand rounds?"

"The Clotho reports it has two, the Alecto one, and we have fourteen type-A warheads."

Again, A'ssia surveyed the holographic representation of the battle. "Disperse them throughout this area here." A'ssia placed her finger in an area through which several groups of gunships were attempting to pass to reach their disabled juggernauts. "Let's force them down the dragon's throat!"

"Acknowledged, Captain."

The ensuing battery of fire and energy trapped the Tarin'Tal craft as they attempted to skirt the conflict and flank the human forces. "Deployment success, captain. They only have one way through."

"Good, let's hold them here. What is the ETA on the rest of their fleet?"

"Forty-three minutes, sir."

"Let's pray that's enough." A'ssia watched the troop ships on her monitor. "Good luck, Captain Ursidae."

15 >> Slaughter

1/20/2454

Location: High Orbit above Lintalla

Status: Heavy Combat

A holographic representation of the battle outside glowed against James's face. He watched as the enemy juggernauts were isolated from their fleet through the superior tactics and weaponry of the human fleet. The juggernaut closest to the raging conflict began to glow as his communications link informed him that his division was assigned to capture the large vessel. He did not know how many Tarin'Tal he would be facing. He did not know what internal defenses they had, and he did not know how he would take control of the vessel once they were inside. But he loved it. Using previously obtained sensor records of the alien craft's exterior hull, he had assigned three different entry points for his division. They would use independent drop ships sporting drill entry adaptations. James's ship would hit the large ship's main docking port and punch through after a salvo from the Pila had weakened it.

"Okay, men, show time! Let's go show those SOBs what true warriors can do!"

The men assembled before him responded with a resounding chant of their chosen battle cry, "Necamus, necamus, necamus!" The men fell silent afterward, saving their energy, bottling any aggression, preparing for the explosion of battle. The only sounds heard in the bay were the stomp of boots, the clank of armor, and the occasional growl from one of the less self-controlled men.

As the massive craft finished loading their men, the side of the troop ship opened to space, displaying an uninhibited view of the massive battle outside. The only thing standing between the assault craft and the cold grip of space was a thin line of energy that glowed lightly as it kept in the oxygen. In one quick moment, the large craft sucked the air out of the bay and released the shields, allowing the drop ships to rocket forward toward the incapacitated juggernauts.

With resounding thumps of acceleration, the three ships of the Fifty-sixth left the Toronto along with the six ships carrying the other two divisions. Nine hundred humans sped toward almost certain doom as the battle raged outside. Many soldiers in the other divisions thought of their own fear and the atrocious kill rate from the previous battle, but not James. The commander of the Fifty-sixth reveled in demented anticipation, the corners of his eyes expanding as they began a quivering dilation. His men partook in their commander's battle lust, and their own desire to fight grew. The room felt heavy with the release of adrenaline, endorphins, and sweat as the men fed off both their leader and each other's growing insanity. With every heartbeat, the men of the Fifty-sixth grew more intent on their prize, and more intent on the battle to be had.

The Fifty-sixth's ships screamed through space, like ferocious bears and wolves charging their prey. Fire belched from the powerful engines of the vessels as they continued to accelerate toward their quarry. As the distance between the human craft and the enemy vessels disappeared, a barrage of cannon fire from the destroyers, covering their assault, flashed by them. Three points along the side of the juggernaut exploded in fire, followed closely by the bone-shattering impact of the drop ships. In a blinding wave of fire and turbulence, James felt his craft punch through the heavy metal of the port, successfully weakened by the plasma from the destroyer's barrage.

The suits protected James and his men from all but the most extreme heat and cold while supplying the warriors with their own oxygen supply, eliminating the need for pressurization before they could attack. The drop ship's main doors slammed open against the edges of a gaping chasm created by the ship's entry into the larger veil. Standing at the edge of an alien oblivion—atmosphere rushing past them into the open space and overflowing with a lust for battle—the elite forces of mankind attacked their alien adversaries.

Their rage was indelible, and their wrath burned like fire. Their blasts of plasma and metal burned in conjunction with the bite of their swords, and they had no mercy. They poured over the first aliens they encountered and easily deflected the Tarin'Tal's futile retaliation.

Rounding a sharp corner, James came across one of the massive creatures. Its movement was restricted by limited space as it wrenched itself at a grotesque angle in an effort to ensnare the much smaller human warrior. Taking advantage of the strain the alien was putting on its own body, James leveraged himself under the beast's belly, moving into the trap at full force instead of backing out like the Tarin'Tal had expected. Twisting, he grabbed one of the creature's rear legs and plunged his sword down the length of its foreleg. James's arms were stretched wide, gripping both the beast's forepaw and its foot behind its back. The monster snapped at James's head, but it could not reach him. Each time it tried harder, it did more damage to its own body. The human youth took advantage of the creature's attack and weight by wrenching both of his outstretched hands back to his chest, completing the brutal twist in the Tarin'Tal's back and snapping the alien's spine against its own body.

As the massive form collapsed, another beast lunged at James, but this time he was ready. Sidestepping the creature's advance, James slammed his shield along the base of its sword arm, simultaneously burning the Tarin'Tal and deflecting its attack. Using both his enhanced strength and the alien's redirected movement, James hurled the beast into the metal wall, leaving deep dents in the wall and the creature's head. The Tarin'Tal reeled back, thrashing with a shattered skull. James ended the beast's misery with a single plasma blast to the alien's already pummeled head. The resulting backsplash of blood and brain matter covered the hall and the human in a grotesque display.

Stepping forward from the carnage of battle, James staggered as his body began to pump dangerous levels of stimulants into his bloodstream. It was ignoring its own safety in its effort to supply him with everything it could to destroy his enemies. His muscles contorted as they filled with blood and the chemicals his body was releasing. He thrashed back against the wall. The black of his eyes began to swell until only a thin band of blue remained between the dark and white. In a sudden wave of unsurpassed energy, he cut loose.

Before, James had fought as a skilled yet wrathful warrior, but now he accessed every ounce of dormant strength within his muscles. He now reacted with a skill ingrained in his subconscious, through training and practice, and the natural elegance of one who has been both bred and twisted for war. Nothing could stop him. His speed and force of attack pushed his cybernetics and body to their limit, risking ripping muscle and flesh from bone and metal. In a blur, he attacked the remaining Tarin'Tal in the corridor. He tore their limbs from under them, blocking every countermeasure they could present with overwhelming ferocity. Without slowing, James disabled the charging monsters with inhuman ease, dragging his burning sword down the length of their bodies as they fell, spilling their alien entrails on the twisted metal deck. His coordination and speed were enhanced by a constant stream of information from both his onboard computer and the ever-present sound of Jessica's voice in his ear, informing him of the status of both friend and foe and advising tactical action. In deference to his berserk state, James continued to command his troops, now as an animalistic warlord rather than a mere soldier. His men fed from his bizarre blend of control and chaos, attempting to mirror their leader's ferocity.

All three of his teams had succeeded in gaining entry to the massive craft, and they quickly converged on the command deck, obliterating all resistance they encountered. Though the surprised aliens fought with stout resistance, they could not stand against the smaller humans' agility and mechanically assisted strength in the confined environment. They melted from their advance like butter on a stove. Each division fought in unsurpassed coordination relying on their operators; the jamming devices the Tarin'Tal used couldn't cut through the powerful signals used by the human warriors.

Several of the aliens successfully barricaded themselves and slowed the human advance with concentrated blasts from their kinetic weaponry, but those who chose to aggressively attack the human forces met quick and grisly deaths at the hands of the soldiers' brutal swords. The human forces mirrored James's attack, using their superior strength to tear the aliens apart with their mechanical hands. The Tarin'Tal could not hold against such a determined and overwhelming force, and they fell in droves.

The alien ship's internal barricades were no match against simultaneous blasts from the human's plasma rifles; the human advance remained unstopped. In a scourge of fire, plasma, and dismembered Tarin'Tal body parts, James and his squad burst into an enormous chamber devoid of resistance. The only alien in the room was not even Tarin'Tal. It attempted to hide its frail form behind a thin terminal.

"Rick! Get that thing locked down. I want to know what it is!" James quickly scanned the walls in the room, intrinsically knowing that one of the bland doors was the portal to the bridge and control of the alien ship.

In a fluid movement, James took a large handheld plasma cannon from one of his squad, flipped the mix ratio of the plasma to its maximum yield, and unleashed three destructive blasts at the door he had chosen. Amazingly, the door stood up to the first two but was burned from its hinges by the third.

"Good choice, Cap…looks like a winner," the soldier commented, as James handed his weapon back.

James sauntered through the charred and cooling remnants of the door flanked by three squads of soldiers, who were all covered in scorch marks, dents, and blood. The blast left the long corridor without lights, but the human warriors' helmets had a complete active scanning display of the path before them. Leaving the corridor, they entered a long rectangular room centered around a single table with displays and panels arrayed symmetrically around a central node. Each panel was equally spaced, equally positioned, and equally manned. The thirty humans faced a room of almost fifty very agitated Tarin'Tal.

With a bellow, the closest alien charged the human force. They slew their attacker with a few arching sweeps of their swords and shields. Rocked from their stunned silence, the remaining Tarin'Tal charged. It wasn't even a contest. James and his men locked their shields together and leveled volley after volley of plasma into the approaching aliens. The Tarin'Tal went down with a methodical consistency, piling on the floor until there were only a few left.

"Cease fire!" screamed James as two of the last three aliens fell. "I want that one alive." His men backed away from the creature, which leveled its kinetic weapon at James and began to circle. "Rick, lets see how good that translation computer works."

Rick responded with a nod, pulled a blocky contraption from his pack, and flipped a switch.

James and the creature continued to circle. There was no way for the Tarin'Tal to survive, let alone win. A ring of human warriors surrounded it, but the alien seemed determined to kill at least one human before it fell. "You cannot win. Surrender and you will live," James demanded. The creature did not react. It continued to circle. "Rick?"

The soldier checked several panels on his machine before responding. "It looks like it's working."

"If you do not surrender, I will break your legs and take you by force." When the machine repeated his statement in the Tarin'Tal's language, the large creature finally responded.

"You cannot disarm me without being forced to kill me, weakling. We will watch as The Will devours you whole, you and all your pathetic Illani race!" As it finished speaking, it sprang forward, unleashing a torrent of superheated particles from its weapon. James absorbed the blast with his shield; then spinning as the creature approached, he slammed the defensive disk into the alien's weapon, melting the muzzle in a wash of fire and energy. The Tarin'Tal threw down the overheated weapon, more in disgust than pain, even though it had charred a good portion of its hand.

In the same motion the Tarin'Tal had used to discard its kinetic weapon, it drew its long, curved sword with its uninjured hand. It attempted to impale James with the savage blade extending from his fist. With the art and speed of an expert warrior, James moved forward into the strike, flowing inside the blade's movement and catching it on the hilt of his own sword. Using the weight of the Tarin'Tal and his own strength, James slammed the beast's weapon into the deck with a wrenching grate of metal. Following through on his sword's movement, James struck three of the beast's knees before the creature could free its sword. James's cybernetically enhanced strength drew a sickening crack from each joint as he struck.

As the creature violently reacted in pain and rage, James stepped back to watch the useless thrashings of the alien. Turning to the large bank of displays and controls, he looked at his men and idly commented, "Take it," and followed up with a hushed, "Told you so."

Responding to orders, seven men rushed forward, leveraging the Tarin'Tal to the deck with the strength and weight of their suits. They bound its arms and legs with thin sheets of metal that they bent to suit their needs. Several men had already begun working at the vessel's controls as the fight had progressed. "Sir, we can't decipher their control systems or mechanisms. We can translate their language and controls, but they are somehow using multiple stations for a single operation. There is a differentiation between stations even on the navigation level. They must use several simultaneous operators…it just doesn't make any sense."

James walked over to survey their work. Across three of the largest panels they had set up a series of displays that translated the information into English. He turned to the remainder of his men. "Squads One through Three, remain here. Seven through Ten, clear this deck. Eleven through Twenty, take primary navigation systems and engines, and Twenty-one through Thirty, take the weapons systems. Each squad, continue to sweep the ship as you complete your tasks. Move out!"

As he turned to his personal squad, he informed them, "You boys, watch my back. I may be out of it for a while."

His lieutenant responded with a curt, "Sir!" and spun to guard the door.

James returned his attention to the panels before him and took a deep breath. "This is gonna sting," he stated, as a series of serrated spikes snapped out from his cybernetic arm. "I was hoping to test this on something a little more human." Closing his eyes, James lifted his hand and, in time with a forceful exhale, he slammed his arm onto the panel, wedging the spikes deep within the enclosed electronics. A pulse of arching energy traveled down the length of the panel and continued through the rest of the stations. All the displays began to flicker as the native systems were hacked by James's cybernetics and brain working in concert. After several long minutes, James's eyes snapped open.

"Get on the horn," he commanded. "We have taken control of the vessel! We have victory."

It came to James's attention that he had accidentally opened a ship-wide omnidirectional communications frequency when his words were met with a resounding, "Victory! Honor! Victory!"

James broke into a huge grin and shouted, "We are the sword and hammer!"

His men responded, "We strike without mercy!"

James looked at the piles of Tarin'Tal unceremoniously strewn throughout the room and muttered to himself in a satisfied voice. "Yes, we are, boys. Yes, we are."

Through the ship's sensors, James was able to see the carnage of the battle. The conflict within the ship had taken the better part of an hour, and both fleets were showing the strain. The Legatus was still incapacitated, floating in the ominous cloud of disabling blue. The tugs had pulled the disabled juggernauts out of the cloud, including his own, and had moved on to helping the Legatus. The fourth juggernaut had been destroyed along with all the gunships that had been incapacitated in the cloud. Using the ship's communication system, James attempted to contact the Legatus.

"Legatus, this is Captain James Ursidae. We have taken the juggernaut. Do you copy?"

A second later, the silence was broken. "Captain Ursidae, this is the Legatus. What is your status?"

James probed the systems of the ship through his link before responding. "I have weapons and some shields, but the engines are still down. We have eradicated almost all resistance aboard ship."

"Excellent job, Captain. Unfortunately, we've lost contact with the divisions who boarded juggernauts one and two. They seem to have almost finished repairs on their weapons and navigation. All our destroyers are engaged on the front, and we need to take them out."

As the officer finished giving James her report, one of the other two juggernauts fired on his ship. The other ships' weapons were barely functional, but James's ship only had marginal shields.

As the energy collided with his ship's shields, the ship rocked and recoiled from the impacting scour of energy.

The weapons onboard James's juggernaut had been one of the systems that had suffered the least damage from the time the ship spent in the cloud, and he put them to full use. In a fusillade of burning energy, James's ship spewed fire over the other juggernaut, shaking the other ship and punching through their shields in several places. His assault was assisted by a flight of Peregrines that dove over the Legatus from the battle to defend the newly captured vessel from its former allies.

The drill of their continuous Gatling fire bore several holes through the large ship, which spewed fire as the air inside violently combusted.

A second round of fire from the craft James had captured finished the ship, and as it lost core containment, the vessel was burned from the inside and out. The juggernaut's charred hulk began to drift out of control, slowly sliding toward the other Tarin'Tal ship that the Third had failed to capture.

The last of the fires on the first ship James had engaged died as the craft was drained of oxygen. Alien alarms blared as the second juggernaut the force had failed to capture prepared to attack. With his shields now down and his engines dead, James had few options left with which to defend his new prize. "Ursidae to Peregrine flight, please respond."

"Flight Seraphim, Captain Abram here. What can I do for you, Captain?"

"Let's have a shoving match with that juggernaut, shall we?"

"Yes, sir. Captain, we have concussion rounds. That should do the trick."

James smiled. "Let's take 'em out!" The juggernaut and the fighters sprayed the dead hulk with fire, forcing it toward the other alien ship, which was still very much alive. The Tarin'Tal quickly comprehended the unorthodox tactic James was employing and began firing on the opposite side of the craft to deflect the floating hulk. The deadly game of inverted tug-of-war continued for several minutes as the two craft pounded the dead hulk with fire and concussion rounds. The superior firepower of the Peregrines, when combined with the more active weapons aboard James's craft, proved more than a match for the other craft. The hulk continued to accelerate.

As the hulk was about to impact the juggernaut, the alien ship's engines sprang back to life, roaring in a futile attempt to escape its impending doom. The ship made it only halfway down the length of the hulk before the dead craft slammed into it. Impacting its engines with brutal force, the juggernaut lost control and twisted into the other ship. Its side tore open, causing a series of explosions within the craft, wrenching it apart in a gore of fire and debris.

James's ship was rocked as chunks of debris from the two dead juggernauts hit his ship's marginal shields as he reactivated the few surviving emitters. As the ship reeled from the explosion, the Legatus descended from its position between the juggernaut and the battle it had been protecting them from, its engines roaring to life. The tugs had freed her from the quicksand, and they now swarmed over the captured craft, tethering her directly against the main docking port of the Legatus. The human fleet withdrew from their engagement, guarding the captured vessel between the Legatus and the swarms of lighter crafts. Already the human fleet had suffered heavy losses. Many frigates had been destroyed, one of the heavy mercenary ships had been torn apart, and the Clotho had suffered severe damage to its weapons and defensive capabilities. The destroyer, however, still had full use of its engines, and it was putting them to work as it accelerated away from the Tarin'Tal fleet.

The fleet pulled itself into a close formation around the Legatus, which had succeeded in reactivating most of its disabled systems. Fortunately for the human fleet, the Tarin'Tal were too disorganized to mount an efficient pursuit. Unfortunately, as the human fleet began to leave the unusual battle zone created by the quicksand, they met an immense Tarin'Tal force that had successfully made its way from the other side of the planet.

Captain Harrington slammed her console and screamed into the communications link. "Attention, fleet! Initiate Cerberus maneuver!" The retreating ships swirled around each other and pulled themselves together behind the Legatus, hiding in her protective shadow as they attempted to punch through the enemy fleet. The fighters that could rushed inside the docking bay of the Legatus while those that couldn't clamped themselves onto the sides of the destroyers. The lighter craft swerved inward toward the more heavily armored warships, and the fleet accelerated at maximum capacity. The Tarin'Tal fleet attempted to get as many ships between the humans and their escape route as possible. An escape opportunity was quickly disappearing, and the Legatus again unleashed her massive cannon in conjunction with her smaller weapons. The space between the two fleets erupted into flame as the humans carved a path to freedom.

The human assault did not go unanswered. The Tarin'Tal flooded space with their own fire. The combined might of three spire ships bore down on the Legatus, and many more waited to sink their teeth in. With a flood of color, the Legatus's shields burst into activity as they struggled to deflect and absorb the lethal force of the alien assault.

A'ssia watched the indicator on the Legatus's forward shields tick away like a countdown to death. "Switch to concussion rounds! Disrupt their formation. Target that flight of juggernauts and clear a path!"

The human warship rolled with its fleet in tow and unleashed a new torrent of fire on a thin point in the alien line. In an enormous crash of men, metal, fire, and alien warships, the Legatus slammed directly into the line of Tarin'Tal ships at full speed, crushing enemy craft. The shields aboard the Legatus began to buckle. Several gunships broke through the shields, but they weren't fast enough to avoid impact.

Several gouts of fire sprang from the forward section of the warship as it emerged from the other end of Tarin'Tal fleet utterly lacking forward shields. "Thirty seconds 'til we leave the gravitational dead zone, Captain!"

"Continue spread and heading. Order all ships to initiate a rear guard action for ten seconds, then have them follow us."

The communications operative looked like she had just sentenced hundreds to death as she confirmed the orders.

In a gallant effort, the remaining destroyers and frigates spun and opened fire on the pursuing fleet. They were outmanned by a thousand to one. The sky burned with fire from the alien fleet as it swept over the retreating humans. The human ships stood their ground, shielding the retreat of the Legatus and her invaluable cargo. They poured a stream of cannon and Gatling rounds into the enemy fleet, which did nothing to change the impossible odds against the human force.

"Sir, the Clotho has just lost shiel...Sir! The Clotho has been destroyed!" The image of the destroyer on her screen blinked and disappeared.

Before her destruction, the Clotho had succeeded in firing their trireme device, which floated backward toward their pursuers. It detonated in a cataclysmic explosion, blanketing the forward ranks of the Tarin'Tal fleet in a deadly wash of antimatter and plasma fire. As the aliens attempted to recover from the detonation, the Legatus activated its GS device, disappearing in a winking absence of light, signaling the remainder of the fleet to complete their retreat. Within a fraction of a second, the human ships disappeared, but they were not safe yet; the entire pursuing fleet jumped into their faster-than-light drives in an unyielding quest to kill the retreating humans.

Fifteen minutes later, the small fleet exited gravity stream in a flash of light. The captain of the Legatus initiated a communications broadcast from her command chair. "A'ssia to Cerberus, this is the Legatus. Mission successful, repeat, the mission was successful. We have a juggernaut in tow. Please be advised, we are under pursuit." Her communications crackled, and a distorted voice came through her panel. "Affirmative, Legatus. Will you please apprise us of your status?"

"We have sustained casualties, the Clotho is gone, and most of the task force has extreme shield damage and power loss. Over sixty percent of the task force's offensive weaponry is no longer functional."

Admiral Hancock listened to the report, while confirming with the information flowing across his display. He examined the damage to the ships and casualty reports and instructed his communications officer to direct the task force into repair stations on the MIC and Princeps.

As the officer finished giving directions to the fleet, he gave special instructions to the captured juggernaut. "Congratulations, Captain Ursidae. You and your men's contribution will not go unnoticed. A contingent of tugs will escort you to the primary docking clamps aboard the MIC. Once the ship has been secured, you will be provided a transport to the surface."

Returning to his display, Hancock examined the cluster of disturbances heading toward the human fleet and Sh'in. They were slowing, and with each reduction in speed his sensors were less and less able to detect them. Any moment, energy output from the alien ships would drop below a level which even the Cerberus's advanced sensors could detect. Fortunately, at the rate the Tarin'Tal force was decelerating, it would be several days before they would fall below the Cerberus's sensor's capabilities. He could only hope that the juggernaut would yield a new way to detect their adversaries before they would arrive.

1/23/2454

Location: Cerberus, High Orbit above Sh'in

Tinek strode down the long hall the Cerberus's main quarters deck. The massive scale of the ship never ceased to amaze him. The largest spacecraft his people had created was a small station above Lintalla, and it had been destroyed during the first hours of the Tarin'Tal invasion. Nilwa, one of Tinek's few remaining guards, and two large human soldiers walked behind him as he made his way out of the hallway and into the transportation hub. He had a meeting with a council of civilians and military officers from the human fleet. Military ranks he somewhat understood, but the civilians were "elected," a concept he had yet to fully understand. He understood how it worked; it was how the humans expected the winner, of what he saw as a popularity contest, to act in the best interests of the people that he didn't get. Illani society had been both feudal and individualistic. They had titles, which had translated fairly fluidly into medieval titles of dukes and counts, while holding many individual rights as sacred.

Any feudal lord from the military or ruling class who attempted to violate those rights would have his lands confiscated, his hereditary title for him and his family revoked, and be publicly executed by the one he offended or their closest kin. They took the issue very seriously. While Tinek understood that these people came from a different history and had different traditions, their views on total democracy were disturbingly similar to the Tarin'Tal's defiled guiding Will.

Five minutes later, the pod came to a stop, and the door slid open to another hub. After a short walk, Tinek and his guards found themselves at an entrance to a large conference room. Inhaling to center himself, Tinek stepped forward. The door slid open, and he walked forward to meet the human leaders in the most important meeting he would ever attend.

There were twenty people in the room; seven wore uniforms, thirteen did not. Tinek recognized only a few people—Admiral Hancock, Captain Harrington, who had been personally tutoring him in both human customs and language, and the civilian representatives who had been present at the ambassador meal he had eaten after he had boarded the Cerberus. Very few of the people in the room looked friendly to the exiled regent.

Tinek had spent the past several days working on a human-style proposal, often with Admiral Hancock and A'ssia. The admiral had explained many of the important points to cover in convincing the "congress" to accept his plan. After all, it was an audacious idea, even to the mind of a born and raised leader like Tinek. The three of them planned to create a unified society of both Illani and human foundations, taking the shattered pieces of both races and reforging them under one cohesive government. He had worked long and hard to find a compromise that would work for both the humans and his own people.

Tinek found himself in the unique position of deciding the fate of his entire race while needing to preserve their core beliefs. If he agreed to any proposal that allowed for any infringement of what his people, and himself, considered their rights, there would be massive uprising, and the legitimacy of both his decision and rule would be utterly destroyed. On Lintalla, there was no concept of a constitution; everything was unspoken tradition, a sacred tradition. As such, there had never been any need for it to be written down. Individual rights were revered with a religious fervor that prevented the legal and linguistic manipulation found in human governments. On Earth, even constitutions were twisted from their original meanings by lawyers and politicians seeking to advance special interests and political gain at the expense of one group or another.

Tinek, however, liked the idea of a constitution. He had always been one to keep records of all the events in both his personal and official life. Too many times, he had seen people twist contracts and laws issued by his father and family. He fully understood that without the Illani's natural view of individualism, the same sort of slow perversion of the law and rights within any government could and would occur.

Again Tinek centered himself, and he began his presentation, using English where he could and relying on the ship's translation devices for the remainder.

"My friends, I have come today not as a foreign leader, but a man in the same situation as yourselves. We have both suffered at the hands of the brutal Tarin'Tal, and both of our races have lost some of the most crucial elements of our society. My people have been subjugated, our cities burned, our infrastructure crushed, and our ruling and military casts exterminated. I am the only individual left who can claim authority over the Illani people.

"You all have lost your homes, support, and land. Even if you do manage to take land from the Tarin'Tal, they will not give it easily or cheaply, and they will be back. Before Lintalla fell, my spies were able to ascertain the extent of their empire; it covers hundreds of systems, many hundreds of billions of Tarin'Tal, and countless subjected races.

"Neither of our races can defend against them alone. Only after we achieve victory and rebuild together can we hope to stand against their might. The only way for such a union to exist, however, would be for both of our races to make great compromises. Your people are accustomed to electing their leaders; my people are accustomed to hereditary rule. One thing that both our people have come to revere is that of individual rights. Our system has not had a major problem defending those rights in over two thousand of your years. Your constitutions have proven an adequate measure to protect your citizens.

"I propose a unified government composed of a regency—what you would call a congress—and a combination of local and magisterial leadership for individual provinces. There would be enumerated rights, but when something is in question, no one must ever be forced to act or give of their own possessions; that is the primary rule of our people. If this rule were violated, there would be chaos. This is why no council, no ruler, no congress, and no consensus of the majority can ever, under any circumstance, define any right or law contrary to this definition."

The conclusion of Tinek's proposal brought a murmur of agreement, shock, and disgust from the sitting members.

"In respect to your customs," Tinek continued, "we would allow free transit between classes, even entry into the ruling class, earning titles by deeds and honor. Your people would be separate from any class but could enter one if they wished. Local governments would be elected but would be, in your terms, checked and balanced by a local lord. Neither could override the other, but either could appeal to a higher authority. There would be a bisected court system for individual offenses, which would be dealt with by your trial by jury. The local lord would deal with offenses against anything other than the state. From the individual to the congress, the traditions of both our races would be respected. Of course, I plan to continue this duopoly of tradition by taking a human wife. I have drawn up a constitution in the style of your people."

At this, several men entered the room, carrying special data pads, each only holding a copy of the document. The murmur simmering throughout the room died for several minutes as the members of the congress thoroughly read the document.

In a huff, one of the members slammed the pad down on the table. "Absolutely unacceptable! There is no way for people to appeal incorrect decisions to a popular vote, and the highest position is hereditary!"

Tinek looked the red-faced man in the eyes and simply responded, "Am I to believe that your people have always been able to appeal decisions like war and rights to the public? Or are they decided by those whom you chose to put in power? Also, I am under the impression that your first nation—United Kingdom, was it?—still had a hereditary ruler when you left Earth. Even if he did not use his power, it was still there."

Not backing down, the man shot back, "Suppose the wrong person comes to office in one of your non-elected positions? How can the people remove him?"

Staring the man in eyes, Tinek responded, "Do you truly believe that a majority should be able to decide a man's worthiness in a glorified popularity contest? My people will find it hard enough to accept your elections. If a problem arises with an appointment, there are two means of satisfaction. The first and most preferable is that the one who is the source of the lord's authority, namely the regent, removes him. The second will use your revered election process. Those whom the people elect locally can choose to condemn the local lord, at which point the national congress can vote to have him removed from power and petition the local lord to strip his title.

"Furthermore, since the lordships are derived from my people's tradition, the penalty for a violation of rights shall be derived from my people's tradition as well."

"And what is that, Mr. Tinek?"

The exiled prince placed his hands on the table before him and stated with a solemn tone, "Death."

The audience began to murmur again. Seeing their attention and respect slipping, Tinek quickly explained, "It is only fitting that if one is given a responsibility for life that the moment he violates that responsibility, forfeiting the trust, respect, and authority he holds, that his life be forfeit as well. If one accepts title and responsibility over others, there are grave consequences."

To Tinek's surprise, there was murmured agreement from the gathered members. The only dissenter was the bitter man with the now broken data pad. He slammed the table again. "No, it is not fitting! What you are proposing is barbarism fit for the dark ages!"

Another member rocketed to his feet across from the first congressman. "And humanity's experiments with popular rule are more fitting today? May I remind you, sir, about the Soviet Union, the South American Federation, the Celestas Travesty, or the Orion Unions? Bloodbaths! Every last one of them was a vile perversion of human nature. What he is proposing is the most balanced idea humanity has ever tried. If we had it your way, we would have a general election on the definition of every political, legal, and religious term! This constitution is solid; it protects everything that human constitutions have protected, possibly better. It lacks the loopholes of the twentieth-century American constitutions, and it is adaptable, preventing a Centari conundrum. And most important, it's not like we have too many choices right now!"

Realizing that any further explanation on his part would cause more problems than it was worth, Tinek sat down next to the admiral, letting the civilians fight out their own problems. After several more hours, the group asked Tinek and the admiral to leave the room. Apparently, the admiral's power over the fleet prevented him from voting in human tradition. Hancock didn't seem to have a problem with it. Tinek turned to the large human commander, both worried and curious. "How long do these votes usually take?"

"It depends. Sometimes minutes or hours, sometimes days. But I think they know that they have a time crunch, and it's not like a better offer will come by anytime soon. I think we put together the best possible proposal. Both of our people need this, and I think the men behind that door understand that."

Tired and contemplative, Tinek smiled and nodded. "I hope so." He spoke entirely in English; he was getting better.

Ten minutes later, the door to the conference room sprang open. As Tinek and Hancock walked back in, Cho, the civilian leader who had defended Tinek's proposal, stood. "As the head of the emergency exiled congress, it is my solemn duty—" his face broke into a wide smile "—to be the first to hail Prince Tinek, regent of both our peoples." The assembly stood and, some less enthusiastically than others, stated in concert, "Hail Tinek!"

A quiet stillness of relief drifted back towards Tinek and Hancock. They had done it! They had created a way for both their races to support each other as one against the Tarin'Tal. Mankind now had the hope of a home, and the Illani now had a hope of freedom.

The fleet had been debating the concept of union between the remnants of humanity and the Illani ever since their arrival. Some thought that the move was too drastic. Others could not believe that a foreign leader would suggest a union after barely meeting an alien race. But others loved the idea; it was aggressive and possible, and they were sick of doing nothing. A strong dynastic civilization reflected the frustration and determination that the surviving humans had been feeling since the Harvester War. It gave them direction in their fight, a goal that would signal when they had achieved their own survival and could focus on rebuilding. The proposal spread throughout the fleet almost as fast as his offer had been accepted. Everyone felt strongly about the proposal, either strongly for or against it. It had only been a few days since the event, and the fleet had begun to fracture along newfound political lines. The news that the alliance had become a union was causing unprecedented unrest, and both Tinek and Hancock knew it.

The congress had voted to accept the treaty and finished signing the new Constitution of Unification. The last signer, the loud pro-unification member Cho, who was now the first minister, stepped back to allow Tinek to sign the document. As the exiled prince engraved his hereditary seal onto the document, the atmosphere in the room changed. As his hand left the page, he ceased to be an Illani ruler and an exiled prince. He became a king responsible for the future of two races. It hit everyone in the room with equal force and disparate impact. In the moments immediately following the signing, the new Unified Council agreed to keep the decision silent until they could make a prepared presentation to the fleet. The decision had been all in favor but three. Those three, however, had left the room furious. The new king knew that if they could have got away with killing Tinek immediately, they would have.

As the members of the Unified Council finished filing out of the room, heading to their ships to prepare them for the announcement, Hancock again pulled Tinek aside. "Your guards won't be enough protection anymore; this is going to cause some really big waves." As the pair made their way down the hall, Cho, who was busy working on a data pad, joined them.

"I doubt we can keep the decision quiet for more than a few hours," said Tinek. "In fact, I doubt Councilman Austin will keep the news from his followers at all." With a slight shudder of disgust, Tinek thought of the divisive man and his contempt for anything other than democracy.

"Then we need to inform the fleet before he does." The admiral input a series of commands onto his armband, looking up after the lights blinked a response. "Follow me. I have a press room established and a public relations officer ready for your appearance."

Forty minutes later, the trio of leaders left the carefully lit room. A uniformed man remained behind, adjusting a series of controls.

"Sirs, the broadcast will air at exactly fourteen hundred hours."

"Thank you. Be sure that it does."

As Cho left to return to his colony ship, the admiral turned to Tinek, whose serious manner did not change when the other man left. He was alone with his ally turned friend. "You said earlier that you knew of a group that would be able to offer sufficient protection. After today I am beginning to agree that my personal forces will not be enough."

The admiral nodded in agreement. "Why do you think this group of yours would be any more immune to usurpation and political discord?" The admiral didn't show any emotion other than a small creasing around his eyes.

"Their leader is unique. He is…not normal. He sees life differently, and his men follow his mentality. You should meet him. He and his division have just returned from a mission and are in medical bay B of the Princeps." While making their way to the Cerberus's main hangar, the admiral handed Tinek a data pad with James's and the Fifty-sixth's statistics imprinted on it. The new king scrolled through the information, his admiration growing as he examined their innovation, kill ratios, tactics, and victories. With one last signal to the command deck confirming a shift change, Hancock and Tinek entered the shuttle. Tucked inside a swarm of fighters and frigates, the shuttle wound its way through the fleet to the Princeps. The shuttle and its escorts flew inside the hangar of the carrier ship, landing on an expansive platform. The medical facilities had been tending to the Fifty-sixth for the past several hours in isolation and decontamination after their exposure aboard the alien juggernaut.

When Tinek and Hancock arrived at the medical deck, the Fifty-sixth had just been released from decontamination. They had lost seventeen men in the engagement, and over half of the division was wounded. Winding through the rows of beds, Tinek made his way to James. One of his legs was encased in a bio-stimulace tube to help his ligaments reattach and mend themselves. He was actively working on his cybernetic arm with his other hand. The cyborg soldier had removed a good portion of his own arm, and it sat on a tray by his bed. Much of the metal was blackened, and the electronics had been melted. The skin around the connections between his arm and the cybernetics had scorch marks and was twisted from burns. Looking up, James acknowledged Tinek by setting down his tools.

The admiral took a look at his arm with more than a little surprise. "Get your hand shoved up one of those kinetic weapons?"

James lifted the now bare chassis of his arm for Tinek and Hancock to see. "No, my little experiment in cybernetic-hardware inter-phone went a little wrong."

"My report said that it worked, and you took control of the vessel. How did you do that with your arm turned to slag?" Hancock asked with honest curiosity.

"It worked at first. The hardware interphase and operational hack gave me access to almost every system on the ship. The problem came when I tried to disconnect. The system tried to pull commands from the connection, and as the connection was lost, the panel overloaded and exploded into all sorts of hell."

Tinek's curiosity with cybernetics was unbounded. He had never seen anyone who had extensive reconstruction before. The Illani race had only achieved small-scale organ replacement, and even then, the equipment was hardly reliable. In a flurry of questions, Tinek lost all thought of the political problems he was facing as his race's natural curiosity took hold of him.

After James had given the new king a description of the basic principles in cybernetic technology and showed him some neural connections on his arm, Tinek started on more serious questions. "I assume you are aware of the potential union between our two races."

James nodded. "I know that you and your men gave us most of the information we have on the Tarin'Tal and Sh'in. I have also heard that you want us to help you liberate Lintalla and kick the 'Tal out of the system."

Recognizing that James was playing the apathetic role, Tinek decided to take a different approach. "How do you like your command, Captain?"

"Honestly, I love it, sir. I get to fight with the best men using the best technology."

"True enough. What about your missions?"

"I get to defend my people and destroy those who want to kill them. What more could I ask for?"

"Have you ever seen a civil war?" Tinek asked.

"No, but I learned about many when I was a kid."

"Then you know that they can be far more destructive to a people than any enemy."

"That is very true. I assume now is where you tell me that there is one about to happen? How can that happen in a fleet of exiles?" James asked.

Tinek knew he was reaching a crossroads with the warrior.

"It would happen if the fleet's view of correct government was violated. Some of your people strongly oppose monarchs."

James thought about Tinek's statement. For a solid five minutes, James didn't take his eyes off him, didn't say anything, hardly blinked. Finally comprehending the magnitude of what had taken place and of what he was being asked, he spoke. "Is it final yet?"

Tinek responded simply, "Yes."

"Is it in writing?"

Again, the same response. "Yes."

"Can I see it?"

"Yes," came Tinek's reply.

James spent several more minutes reading the document on the data pad Tinek and Hancock had brought with them. Without a word, James handed the pad back to the admiral and closed his eyes, taking a deep breath. James pushed the mobile workbench with his cybernetics away and forced himself to sit up. Dragging his healing leg under him, still encased in the tube, he pulled himself to the side of his bed. With a surge of determination, he leveraged himself to stand next to his bed. Slowly the skeletal frame of James's cybernetic hand closed into a fist, which he raised toward Tinek. The admiral tensed, his hand dropping to his sidearm in dread that he had misjudged the young soldier. The two guards behind Tinek leveled their rifles. In one powerful movement, James slammed the fist into his own chest, slightly bowing. "Hail Tinek, I pledge my loyalty to you, and I pledge my protection and service unto death. You have my allegiance."

Tinek's posture shifted, and a great weight lifted from the room. Tinek had not realized how much or why he cared that this boy personally accept his rule, but he did. His acceptance gave the new leader strength. As James came back erect in the jerky motions of his restricted muscles, Tinek grabbed his cybernetic arm just below the synthetic elbow and raised his own fist in a similar gesture. "And I am honored to have a warrior such as you at my side. There may be hope for our people yet, Captain Ursidae."

To his great objection, Tinek and Hancock helped James back onto his bed. "I know you are still healing, James," the ruler said, using his first name, "but for our unified races, I need your help already. Your division is the most capable group of men in the fleet. My guards are either dead or exhausted beyond their physical limits, and Kincaid's units are neither trained nor proven in combat or loyalty. The only unit we can count on to keep the highest members of this new government safe is yours. I offer you and your division the position and title of the royal guard and assault force. You may choose the name and colors for your unit. You will be entirely separate from the chain of command, responsible only to myself and the admiral, and you will prevent this fleet from doing damage to itself."

James flushed with the honor and responsibility he was being offered, but he didn't hesitate to consider Tinek's offer. Looking the new king straight in his eyes, swirling with the grey and red of uncertainty, James stated, "The Imperial Hammer is at your disposal, Your Highness. You need only command me."

Taken aback for a fraction of a moment by the speed of James's acceptance and the name he had given his unit, Tinek simply nodded his head in thanks.

Reaching over to the table that had been moved back to its previous position, James pulled a device from the scattered parts and activated it. "Rick, Sam, Hilben, get over here." There was a scattering of movement from a curtain nearby, and the three men came quickly into view. "I assume you heard all that."

The three hardened warriors grinned and nodded in assent. "I have trained you well. What do you think?" In unison they mirrored the homage that James had created a few minutes before, each swearing their loyalty to Tinek, and each received the same response.

"Good, now let's get to work. Rick, Sam, suit up and get yourselves back here ASAP. I know that the medics have your suits nearby. Hilben, contact the men. Organize a meeting at the main barracks commons in camp. I believe half the men are there already."

Each of the men pounded his chest, using it as a new salute. "Sir!" they stated curtly and powerfully. They sped off to complete their assigned tasks.

Turning to Tinek, James somberly stated, "I am going to have to ask you to remain here until my men can return and provide protection, Your Highness." Tinek cringed slightly at the title James used to address him. It translated fairly directly into his language, but he could not stand the thought of his personal warriors addressing him with such formality. He had hated formality before and hated it now. The only difference was that now he was the king and had the power to change the protocol.

"Thank you, James. I can wait," Tinek said as the men left. "I hate to do this already, but I have a direct command for you and your men."

James's eyebrow rose. "Yes?"

"You and your men don't have to use any honorary titles when addressing me. You all may refer to me by either my personal or family name. I want friends and warriors, not servants."

While Hancock seemed annoyed by the statement and disturbed by the sentiment, James loved Tinek's personable nature in command.

"Yes, Tinek. It shall be done." Tinek chuckled in a very human fashion at James's informality. The two spent a few minutes talking about the scheduling of guards and the entry of Tinek's original guards into the Imperial Hammer before the two soldiers retuned in full armor. "Please stick with Tinek until I send replacements," James ordered. Giving James and then Tinek the new salute, the two men followed Tinek and Hancock out of the room as they left to prepare for their presentation to the fleet.

17 >> Retrospect

1/20/2454

Location: Cerberus, High Orbit above Sh'in

Jessica walked down the dusty path as it snaked its way to the town from the new base. It was morning on the planet. The military was still operating on a twenty-four-hour clock, which meant that shifts were changing all over the fleet and planetoid. The base had been filling with grumpy, hungry, and tired men for several hours as Cormac's men came back from a training exercise and James's men began arriving from the Princeps. They hadn't let her into the Princeps's medical bay to be with James when they had returned from the battle. She didn't mind so much. She had been aboard the troop ship for her control duties in order to prevent interference from the quicksand charges and had been able to help James when the console had overloaded. Even now, her cybernetic link with him allowed her to talk to him whenever she wanted.

After the battle for Sh'in, she and James had developed and installed direct-line communication devices in their neuro-cores. They were based in large part off the hardwiring she had done to herself when James was unconscious on the battlefield. They used the nervous system of both people and served as an innate connection between the two communicators. It no longer mattered if one of them was unconscious. As long as they were still alive, they could find each other. The connection was so deep that if they both concentrated, they could mentally communicate over long distances. That took an excruciating amount of energy, but she knew that James was safe, so she was happy.

The outskirts of the new city were separated from the base by a small stretch of grassy terrain but connected by a newly paved road. The road was made from dense clay, which when mixed with crushed stone and a few benign chemicals provided an extremely adaptable surface that was both tough and durable. It was like a hybrid between a dirt path and a paved walkway. She loved how the substance wasn't as artificial and rough on the feet as the cement and asphalt that blanketed large parts of the old colonies. Jessica enjoyed the clean, earthy air that blew solidly across the stretch of ground as she strolled toward the growing city.

The skeletal hulk of the Explorator was partially obscured by the looming shape of a second colony ship that had landed only a day earlier. The population of the ship had been on the verge of a full-blown riot when they were initially denied access to the planet. When Hancock addressed the situation personally, he realized that there was no way for the conflict to end peacefully unless he let the people on the colony ship land. No one could blame them. They had been cooped up aboard the stinking ship for months. The crowding had been worse than many other ships. The average refugee had less than four square feet of space; in short, it was horrible. The people from the ship wasted no time in joining the growing society on the ground.

In one day, the planetary bazaar had doubled, and countless buildings had sprung up over the landscape. Jessica understood why so much construction was taking place. The new colony ship could provide its own and the Explorator's colonists with more building materials; the Explorator's stock had been greatly depleted by the immediate construction of the abe ranches. The colonists had even progressed fairly far in dismantling the ship itself for material. The result of both colony ships landing in the same area was the beginnings of a small but true city.

The bazaar extended through the length of the city, neatly bisecting it with a fledgling commercial district where anyone with skills, salvaged items, food, or services gathered to seek the limitless opportunities that came with a virgin world. And find them they did.

Jessica entered the rows of businesses in prefabricated shops. Some of the first shops she passed were labor suppliers, essentially a series of rudimentary temp agencies. The signs advertised skills from pilots to construction workers and metal workers. Men obviously from other fledgling businesses were haggling with patrons and clients over wages and workers. Further down, she reached a series of shops filled with meats and grains from the planet's natural supplies. Even though there was only abe meat and lax grains so far, the people in the city seemed to have no limit to their imagination as to how the new foods could be prepared. There was smoked meat, barbecued meats with spices found around the planet, dried meats, and raw meat for other shops to buy. Stalls sporting the local grain had uncooked lax, baked sand nuts, roasted sand nuts, pit-smoked sand nuts, boiled sand nuts, and sacks of powdery ground sand nuts that looked incredibly similar to flour.

Each member of the military had been given a small salary of credits to use on the planet, which afforded Jessica the luxury of purchasing power without needing to take out a fleet loan. Most of the businesses established so far were based off credit from the fleet, and individuals who wanted to remain debt-free could work for those who had taken the loans until they had enough money to start on their own, which explained the temp agencies. Thankful she didn't have to think too hard about financial matters because of her position, Jessica moseyed through the meat shops until she found some spiced, smoked meat that she liked.

As she continued down the line, slowly chewing on the tough meat, she watched people running around preparing for dinner. Some were buying cooked foods, some were buying material for their own specialty shops further down the line, and others were buying raw foods to take to their new homes. Continuing to gnaw on the piece of meat, Jessica walked further down the shops. The delicious smell of cooking meat and grains filled the air.

After a while, the shops grew more spread out, creating a courtyard filled with tables and benches. There was even a public fountain. Jessica finished the meat and began to look for something more substantial. Following her nose, she found a shop that was cooking long strips of meat in a sauce that smelled like tangy barbecue. They were also making circular pita-looking patties, which were lightly frying in grease from the local meat. When both were finished, the meat was wrapped in the bread, which looked almost like a crispy meat burrito. The taste, however, was different. It was smoky and rich. The meat and bread complemented each other well, and Jessica loved it. Her nose hadn't led her astray, and neither had the sign above the shop, which read: "Best Sh'in wraps period!"

Making her way back to the fountain, Jessica sat down. "Good, aren't they?" came a familiar voice from the other side of the table. Jessica looked up to see hers and James's best friend.

"Well, if it isn't Colonel Cormac Kincade. What are you doing so far from those little boys you've been tutoring?"

Cormac laughed. "Oh, they're hardly boys anymore, and they are comin' along quite nicely. Not so sure about the armor the MIC is crankin' out, though. I'm gonna need James to take a look at it." He dropped a panel from the arm of one of the suits on the table.

Jessica forgot about her wrap as her love of cybernetics took over. Flipping a small device from her belt, she instinctively worked on the panel, prying off circuits and reattaching them where they suited her. "Simple problem, really. They are trying to use too much redundancy. Everything from power to fluids in these machines needs to flow like veins, and when you try to force it into a grid, it fights against itself. Everything slows down, and the whole machine acts gummy...that should do it!" She tossed the panel back to Cormac and began eating again.

Cormac whistled in astonishment. "You realize I had every engineer in three divisions and the guys from the MIC working on a problem you just solved between bites of food!"

Jessica smiled an overly sweet smile and attempted to impersonate James's voice when he was on a rant. "Those high-tech loons just don't realize that you can't make cybernetics and robotics like you do ships. Things just don't work the same. It's more alive, and if you treat them like they aren't, then they won't be!"

Cormac smiled as he sat down. "Yep, that's what he's always saying. I don't know why Casey doesn't take his word for it. James is the best cybernetics engineer I know of."

Jessica ignored Cormac's business talk, becoming too engulfed in the flavor of her wrap to care about the stubbornness of other men.

Cormac stretched, yawned, and looked at his food. "You're right, better things to do right now." He tore into his wrap with wild enthusiasm.

Several minutes later, the pair sat, licking their fingers and watching the hustle and bustle.

"It's good to see people being people again, isn't it?" Jessica mused.

Cormac nodded his assent. "After the exile I didn't think peaceful things were possible anymore, and here we are standing on solid ground, full bellies. There is a soccer màtch starting right over there," he warned, as a checkered ball flew toward them. With instinct and precision, Jessica caught the ball in the crux of her foot, then flipped it onto her toe, where she balanced it. The superior stability of her cybernetic foot wowed the group of children. After she removed her shoe and showed them that her foot was synthetic, she tossed the ball back to the group of thoroughly impressed children, and they ran off squealing to continue their game. Jessica sat for a long while, watching the group play in the low light of the planet's long dawn. The air that flowed down the length of the bazaar was not hot, but warm and refreshing. She sat pleasantly basking in the breeze.

"This is good," Jessica murmured to herself.

"Yes, it is," Cormac replied. The big man had propped his bench along another and was using it as a lounge chair with his feet on the table. He and Jessica soaked in the morning, realizing that for the first time in months, they were enjoying life rather than thinking of ways to survive.

"I wish James were here," Jessica pined.

"Oh, that reminds me," Cormac said. "He asked me to pick you up for him. He said that he has some big news but needs to take care of some things first. Said that both of us should be there. He said that it would change everything."

Jessica seemed disappointed as she gazed at the sky, a few reflecting glints giving away the positions of some of the largest ships in orbit. "I wish he would stop looking for danger. He keeps taking more and more responsibility. It's like he looks for it around every corner."

Cormac cocked an eye open at her disheartened remarks. "It's his nature. Your boy's a leader and a fighter. If he stops, he'll die." Cormac paused for a contemplative second, enjoying the feeling of the breeze before continuing. "It's not like you need to look for it right now, though. Three months ago, I was a lieutenant in a division rotting on a rusted hulk. Now I am a colonel training an elite force for an invasion of an alien planet to free a people I've never met."

Jessica looked a little puzzled. "What do you mean?"

Cormac closed his eyes and inhaled the smells of the new planet. "It means that it doesn't matter where you came from or who you are anymore. If you have a skill or talent, you will be asked to use that skill in as many ways as you're able. James is the best warrior I have ever seen, and people follow him without question, like some sort of prophet. Mankind needs that. Our humanity needs that. He understands that need, and he will take that duty and fight for it. That's what he is."

Jessica stared at the sky, taking in Cormac's words. She understood, but she wished she didn't. She simply wanted to be with James, to be happy, but that was impossible. He never stopped moving, never sat still, and was only happy when he was building something or fighting. But she loved him anyway. Jessica was almost in tears wishing that James would stop putting himself in danger.

Cormac understood her desire to see James at peace, but he also understood what drove the young warrior. He had seen the boy in battle, and it was horrifying. He would have deemed him a monster had it not been for two things: the source for his rage and his reasons for fighting. After months of teaching James how to fight with an expert's grace and power aboard the Santa Monica and spending many nights designing and building the new tools and armor that eventually led to the battle suits, Cormac had come to understand James's motivation was personal. He blamed himself for the death of his family, especially his sister.

Somehow, he knew that James also felt responsible for the entire colony that was destroyed. He had bottled his anger, wrath, and grief inside, only releasing it through battle and his work with cybernetics. The responsibility he felt for those tragic losses did not die with time; it only grew. Eventually, Cormac had come to see that James blamed himself for anything that happened to others, foolishly taking responsibility for that which he had no control. The result was dangerous. He had tried to help James work through his issues of responsibility, but to no avail.

If anything happened to anyone James felt responsible for, his anger grew, and his need to protect what he considered to be his people grew, feeding a never-ending cycle. Cormac hoped it would not lead to a cataclysmic mental meltdown. He hoped that he would attach the responsibility onto something or someone other than himself, and eventually allow the man to deal with the guilt he felt for his sister and family. Cormac knew, however, that it would not be a normal resolution. He was attempting to relieve his guilt through the spilling of blood, something at which James was already instinctively an expert.

Cormac only wondered what would be left of his friend when it was all over. He hoped that he and Jessica would be able to be there for James when it happened.

Getting up from his lounging position by the fountain, Cormac shook the dark thoughts about his friend from his head. "Come on," he said to Jessica. "We should head over to the spaceport. Our shuttle leaves in thirty minutes." The pair began to walk through the city; the sights, sounds, and smells of life woke them from their dark fears about James. As they walked, the pair was treated to a wide range of shops and merchants.

A leatherworker was making some clothes from the skin of an abe, which from the looks of it was tougher than buffalo leather. While his shop was recessed into the prefabricated building, he was working in an open-air awning to both demonstrate his skill and take advantage of the pleasant breeze.

A slow clanking and whirring sound came from a metalworking shop that had all sorts of construction material piled outside with smaller fastening equipment in the window. Even more unusual for a bazaar was a shop sporting full-sized variations of the cowboy skimmer used to harvest the abes. Apparently, the ranching and farming industries had taken off so well that the MIC only needed to continue production of the chassis. It had begun receiving raw materials from some basic mines near the new city, and the specialized businesses on the planet were outfitting them. This allowed for increased diversification and usefulness in the vehicles. Some continued to use the tentacle approach for dealing with livestock, some used specialized low-level adjustable mono-directional shields to engage in construction, and still others were outfitted with water delivery piping and farming gear for fresh lax farms. Stranger still was a shop that simply advertised "Animals." It had pictures of domestic pets such as dogs and cats on the window along with Earth farm animals. In front of the shop, a young boy, about twelve years old, sat next to a pen with a dozen baby abes.

Curiosity drawing her inside, Jessica saw that the owner had got ahold of a bank of bays from one of the colony ships' biogenesis and Earth animal population bays with a full library of genetic profiles and frozen embryos. The setup made producing a viable herd of livestock as simple as sticking an old-style burrito in a microwave. The enhanced gestation of the animals in the tubes, when set to maximum acceleration, would only take days instead of months to rear. The result was an animal with long-term atrophy; they didn't taste very good, but their offspring would be entirely normal.

Wow, she thought, *that woman must have taken out one massive fleet loan to get all this.* It was, however, one of the busiest shops in the market, and Jessica was sure that the woman would have her loan paid off within a month. As she left the shop, Jessica noticed a map above the door that displayed the valley and surrounding mountain ranges. It showed which ranch had animals from the shop and how many. An impressive volume from what she saw on the map.

Cormac had to duck into the shop and almost drag Jessica away from the bio-mechanical tubes before she could pull them apart to see how they worked. "Jessica, if you spend any more time here, we will miss our shuttle." Coming back from the brink of techie insanity, Jessica pulled herself from the shop and continued with Cormac to the spaceport.

The remaining shops were of little interest to either of them once they were informed that the launch time for the shuttle had been moved up by another five minutes. They arrived just in time to flash their identification tags and climb aboard.

The military shuttles had been called to the troopships for some reason that neither Cormac nor Jessica had been informed. The shuttle that picked them up was one of the first civilian operations that had recently been finished, having been overhauled on the surface. As the shuttle left the ground, Jessica wondered what was so important that he had to tell her in person.

Cormac had an idea, but he wasn't sure if it was right; if it was, he couldn't risk telling anyone. He had been informed that the admiral would be present. He had been ordered to send the best squad from each of his divisions ahead and had been asked to facilitate Sergeant Hilben in convening a meeting of the entire Fifty-sixth. This was about to get really interesting really fast, and he knew that James was right in the middle of it. Cormac wondered what he had got the young warrior into when he gave him command of the Fifty-sixth.

1/22/2454

James sat in the meeting with Tinek and Hancock; he had finished the repairs on his arm and had reattached it. The leaders discussed the dissemination of information throughout the fleet and the political ramifications of a potential power play. James hated the politics of it, but he listened intently, knowing that any political controversy could cause a threat to Tinek. The two leaders didn't mind James working on his arm while they talked. They both knew that he needed to be fully functional by the time the broadcast reached the fleet. James's injuries had healed after Hancock had ordered that he be put in a full regeneration chamber, which normally was reserved for critical patients and time-sensitive cases. James had protested that there were people with far worse injuries than his, but Hancock's order was final and James was moved to the beginning of the queue for healing.

Through her cybernetic link, Jessica had informed him that she and Cormac had arrived aboard and were waiting outside. Wrapping up their conversation by deciding to make the final announcement in two hours, Tinek left for his room, flanked by two of James's armored warriors. Everyone knew that they would need as much rest as possible before the announcement.

Pulling his two friends inside the meeting room, James and Hancock explained the situation to them. The admiral wanted to get as many armored soldiers mixed throughout the fleet as he could before the announcement, which is why he had called Cormac. Jessica had been given access to all information because James had tasked her to inform and update controllers for his division. He had told Tinek that he needed her for statistical and tactical support. Cormac took the information with the stoic nature of one who had both seen it coming and comprehended the heavy weight and ramifications of the task that had been set before them.

Jessica, in contrast, was excited. The new government didn't matter much to her, but she was really excited about James's new position. Jessica answered several of the admiral's questions regarding the logistics of controlling squads spread throughout the fleet, acting as backups for the security forces and regular troops. Satisfied with her answers and finishing a few details with Cormac, the admiral left the room as well. He intended to get at least a little sleep before an entirely new hell broke loose.

On the way back to the Cerberus's main hangar, they continued discussing the new situation and what it meant. Cormac was worried; he had suspected that something like this was about to happen, but he didn't know if his men were ready for anything so delicate so soon. *At least they aren't going into combat,* he reassured himself. *Just a bit of crowd control.*

"So, Tinek made you and the Fifty-sixth his personal guard. Quite an honor," Cormac said, smiling.

James smiled, trying to remain humble. "It's the division, not me."

"Oh, but you are its commander and most successful warrior. Something tells me you were part, if not all, of the decision."

"Of course, he was!" Jessica cut in. "No one can protect the emperor better than James." Her tone was completely emphatic, and Cormac's eyebrow went up.

"I am not so sure you should be calling him that. It, uh… has connotations."

Jessica put her hands on her hips. "Then what should we call him? King sounds dorky. He clearly doesn't qualify for prince or regent anymore. He is the final authority for two races, so I think that qualifies for imperial status."

Cormac didn't look pleased. "I still don't think it's appropriate, especially in this situation. If people who don't support the union start hearing others call him the emperor, it could cause unnecessary unrest, maybe even violence," Cormac said, clearly worried.

James was annoyed by the idea of civil unrest. "Oh, lighten up, Cormac. It's not like anyone will want to fight about what we call him, and if they do, that's what me and the guys are for. I got to name the unit; it's my right as leader of the guard. I called it the Imperial Hammer, and he didn't object."

The unhappy look on Cormac's face turned even more sour. "Maybe he just let it slide, hoping you would come to your senses and pick another name."

Too offended to talk about it anymore, James sat in silence through the remainder of their flight back to the planet. Jessica and Cormac continued to argue, mostly good-naturedly, about how Tinek should be addressed in the new society.

After their flight landed in the base's military spaceport, James and Jessica made their way to the command building while Cormac went to prepare a briefing for his divisions. Inside the command structure, Jessica checked the locations of all the divisions' troops through their sub-dermal implants. "They are all in the barracks, James."

"Good, I have the mechanics painting the imperial seal on the suits right now," James said, as he finished inputting commands in a console. Leaving the command structure, he crossed the small patch of dirt that passed for a quad in the center of the complex of buildings and entered the barracks. The entire force of active duty soldiers in the division were present, minus the two James had left with Tinek. Even the support crews and controllers were there beside the warriors in the massive structure.

Standing in front of his men, James prepared to inform them of their new role. "My brothers of the sword, an event today has changed everything we know. We have fought the Tarin'Tal together and forged victories from their ashes. We have shown that their strength and numbers mean nothing to us. My friends...you are elite! You are the best soldiers at our race's disposal, the hammer that protects our people from those who wish to slaughter them. On our shoulders we have borne the brunt of two battles crucial to the survival of our people. Now we have been called to yet another task to ensure the safety of our people.

"We can no longer exist as exiles. The Illani, a noble race, like ours in innumerable ways, have joined us against the Tarin'Tal. Their leader, Tinek, has given us vital information and support at every turn. And now, he has given us an opportunity that seemed impossible only a short time ago. The fates of the Illani and human race have been entwined into one. In both defense and survival we cannot afford to live apart. We have been joined into one great empire!" Behind James, a holographic projector displayed the Constitution of Unification in huge letters that everyone across the field could read.

"Both the authority of our military commanders and the duly elected civilian representatives have ratified this government. We are one people, and Tinek is our emperor. You, each of you personally, have been called to protect this empire. You are the only ones capable of maintaining unity, and you are the emperor's personal force. The Imperial Hammer! And we shall lead our unified races to victory and honor yielding a lasting survival, peace, and freedom to our people!" As James finished his speech, there was a moment of silence throughout the mass of men, followed a second later by a rhythmic clashing thump of fists hitting chests.

One of the soldiers in the front, Thomas Hilben, shouted, "Hail Tinek, Tinek through Ursidae!" His shout was picked up by the hundreds of men assembled, all declaring their loyalty to their new emperor, and, to James's infinite surprise, their commander as well.

The group did not dissipate when they were dismissed; they were abuzz with excitement. Their enthusiasm was almost on a delusional scale.

James went to the command structure to prepare troop distribution and security organization with Nin Serbel and several ranking security officers from the fleet. The organization of men still assembled outside, however, had devolved into an impromptu celebration. It was a good thing that there was no alcohol left in the fleet or the party would have got out of hand; the men would have been rendered useless for the new role they were celebrating. After a few minutes, Thomas succeeded in calming the men down. He explained everything he could about their new role, and even showed them their new salute.

Their attention was taken from Thomas, however, when their newly painted suits came out from the maintenance building. They were rolled out on long racks ready for them to be equipped. The imperial seal, which had previously been the hereditary seal of Tinek's family line, further stylized by human artists, was boldly emblazoned on the metal chests. One of James's lieutenants, Sarah Michelson, ran her hand along the freshly dried paint; the swirling flames in the center were flanked by a vicious-looking Illani animal on one side and an Earth-style dragon on the other. Both were surrounded by the outline of a rectangular shield which stood out starkly from the pitch black of the suit. The radiance of the dark-red and silver paint contrasted with both the white inside and black outside the symbol, and she thought it was beautiful. The only part of the suit not painted pitch black was a triangular slab of metal along the face of the helmet, like a knight's visor. It was solid metal and painted pure white. The entire division stood silent, admiring the impressive new uniform colors blanketing their armor. With a whoop, one of the soldiers in the front of the group rushed forward to put his armor on. The remainder of the division, each eager to sport their new colors, followed him closely.

Even though the Illani did not use flags on their world, preferring to paint massive seals on walls and doors, James had insisted that his division use flags bearing the same imperial seal as their banners. Although Tinek had been hesitant to employ the human tradition, he obliged James's enthusiastic requests. Each squad was given a flag on a short pole that allowed the bottom of the flag to hang just below and behind the warrior's head.

As James came back out of the command building, the division's lead lieutenant, Judas, signaled the entire division. "Atten-tion!" In a flash of movement, the sea of black came rigid. "Present colors!" Washing color across the field, each division unbound their flags and raised them diagonally across their chests. "Present arms!" Rasping metal against metal, every warrior that did not bear a flag unsheathed their swords, pulling them from the right hand side of their back and around to stand vertically along the center of their armored bodies. The force stood arrayed in armor and arms prepared to stand with their new leader in presentation to the fleet. Infinitely pleased with his arrayed men, James gave them their new salute, slamming his fist into his chest and holding it there as he made a slight bow. Reverberating across the entire valley, the warriors mirrored the salute, impacting their powerful fists into their armored chests.

James walked to the front and center of the division, to the last waiting mobile armor alcove. Standing in front of his men, James stepped back into the station. A sheet of metal slid in front of James, partially blocking him from the view of his men. It slid backward onto him and encased him in the frontal armor. As the joints locked down, he raised his arms, which were tracked by the computer and encased in their own armor in a swivel of movement. All the suit's connections hissed a cloud of gas as the suit pressurized, and a series of cables popped off and sipped back into the alcove.

James stepped down onto the dirt to face his men. There was no difference between the exterior of his suit and that of his men's; they didn't need any. Their face displays informed each warrior of each other's name and rank whenever they came into another's view. Standing on the dusty soil, James whipped his sword from its sheath on his lower back, spinning it in several skillful strokes and re-sheathing it in one clean motion. "Let's go crown an emperor."

His force spun their own swords into their sheaths as well, the rasps of metal entering metal followed by a loud cheer. "Hail Tinek, Tinek through Ursidae."

The division turned in fluid order, the precision of their cybernetic armor allowing them to synchronize their movements within a fraction of a second. Moving into the large transport stationed at the landing pad opposite the command building, the men began their journey to serve their new emperor. When the transport was full of the warriors and their controllers, it rose in a wave of displaced air as gravity manipulators and thrusters pushed it into the sky. The trip did not take long; it never did. Breaking atmosphere in only five minutes, the shuttle swiftly wound through the fleet until it arrived at the Princeps. The emperor was going to make his announcements from the invulnerable carrier instead of the Cerberus because of its huge hangar where thousands of people could gather at once.

During the flight, James had wirelessly transmitted his orders into each individual warrior's armor. He kept his lines open in case any of his men needed further clarification. They didn't. His men exited the shuttle, broke into their squads, and scattered across the hanger and the surrounding deck. James found Tinek exactly where the new emperor had said he would be. The sub-dermal implant he was now sporting, as well as the signals from his two guards, Rick and Sam, didn't hurt either. The other eight members of James's personal squad trailing him as the commander of the new Imperial Hammer division approached the emperor. "Emperor Tinek, I have brought the entirety of the Imperial Hammer aboard. They have spread throughout the area. If there are any problems, three hundred men are at your disposal immediately."

"Very good," Tinek said, impressed. "Only a few hours ago you were having trouble standing, and yet again you stand as a leader of men. By the way, what is this title 'emperor'? The translator is not turning it into an Illani word."

James was surprised. "You mean that you are the leader of your race and you don't have a word for emperor?"

"No," Tinek responded simply. "We have words that translate into leader, king, and regent." Tinek used the English words; James was still shocked at the man's ability to learn languages so quickly.

James explained the significance of the word *emperor*. "An emperor is the title of someone who rules an empire. He is a highest-level ruler, many times a king over other kings." Tinek seemed to understand the warrior's meaning.

"We do have a term that translates vaguely into empire. But that word—it sounds so much stronger." James understood the concern that Tinek was expressing about the nature of the term. "Do human emperors tend to infringe on the lives of citizens? I do not wish to convey that image to both your people and mine."

James thought about it for a minute before responding. "Some emperors have slaughtered millions and devastated cultures, and others have been the best thing that ever happened to their people. I don't think that the nature of the emperor's power or whether he uses it for good or evil is what defines his position. It seems to me more like it is a description of the extent of the realm and number of inhabitants. What I think is most important is that it has an extremely strong connotation of power, the immovable, unstoppable power of a people. If we look at ourselves as an empire, it shows the people that we know that we can defeat the Tarin'Tal and give them a strong unified identity."

Considering the definition James had given him, Tinek was still not convinced. "I will discuss this with Hancock and the council and receive their opinion on the title. Until then it would be a good idea to keep such titles as low-key as possible," Tinek said, slipping back into his native language and letting the computer translate it for him.

Not liking the direction their conversation had taken, but respecting the new leader too much to argue, James responded, "Of course," and let the matter drop. He may be a combative and opinionated man, but he knew better than to start an argument with Tinek on such a pivotal and uneasy day.

Tinek returned to his notes and continued rehearsing his English as James proceeded to ensure the security of the bay. Jessica had routed the entire division's mapping and personnel information into one of her screens, which she passed on to James. This allowed both of them to identify potential threat locations, troop deployment, and optimal stations for his men. It was under twenty minutes to the presentation, and the room was almost full to capacity. It was not so much a room as an expanse; the bay extended the length of nine football fields in every direction and was over three hundred feet tall. It was one of the Princeps's main hangars, but all its crafts had been crammed into the other three hangars to make room for the event. The room was so large that the individuals at the back saw those on stage as blurry specks.

Ten minutes before the beginning of the presentation, Hancock and Cho joined Tinek at the elongated podium and flanked him on either side. James and the rest of the squad, having returned from their short break, took position behind the three leaders, fanning out behind them and stationing themselves like ancient suits of armor in old Earth castles. The group struck both an imposing and inspiring image; the line of black armor behind the three leaders gave them a sense of power while at the same time made them look more human. As the timer James had running in his helmet ticked down to zero, the lights in the room dimmed, and a gigantic holographic projector fired up behind the stage. The prerecorded presentation that the three had made only hours earlier began to play.

The same image was being shown throughout the fleet. Everything from the frigates to the massive colony ships had active screens. On the planet, several hundred thousand civilians gathered around massive projectors to hear the announcement that had been promised to be the most important one they would ever hear.

As the recording wound to a close, stunned and dynamically different reactions swirled throughout the fleet. Some were mad as hell. Some were overjoyed. Some were just glad to have a final destination. The vast majority viewed the turn of events with reserved skepticism, wondering if such actions were warranted or rash while at the same time understanding that something needed to be done. After everyone had recovered from the initial shock at the magnitude of the event, Tinek, Hancock, and Cho opened the floor to questions. And there were questions.

19 >> Sedition

1/28/2454

Very little had been accomplished over the past few days. There had been several outbursts of violence throughout the fleet, but the armored troops and the Imperial Hammer had kept them to a minimum. While Tinek had insisted that he be referred to as regent or king, a popular imperial movement had swept through the military and several civilian factions who supported Tinek. They had almost forcibly changed the vernacular from a king to an emperor. Whether it was out of a sense of unity, because of the strength it conveyed in contrast to their exiled status, or because they just like the sound of it, no one quite knew or cared.

Councilman Austin, despite having sworn his fealty to Tinek at the time of ratification, had recanted his loyalty, and a movement was spreading among his supporters demanding Tinek's impeachment. Two other councilmen had followed suit, gathering supporters on two of the colony ships. While almost the entire military had grown to accept and even prefer the new structure of command, several groups in the civilian population did not see similar unanimity.

Rather than implement further controls that would seem like martial law and vindicate the fears of those who opposed the new government, the leaders of the fleet had allowed the new "Pure Democratists," as they preferred to be called, to freely gather aboard the two ships. The Democratists had been transferring between the four colony ships left in orbit. The two ships full of men either ambivalent or supportive toward Tinek and the new empire had agreed to be patient and settle on Lintalla to help the rebuilding economies in exchange for large, low-interest, long-term fleet loans. The Democratist-dominated ships, however, were demanding that they too be allowed to land on Sh'in far away from the new city and imperial control.

In stark contrast to the vaunted ideals that he used to condemn the new government, Austin was demanding that he be made governor without even a proper election. He continually appealed to his election as councilman as justification of his actions, stating that he defended the will of the people.

Austin's supporters had begun running not-so-subtle propaganda throughout the fleet, mostly aboard the two colony ships they had occupied. Normally their message was aimed at destroying the reputation and authority of Tinek, Hancock, and the new government. Intermixed, however, were posters featuring Austin as a "champion of democracy" and saying it was "the will of the people."

Karen swiveled back from her desk as a new stream of civil registrations scrolled through her holo-display. The governor and her staff now occupied one of the city's new central towers, which dominated the valley skyline. The colony ships had been designed with several towers meant to be anchored into the ground as the rest of the ship was dismantled, creating instant centralized structures for a new city. Contrary to most colonization efforts, which landed one colony ship per city and very few per planet, the fleet had landed two ships in the same location. The resulting assortment of structures and infrastructure machinery allowed the new city to grow at an exponentially impressive rate.

After only a few weeks, the valley floor had been covered with sturdy prefabricated buildings, several towers, a fledgling industrial sector, and a booming construction industry. Further from the city center, there were rows of new buildings made from local materials that the colonists had recently begun to mine.

All this development meant a lot of work for Karen. Initially the fleet had established a homestead policy for land occupancy and ownership, but it had quickly proven inefficient with such a quickly growing urban center. Karen had eventually established a fleet loan system for commercial and industrial development, mainly concerning land within the valley, the city's de facto limits, and a separate system resembling the old homestead system for those in residential areas. The problems for the new governor seemed to be coming, not from people wanting to do business and build lives on Sh'in, but from those who had a problem with the way it was being done. She constantly received complaints about property rights, why there wasn't a representation system yet, why there weren't more public utilities yet, why people didn't get this, that, and the other thing.

She didn't know if the recent behavior was a result of being cooped up on a refugee ship with everything taken care of for them, or if she was simply dealing with morons. Whenever she came up with a solution, which normally included a fleet loan and an entrepreneur supplying something that most Earth governments had come to provide, she was bombarded with complaints and demands. It didn't matter how well someone ran or implemented a new communications net, someone was always demanded more service, fewer costs, and easier use for whatever they deemed a "life essential."

Sheesh! Karen thought. *Just a few weeks ago, they didn't have a room to themselves, and now they are lobbying for better holo-comm service. These people are some of the most ungrateful idiots I have ever seen. And I ran the Takus mining operation!* The recent development with the Democratists was not making her job any easier.

Recently, Karen had been receiving demands from the new Democratist faction. They had insisted that they be given land and resources for the construction of a new city on the opposite side of the planet closer to the polar region. They had also demanded diplomatic and governing independence as a separate entity from Karen's authority. Even though she had insisted that she did not have the authority to give either land or title, the Democratists still hounded her. Karen and the gubernatorial staff were slightly isolated from the volatile political problems of the fleet by both her responsibility and the fact that the people under her authority were primarily concerned with getting their lives restarted. Even with the malcontents' continual griping, her job had been relatively stable and sane compared to the controversies Hancock and Tinek endured. But that was about to change.

Karen continued through the lists of requests: additional fleet loans for more equipment and labor, homestead applications, mining applications, and so on. An annoying whine from her communications console interrupted her. Tapping a button, she accepted the high-priority call. A man's worried voice came through the speakers. "We've got a situation here, Governor. A protest is forming in sector thirteen. They are calling for the removal of Tinek, Hancock, and yourself. They aren't violent yet, but at the rate the crowd is growing, their peaceful demeanor could change in a hurry."

Closing her eyes and releasing a breath in frustration, Karen pondered her possible responses. "Contact Cormac...request a division for a possible riot situation. We can't risk damage to our limited supplies of planetary capital. Set up a perimeter with both local divisions, and keep non-protesting civilians away from the target area. Don't interfere, do not attempt to disperse them. Pick five men and wire them for covert surveillance. Have them enter the crowd as protesters to search for ulterior motives. If they become violent, use stun weapons. Understood?"

The voice on the other end was reassured by her confidence as he responded curtly, "Yes, sir." Pushing herself back from the desk, Karen swiveled her chair around to peer out the huge window of her office, which had once been the captain's quarters. Slowly she inhaled and exhaled again, knowing that she would need to center herself. This type of problem was exactly why she hadn't wanted the job in the first place. *But nooo,* she thought, Hancock had insisted, and he just wouldn't take no for an answer. *Big jerk,* she thought, letting trivial thoughts settle over her until she found herself ready to confront the new crisis.

Several minutes later, Karen stood in the recently constructed planetary situation room with several personnel and Commander Taft, who had been promoted and assigned to planetary security. The central display projected an aerial view of the growing mob. The demonstration, which had started near the central spaceport, had quickly grown in size and strength. Being unprovoked and completely accommodated, Karen quickly assumed that the crowd's borderline violence and ferocity was motivated by something other than that of a normal political demonstration. Then again, everyone in the fleet was a refugee who had barely survived the annihilation of their civilization; nothing about them could really be called normal.

Tapping a panel on her arm, Karen asked, "Infiltration?"

A muffled voice came back over the communications array. "Successful. However, we still don't know the crowd's motivation other than their stated goals." The local troops had begun moving onlookers and pedestrians out of the way of the marching group. They had even gone so far as to block traffic and establish a region of restricted airspace along their projected path. The group watched as the demonstration slowly turned into an aggressive mob. Their movements sped up as their path led them to the central authority, the building from which Karen currently watched. For another fifteen long minutes, the aggressive throng continued its advance. The group locked in the situation room could do nothing. They didn't want to provoke a violent reaction or give the appearances of martial law, but the group's demands were ridiculous, and they were acting inherently violent.

A gaggle of drones buzzed over the mob. Until now, the protestors had ignored both the mechanisms and the soldiers bordering the roadway. In a flash of movement, the mob, which had slowly evolved from the demonstration, turned into a riot. The guarding soldiers responded with precision, snapping their shields on with a crackling hiss. One of the mob members walked forward and threw a large mass at the building's main entrance. A squad of soldiers rushed forward and stepped over the object, shields raised against the violence, then retreated back into the building slowly, taking the object with them. Inside the building, it was scanned by a combination of hazardous material and explosive detection devices. When they received the all-clear sign, the hard mass was brought up to the situation room.

Setting the object on an analysis table in the corner of the room, the guard stepped back as the machine went to work. Pinpoint gravity devices levitated the circular object and sent it slowly rotating, giving everyone a full view of the object. A mechanically generated voice came smoothly through the system's speakers. "The object appears to be a holo-pod. Preliminary data scans indicate that it contains nothing more than a holographic presentation. All signs say that it's safe."

Nodding, Karen assented to its recommendation. "Activate it," she said.

The pod ceased its rotation, and after extending a tripod, it fell on the platform. The top opened a series of narrow slits that emitted a hologram. A human shadow appeared above the ball and began to speak. "Your constant violations of our rights have driven us to this. You have refused to let democracy speak, and this is what happens. We know that the corrupt officials in the fleet will not step down, so we have kept our demands to a quandary minimum. We must have recognized space for a new colony, supplies, and support from your government. We must receive construction assistance and full trade rights.

"Furthermore, if we are not granted full governing autonomy, there will be serious ramifications. We are not accountable to any emperor, least of all the alien Tinek. The representatives from the fleet had no right to force us into an empire and kill democracy. Finally, we must have free entry into our domain, no blockade, and no ramifications. If you do not comply with a document agreeing to our terms signed by the ruling triad and Governor Karen Emerson, we will tear down your colony and separate ourselves by force. This is your only warning!" The device resealed itself, pulling its tripod inside and closing its emitters before rolling over on its curved side.

"Well," Karen said, "I sure didn't expect this!"

James walked down the halls of the Legatus. The ship's repairs were finished, and it was again fully functional. There were, however, still maintenance crews busy throughout the vessel, giving the ship a new paint job. Hancock had insisted that the Legatus be made the imperial flagship, stating that they needed to keep the Cerberus for the heaviest engagements, holding the cruiser in reserve. Tinek, on the other hand, was still fascinated with the concept of a flagship. His people, having neither a strong military or naval tradition, had never developed the concept.

Tinek had been dealing with political crisis from throughout the fleet for the entire day. James was impressed by the man's tact and efficiency in putting out even the most severe political fire. James knew that he never would have had as much patience as the new emperor.

Tinek, Vilnir, and James sat down in the imperial office, which had been converted from an old conference room aboard the Legatus. The three other warriors who had been following the trio from a distance took stations outside the door. One stood on each side of the entrance, and the other stood across from the door. Their pitch-black armor let passersby know that they should simply move along—as quickly as possible.

All three men were tired from their most recent situation. Tinek had solved it by making a personal appearance and answering several questions from some local leaders aboard a large freighter-come-refugee transport. Their questions had been thorough but fair, and Tinek had been able to satisfy them. It had been one of their more normal runs: simple questions about fairness and accountability under the new system. The answers were all in the constitution and several documents that had been released explaining them, but people still wanted to know personally that the emperor neither wanted nor had the power to supersede the safeguards for personal freedom.

No sooner had the trio sat down to recover than both James's and Tinek's communications devices went off in a shrill of light and sound. While Tinek began a three-way conversation with Hancock and Cho over their holo-comms, James tapped a device behind his ear. He had streamlined his communications device; the volume of calls he now received had begun to necessitate an implant, something he was not adverse to.

"Ursidae here."

A crisp voice spoke straight into the warrior's ear. "We have multiple situations, sir!" the soldier on the other end said, panicking. "Reports are coming in from throughout the fleet: rallies, demonstrations, riots, and some explosions of unknown origins."

James's jaw clenched. After all the recent problems, this turn of events was not unexpected. "Keep me informed as the situation develops. Activate the entire Hammer and get them here now. Diversify the transports and methods. I'm willing to bet they're after Tinek, and hence us."

"Yes, sir!" the voice snapped. The communication ended as the man went to fulfill his commander's orders.

"He's right," Jessica's voice hummed, seeming to come from his own subconscious. She was using their direct link. Both James and Jessica were on the Legatus, so the connection wasn't hard to maintain. "The fleet is degrading into chaos. Here, I'll show you." James closed his eyes and concentrated on Jessica's, pushing the link they shared into the forefront of both his conscious and unconscious mind. In a rushing sensation, James saw what Jessica saw. A holograph of ships listing controllers came to his "vision."

He saw security cameras of shipboard riots. He saw the mob on the planet. He saw brutal beatings and the destruction of irreplaceable equipment. He also saw the two colony ships pulling from their positions in the fleet and accelerating toward the planet. "Yeah...this is a problem." James spoke into Jessica's mind. "Gather the controllers; we have work to do."

No more than ten minutes later, Tinek stood in the command deck of the Legatus as Vilnir and Harrington provided him with a stream of updates and information. The main display pulsated data from throughout the fleet. Admiral Hancock's image rose from one side of the holo-display, and the two began to discuss possible threat scenarios and ramifications. Tinek had prepared a quick presentation to the fleet after it had been determined that the disturbances were not only inspired by but also instigated by Democratists in a fanatical separatist movement.

"Damn!" Tinek swore in English, in a very human manner. "Austin knows full well that we would have given him permission to land the ships if he and the people wanted it enough. What's his game?" Vilnir stepped forward with a data pad, which he inserted into a console, causing another stream of information to flow through the display.

"It appears he is employing a PR tactic designed to throw your rule into question from two separate perspectives. One: to give the impression that you would deprive people of the freedom to choose where to live and how to live, hence making you look like a dictator. And two: your affiliation with the military headed by Hancock cannot be trusted to protect his skewed view of democracy or the peace. By the looks of the fleet, it seems to be working," Vilnir said, as he backed away from the console to converse with another group of representatives from the fleet.

"I agree with Vilnir," Hancock said. "He knows that his actions are unnecessary and needlessly destructive. He is able to fortify his position while we are forced to concentrate on damage control. If we make any aggressive moves, we will confirm the doubts he is sowing throughout the fleet."

"Damn," Tinek repeated, "he is good."

James had plugged himself into the communications console, giving him the ability to monitor troop, population, and ship movements and still keep an eye on Tinek and the room. The two colony ships continued their descent to the planet's surface. They had finished their haphazard movement through the fleet and were about to enter the planet's atmosphere. Hancock had ordered every ship to move out of their way, reducing the risk of a collision caused by the speeding ships. The only military activity that had been taken in response to the space-borne insurrection was a trail of two destroyers, ten frigates, and ten Peregrine squadrons for each ship. Their movements had been reserved and cautious, trying not to panic the isolationist Democratists but still letting them know that they were being watched closely.

Similar reservation, however, was not shown to the rioters and violence within the fleet. Cormac's men, having been stationed throughout the fleet since the announcement, quickly moved in, in conjunction with normal military troops. The rioters' advances had been brutally stopped by columns of metal and man as the armored soldiers suddenly bore their way in. In defense of the innocents the rioters had targeted, soldiers tore into them. Their armor made short work of any defense while the cybernetic precision allowed them to prevent any major injuries to the rioters.

The regular troops formed a shield wall, their glowing energy defenses forming a luminescent barrier between the violence and the retreating civilians aboard dozens of ships. Then as suddenly as the violence had broken out, it was over. The instigators who could escape fled to the darkest recesses of the massive ships. Those who could not were captured by the heavily armored warriors and swarms of lighter soldiers. Try as the Democratist leaders did, they could not continue the fight. They had not anticipated the shear immovable masses of the armored divisions. They struck fear in the hearts of those who stood in their way. They had stabbed, swarmed, shot, and even crushed the armored soldiers by machinery, and still they would not die. To the rebel Democratists, they seemed immortal. To some they were angels of salvation; to others, demons of death.

Aboard the Cerberus, Admiral Hancock commanded the detention of the remaining rebels and orchestrated the delivery of the remainder of Cormac's troops into the fray below. Tinek and James observed the battles as they came to a close. They began to weigh their options through a sea of information pouring across their screens, far more than any human or Illani could process.

Austin's plans had been cut short. The colony ships were headed to the ground—that would have happened anyway—but the fleet lacked the chaos that he had been hoping to blame on Tinek and Hancock.

Cho walked back into the room, followed by a stream of officials, all of which held data pads, recording devices, and other tools of the PR trade. As he reached the holographic display, A'ssia motioned to one of her officers, and two of the chairs slid into the deck and were replaced by a long desk. Buzzing through the room, the techs and experts worked on ways to minimize the effect of the recent incident on both popular opinion of the new government and the general morale of the fleet.

A man with a large bundle of equipment set up a recording system attached to the end of the table. James didn't know if the man was inept or simply unobservant; he had switched the camera to not only record but to broadcast as well. The young man, probably just out of college at the time of the exodus, then walked around the table to ask his superior some unimportant question.

Tinek, meanwhile, had been in a heated conversation with both Cho and Vilnir about how best to proceed. Cho had wanted to present a strong military presence in their broadcast. Vilnir advocated a balanced approach. Tinek was fearful that almost any action would be interpreted as militaristic and dictatorial. He had convinced himself that he was now in a no-win situation and was beginning to crack under the pressure. A'ssia discerned the young ruler's breaking point even through delivering orders among her forces. Pulling him aside, the young captain attempted to reassure Tinek and help him understand the human viewpoint on such a situation. The Illani had some precedents to such political controversy, but never in such a powder keg situation involving the entire domain. In only a few minutes, she was able to calm Tinek down, and he came back to his rational self.

Disturbed by a shout from one of the stations, Tinek and A'ssia spun toward the holo-display. The same boy who had set up the devices earlier burst through a group of men, pulling a long dagger out of a shattered implement. The guards in the room swung around to blast the assassin, but they were too late. He threw the dagger with blinding speed and precision, and it spun through the air toward Tinek. He saw it coming but knew that he couldn't move in time; he would die. He would die without saving his race. He would die without fulfilling his new responsibilities.

In the blink of an eye, everything went black, but nothing happened. The darkness vanished, and Tinek realized James was holding the offending knife less than a millimeter from the young emperor's forehead. With an ear-splitting roar, James returned the knife to its sender with more than a thousand times its original force. It exploded in a pink mist of bone, brain, and blood out the back of the assassin's head and buried itself into the console directly in front of the camera the would-be assassin had set up.

Tinek was in shock; someone had tried to kill him! He realized a second later that he had pressure on his shoulder. It was A'ssia; she had gripped him in a protective embrace. She slid down his side with an ugly groan. In horror, Tinek realized that his hand was covered in blood; there was another knife in her back. A gurgling crack from the other side of the room confirmed the existence of a second assassin as Hilben dropped a man's limp form from his armored hand.

Weakly A'ssia demanded to know if Tinek had been hurt. "Shut up!" he stammered. "Be quiet and try not to move...Medic!" he screamed. "Get me a damn medic!"

Before he could finish his demand, a team of medical personnel buzzed around the Legatus's captain. They brushed Tinek aside.

"Emperor or not," Cho stated sympathetically, "they need room to work," he said, as he pulled the man away from the mass of personnel.

Tinek turned to James and Hancock's helpless images in the holo-comm. "They will burn for this! You hear me? Burn!" He shouted wrathfully in English, his accent almost nonexistent. "Convene the council. Admiral, come aboard the Legatus." He turned to Captain Harrington's second-in-command. "Unfurl the colors and take the ship to full alert, put us in orbit directly above the landed colony ships, and send an ultimatum to Austin. He comes to account for his actions or he dies! He will not use more innocents as shields. I will not play the pacifist anymore. I will learn from your violent human history. I cannot be an Illani ruler only. I must act human, be human, and defend my people with lethal force. Humans are a warrior race, so I will not rule as a pacifist. Mankind has learned to fight fire with fire. I will take this lesson to heart. Anyone who harms my people will burn!"

Anger dripped from every word, and his eyes swirled black with wrath. The essence of vengeance oozed from every pore; he did not seem like an Illani. He did not seem like a human. He was an emperor. He turned to Cho and grabbed his collar. "Convene the council now!"

"I will go," Cho said, giving a slight bow as he quickly left the room. James stood in shock at the strength and wrath of the emperor. His respect and loyalty for the man grew beyond measure. He saw the same unyielding drive to protect his people who lived unendingly in himself. He had finally found a man who could protect his people. Turning to view the remaining techs with lethal suspicion, James noticed that the recorder was still broadcasting. With a quick flip of his wrist, he deactivated it. He followed his emperor from the room after the levitating gurney that held the still bleeding form of Captain A'ssia.

1/28/2454

The fleet had been brought to full alert as they waited in geosynchronous orbit above the site where the two rebel colony ships had landed. A few frigates and mercenary ships had joined the Democratist rebels during the confusion, and an entire division of fleet weaponry actively targeted every last one of the traitors. Admiral Hancock had returned to the Cerberus and agreed with Tinek that any further rebellion would be met with lethal force. He held the fleet ready to make good on the threat. James stood on the command deck of the Legatus with Harrington's second-in-command. He paced back and forth, staring at the holo-display of the new rebel colony from orbit. A dark cloud of anger veiled his face as he stared at the usurpers miles below. Tinek was still in the ship's medical bays with A'ssia. James still had no clue whether she would survive or not; he had seen many men on the battlefield die from less. The blood from A'ssia and the two assassins had been cleaned, and a tech was repairing the communications station from which James had ripped out his still connected arm to reach Tinek in time.

The entire Imperial Hammer was now on board the Legatus; he had even brought up the full complement of techs and controllers. James had posted two entire squads to accompany Tinek at all times; the remainders were spread throughout the ship at strategic locations. The lead squad, James's personal men, stood silent with him on the bridge, sharing their leader's thirst for revenge. Tinek had placed the ship under James's command in his and A'ssia's absence, and he itched to bombard the ships and rebels below. He found the very existence of those ships to be an abomination and a personal offense. The seconds turned to minutes and minutes to hours as he waited. Through the holo-display, he watched events unfold throughout the fleet.

On the planet's surface, the riot had turned into a full-blown battle until Cormac and his division had arrived. His troops had dispersed the rioters as easily as they had in the fleet above. The people on the planet, however, were not as forgiving as those in the fleet. They had turned on the rioters as the battle came to a close. They took a brutal vengeance for the damage and death they had tried to spread in their new home. The city had bonded in their revenge, and they slaughtered the rioters in a wholesale massacre.

As the streets were cleared of bodies, the city held a series of elections and official actions. They had elected a local council and mayor; the settlement's name, New Carson City, was finalized; and they had bestowed honors on their governor, Karen Emerson. In an act of loyalty, Carson City drew up a new charter in which it declared itself to be an "imperial city" and condemned the Democratists' landing as an unwelcome and hostile presence on their planet.

In the fleet and in orbit, there was complete outrage at the actions of Austin and his supporters. Following the dispersal of the riots, the majority of the instigators were captured and moved to secure facilities aboard the Cerberus. The council had convened, and a series of decisions were reached. The council stripped Austin and his compatriots of their titles; the entire fleet had already demanded that he be stripped of all rank and authority. Most demanded that he be imprisoned. Some thought that he should be executed. James had read the Illani beliefs on the betrayal of power, and he had come to the same conclusion that their culture had—you betray the trust of people and infringe on their lives, you forfeit your life. But James had vowed his loyalty to Tinek, and he now considered such decisions to be under the emperor's authority.

The rebel colony, however, was left unmolested as the orbiting imperial fleet waited for a response to their demands. The men on the planet had not been idle. They had already begun construction of prefabricated buildings and an industry mimicking the plans that Karen had established for New Carson. James watched as they kept building and building, ignoring the fleet above. He wondered how they expected to survive after such a violent rebellion. Did they expect the fleet and the emperor to stand by and let their actions go without repercussion? They were naive, prideful, and stupid, and James hated them for it.

James saw a frigate attempt to skim away from the fledgling city, possibly converted to one of the new abe designs. James remembered Tinek's orders: "Nothing leaves or enters their landing site." Stepping closer to the display, James enlarged the view of the craft with a flick of his wrist.

"Commander, destroy that frigate with three simultaneous cannon bursts. Make an example of it."

The officer at one of the weapons stations acknowledged James's command with a simple, "Sir," and executed the order. The side of the behemoth warship roared as three of its capital plasma cannons unleashed a salvo of death on the planet. Their aim was perfect, and James watched with satisfaction as an area a mile wide erupted in flames.

"Confirmation?" James asked.

The same officer responded. "Target has been destroyed, and sensors indicate that nothing larger than a millimeter survived the detonation. Your message is sent, sir."

Though the rebels had yet to respond to any of the fleet's demands, emperor's summons, or calls from the council, they did respond to James's actions. Too soon for their message to have been prepared after James's strike, the fleet received a closed message to the Legatus. The communication demanded compensation for "a wanton act of destruction against a peaceful agricultural expedition," continuing to insist that they be delivered—"a ship to replace the one destroyed and the head of the commander responsible for the violent attack on the sovereign state of Free Sh'in."

James sat down as he heard the message. Leaning back in the command chair, a slight smile of disgust and disdain crept over his face. Pressing a button on his arm, James spoke into it. "I assume you heard that, Admiral."

Hancock's voice returned, only slightly distorted, through the ship's communications grid. "Indeed I did. Feel free to send a response."

James could hear a cruel tone in the admiral's voice that matched his own mood. "Thank you, sir. I am going to enjoy this." James turned off his communicator and walked over to the commander whom he had ordered to strike the frigate.

"Move over, Commander. My turn." The happiness in the warrior's voice sent chills down the officer's back as he watched James prepare to rain death on the rebels below.

James focused a moment on his cybernetics before inserting his arm's plug into the console. In that moment, Jessica's thoughts came through to his.

"Ooooh! Can I help?" she chirped.

"Sure," he responded, and he allowed her to slip deeper into his consciousness. Together they picked the flashiest targets on the ground and began to dance the ship's massive armaments on the traitors below. From the ground, the only warning was a series of pulsating flashes from the dawning sky before streaks of fire and explosions erupted throughout the colony ships and surrounding construction sites. James didn't use the large capital guns, instead favoring the ship's smallest cannons. He was sending a message, not engaging in mass murder. In a swelter of fire, sound, and smoke, the ground was turned to chaos. With skill derived from linking the ship's sensors directly into his mind, James and Jessica avoided actually hitting anyone, while still terrifying everyone. The barrage continued for only two minutes. It stopped as abruptly as it had started. It was a not-so-subtle reminder that the continued survival of the rebels was a generous toleration by the fleet above, not a given right—not anymore.

Again James waited, pacing back and forth in front of the display. The room was silent, partly out of fear of the man, partly out of a respect for the seriousness of the situation, and partly out of respect for their injured captain. Time ticked by, and again James began his long wait for something, anything, to happen.

Before he could drive himself back into the recesses of his mind, however, he received a communication request from Cormac. "How is everything over there, James?"

"Other than a rebellion, a near-dead captain, and an emperor who won't take a decent nap, not much. You?"

"We've captured what we think are the last of the riot instigators, and I have been assigned to their security aboard the Cerberus. It's going to take most of my time. Just thought I'd check with you. You don't need any help?"

James looked behind him at his men, still fully dressed in their armor. He had most of his on, but his helmet and forward arm plates sat on a chair around the display. "I'm good, thanks."

"Okay, just checking. Let me know if I can help." James was about to switch the display back to the planet but stopped with his finger on the panel.

"Thanks for calling," James said sincerely, before he hit the trigger, sending the display back to the dusty planet. James would never admit it, but he valued Cormac's opinion like a father's. They hadn't spoken since their argument about the emperor's title, and it helped his state of mind to know that his friend still cared.

No sooner had James switched his display back than the main door to the command deck opened and armored warriors began pouring through. The first ten soldiers of the two divisions James had assigned to Tinek came through the door and took up positions around the room. A horde of medical personnel followed them, carrying A'ssia on an anti-grav bed. She was protesting adamantly that she was in no position to be in the bridge, that her bedridden and disheveled state was embarrassing and would destroy the respect of her men. She was wrong. The murmuring that had begun when the soldiers entered ceased when they saw her.

Every last person in the room came to attention, including James. Led by an unknown force, they all gave her the Hammer's salute. Not only did they reaffirm their loyalty to their captain and their emperor, but the ship also embraced its role as the imperial flagship, new home of the Imperial Hammer. The men did not lift their salute but waited for Tinek, knowing that he would not be far behind their captain. The emperor came into the room surrounded by the second squad James had assigned to him. Even with his nose buried in a data pad, he carried a new presence and strength that did not leave any doubts that this man was the emperor. Not a stagnated leader, not a young idealist, but a vibrant ruler bent on the survival and prosperity of his people—a true emperor. Tinek saw the mass salute and returned one to the men. Together, both the emperor and his men released their salutes, and the bridge exploded in activity.

"Call up six squadrons of frigates and twenty-four squadrons of Peregrines, four squads of fighters per frigate. Have the speaker systems been mounted as I ordered?" Tinek asked.

An officer at a console in the corner of the room swiveled in his chair. "Sir, they are putting the finishing touches on as we speak; they will be in space momentarily."

Tinek acknowledged the man's report with a satisfied grunt as he swiveled back to the display. "Signal the Cerberus, the Leviathan, and the Princeps to begin the prison maneuver."

The communications officer turned to the emperor. "All ships acknowledged, fighters and frigates are space borne and are beginning their descent." Pleased, the emperor leaned back in his chair. He reached over, took A'ssia's hand, and waited for it to begin.

The four ships made a gigantic box over the area in which the rebels had landed. In a swivel of their massive shield projectors, they aimed their arrays at the ground surrounding the Democratists. The enormous projectors were activated, and a shudder of blue irrupted as the shields made contact with the planet's atmosphere below. From the ground, it looked like a gigantic box had been dropped over them from heaven, smiting them from light, wind, and even existence itself. The only thing visible in the shield prison was the light blue blur of the shields; the only sound that could be heard was the light hum of the shields' constant contact with the atmosphere and the screaming of terrified rebels.

Only a few seconds after the shield walls activated, a swarm of frigates and fighters blanketed the surface of the fledgling city, calling for surrender. With the force of speakers that could blow out the windows of an entire skyscraper, they demanded the surrender of the rebel leaders and the delivery of the former councilman Austin, bound and in custody. The swarm's torrent of demands continued for twenty minutes before they were recalled; any further attempts would be useless noise.

The emperor and his personal force waited aboard the Legatus, hoping and praying that either the rebel leaders or those they had led to the surface would do the right thing. But their hopes were futile. Even after James's display of resolve, even after the massive display from the fleet, and even after their imprisonment, they refused to surrender. Either that, or their leaders were keeping control long enough to use the people as a shield for their own skins.

"Still no response, sir," the officer reported. "I am reading a lot of activity down there but no signals and nothing that could be interpreted as surrender...wait, I am getting something...I'll put it on speakers." The holo-display crackled slightly, and the smug features of Austin came into focus.

"Greetings, this is the president of Free Sh'in. We humbly request that you cease your unprovoked aggression toward our peaceful people. We only wish to live our lives unmolested. If you would like to orchestrate a meeting, it can be arranged on our planet. You may even bring a secure—"

"Shut it off," Tinek snapped. "What gall! Is he completely mad? Record the rest for analysis. Then reply with a repeat of the ultimatum."

Tinek's eyes closed. After sitting and thinking for several minutes, he said, "Convene the council. We may need to take a more aggressive path to our solution. Begin a light exterior bombardment. Do not hit anything in the city, but don't give them any rest." Tinek stood to leave the command deck. His guards followed, and they stopped when he passed A'ssia, who was being led back to her quarters where she could rest. Leaning to James, Tinek spoke in a hushed tone: "I want an entire squad with her at all times."

James smiled, clearly happy with himself for anticipating the emperor's orders. "Already done, sir!" The young warrior tilted his data pads to Tinek, showing that he had already deployed two squads to the captain more than an hour earlier. They were waiting just outside the doors for her. Tinek clasped his friend's forearm and shoulder, thanking him with an intense look in his eyes. The emperor was beginning to think of James like more of a brother than an ally or a subject.

As the emperor left the room, James signaled to the rest of his squad. He hit a button on his arm and activated a series of commands he had given to his men earlier that they were already waiting to execute. Three squads of his armored soldiers met him when he reached the Legatus's hangar. Other than the commanders of the four squads he had directly assigned to Tinek and A'ssia, the men standing before him were the most trusted—and the most powerful—warriors under his command. His men had come in a specially renovated mercenary ship that Tinek had requisitioned for him, obliging him with a "special project."

Although it was tight, all thirty-three of his warriors and controllers fit in the craft. One of his unit's controllers had been a pilot before the exile, and she took the craft out of the hangar and sped toward the planet. The Imperial Hammer identification signal prevented any officials who noticed the craft from asking any questions other than, "Need fuel?"

The craft's speed and agility brought them down to the planet's surface, darting through the shield screen with barely more than a whisper. Their emitters harmonized and disconnected when they passed through. In the roar and flashes of the bombardment, the small craft went entirely unnoticed as it made its way to the city below. Using the telemetry of the fleet's sensors, James was able to identify the areas that were the greatest likelihood of finding Austin and his compatriots. They landed hard on the top of one of the colony ship's towers now functioning as one of two hilltop spires. "Move!" James commanded.

The battle began.

Part of the reason James had chosen this particular grouping of towers was their high concentration of weapons signatures. Austin's supporters had succeeded in securing an impressively large number of powerful small-arms weapons, which they used in a desperate attempt to stop James and his men. Their blasts glanced harmlessly off the warriors' shields as they advanced at full bore. The rebel security was scoured off the roof before they realized the power of the forces they were up against. Only fifteen personnel had been posted to the roof of the building. Compared to how many trained personnel had joined Austin, it was a large deployment. The guards had successfully warned the security personnel among the rebel fleet, and by the massive number of men flocking to the adjacent tower, James knew he had been remarkably close to choosing the right spot. James would have taken the frigate to the top of the next tower, but the number of anti-air weapons on the roof would have made the approach more trouble than it was worth. The odds were more favorable for the Imperial Hammer warriors in a straight-up battle than an aerial assault.

The fight was an easy one. James and his men blasted their way down the halls and stairwells to the base of the tower so they could scale the other in search of Austin. He had left one-third of his men with the frigate to defend their escape route and their controllers. That left him with twenty men against the entire mass of the rebel security forces. The battle to the floor of the tower was easy; the rebel resistance was swept away. James and his men let anyone who ran or surrendered live. They immediately killed anyone who continued their treasonous fight. In minutes, James's force began their assault of the lowest level of the building. The resistance in the tower's exit shattered almost as soon as the fight began; the rebel personnel scrambled out of the building, running for their lives.

As the group stood on the ground floor, which was also a security terminal, they attempted to hack into the computers to find Austin's location. Even James's cybernetic hack yielded nothing on the rebel leader's location. Retracting his spikes with a rasp of metal, James turned his attention to the building's large exit. "Looks like we're gonna have to do this the hard way," he stated, no disappointment showing in his voice. He pondered the coming battle. There was a murmur from across the room as the armored warriors agreed with their leader. Even though the faces of the metal men could not be seen behind their solid faceplates, their body language and voices spoke volumes. With several gestures and commands, James arrayed his warriors to assault the courtyard outside the building.

More than five hundred heavily armed rebels had gathered in the courtyard. Some of them carried shields, most carried plasma rifles, some even carried plasma swords. All of them thought they could stop a simple attack of twenty imperial soldiers. They stood, staring at the door to the building, their shear numbers barring the way between the tower James had landed on and the one holding their leaders. There was silence; the noise from inside had stopped as they waited. The ground began to shake, and a length of the wall on either side of the door the rebels expected to be attacked from began to crack. At once, the entire stretch of building collapsed outward, crushed and pushed aside by the unyielding shields and massive weight of the armored warriors. Shocked, the men standing in the courtyard froze. It was a lethal moment. Taking advantage of their enemies' hesitancy, James's warriors attacked. They leveled the first ranks with a series of devastating volleys from their rifles before reaching the lines. There was no stopping them.

The warriors of the Imperial Hammer smashed into the rebels with the force of a cannon barrage, throwing men and machines in every direction like wrecking balls from hell. The rebels were struck with an equal measure of fear as the armored men plowed through them. They quickly broke, shattering like dried and broken earth dissolving into the wind. The obliteration of the rebel forces was complete and final. Nothing could oppose James and his men; those who tried died in a zephyr of flame and blood.

With the Democratist's forces fleeing in every direction, James approached the last group of resistance. They fired volley after volley at James, which he easily absorbed on his shield and armor. Sheathing his sword and locking his rifle behind him, James walked through the men, snapping arms and necks when anyone got in his way. Finally, he reached the leader of the rebel forces. James grabbed him by his chest, lifted him up, and slammed him into the wall. The sound of ribs cracking filled the silent dawn, followed closely by the man's futile attempt to catch his breath.

James dropped the struggling man, allowing him to gasp for air on his hands and knees. Squatting next to the prostrate rebel officer, James leaned over next to his ear. "Where is the king of traitors? Where is Ethan Austin?"

The man shuddered and gasped for breath. "Ne-never, you d-a...you damned Imperialist!"

James didn't respond. Instead he reached over and squeezed the man's shoulder, crushing it completely. The man screamed even through his damaged lungs. "I promise," James said. "I promise that if you give me Austin that you will not stand trial, you will not be dishonored, and your death will be quick. Your precious leader has killed many and betrayed the emperor he swore loyalty to. You owe him nothing."

The man's wide eyes didn't blink, didn't shut. He didn't breath, didn't even move. "C-on-trol r-oom main build-ing."

"Thank you," James said, as he crushed the man's head into the ground, killing him painlessly and instantly.

"Not very imaginative," Lieutenant Judas stated as he walked up.

Hilben walked over as well. "They're makin' it too easy, not even hidden."

James stood up from the corpse of the rebel commander. "I know, Thomas. He's a deluded madman, and he truly believes he has a right to rule." The group turned to the building before them and resumed their assault. The remaining defenses were too weak to even slow James and his men. On the command deck, the Imperial warriors found almost the entire leadership of the Democratist rebellion, and without ceremony, every one of them was executed by beheading.

The Exile Empire

Before each Democratist died, James and his men told them the following as they screamed for mercy: "For your crimes against the empire and your treason, you are condemned to death." Austin, however, was not in the room. James again inserted his hack into the main computer, this time finding that one of the main pressrooms was in active use. It was a long narrow hallway with a camera at one end, a table for presentation in the middle, and a large banner in the back that the presenter entered through. James made his way to the pressroom. Jessica informed him as he walked that there was no sign that Austin was aware of the assault. He was apparently fully engaged in his presentation. The entrance to the room was large and draped with a dual-sided tapestry with a unity symbol emblazoned with the statement: "All is equal."

James cut his way through the thick fabric with his sword, the superheated plasma igniting the tapestry, which burned brightly and quickly. As he walked forward, bits and pieces of the burning material fell onto him, some sliding off in a continuous rain of fire onto the ground, others sticking to him, leaving streaks of fire on his armor. Emerging through the other side of the fabric, James saw Austin delivering a fiery speech into a recording device.

"Ethan Austin. Traitor, coward, and murderer, it is time to account for your actions. For your crimes against humanity, conspiracy to murder, incitement to revolt, rebellion against the empire, and your attempt on the emperor's life, and by the authority vested in me as the Imperial Hammer, I sentence you to death!" James's words were slow and exact as he walked toward the rebel leader, strips of flame flowing off him. With smooth precision, James unsheathed his sword. He spoke the word "death" as he impaled Austin through the chest with his sword, lifting him into the air and pinning him to the wall of the presentation room.

The camera had been giving a live feed to the entirety of the rebel population at the time of James's entrance, and it had not stopped. Austin's death had been broadcast to several hundred thousand people. He thrashed and whimpered, trying futilely to flee. James left the room through the last burning fragments of the rebel banner, and the people watching the broadcast were left with a view of an empty hall and the hilt of a sword half visible from the side of the room. They heard the last sounds of a dying man. With that last execution, James Arellius Ursidae had ended the rebellion.

1/28/2454

Location: Sh'in

The fleet was buzzing with excitement and confusion. The signal had been running locally when James had executed Austin, and it had been turned and rebroadcast to the entire fleet. Everyone had seen the execution. Everyone. No sooner had the video played than the rebels opened live feed, which was played to the fleet. The remaining instigators of the rebellion that James and his men had missed before returning to the Legatus kneeled, tied and beaten before a group of civilians. One of the civilians stepped forward to speak. In front of the camera, he and the other civilians bowed, going to their knees.

"Emperor, we swear our loyalty to you and renounce the actions of the traitor Austin and his allies. My friends and I were not willing participants in their rebellion, and we have captured the remaining conspirators that your men did not rightly execute. We offer them to you with our most sincere apologies and the surrender of the entire rebel population. My friends and I that you see here were not the only ones who were taken down against our will when the ships descended; our allies throughout the colony have taken control. The entirety of Sh'in now serves you, Emperor Tinek. We ask only that you allow us to form a local government and execute the traitors on the ground they believed themselves worthy to rule."

Tinek signaled the communications officer to open a frequency to reply. "I accept your surrender and your loyalty. The council will decide the fate of the traitors you have captured. You must open your colony to full imperial control until the governor determines that the city no longer holds a threat of rebellion. Even so, you may begin local elections and set up a local civilian government that will report normally up the chain of command. Is that clear?"

The people on the screen rose from their knees, giving another slight bow, not raising their eyes to meet Tinek's. "Yes, Your Majesty," they said. They remained motionless, waiting for the connection to be cut from the other end.

Tinck sat back, exhaling long and hard. It was over. The rebellion was over, and his new people had finally stopped killing each other.

Below, the imprisoning light show of the shields cut off, along with the prolonged artillery barrage, leaving an eerie silence over the landscape. Everyone refused to believe that their slice of hell had ended; most refused to leave their shelters. The silence was finally shattered by the roar of descending ships— hundreds of them—flanked by waves of frigates and fighters. All manner of military personnel and civilians were coming to ensure order. Many of the governor's staff and support personnel came from New Carson to aid in the unification processes on the planet, increasing the already growing bustle of the area. Tinek continued to watch the activity on the ground for several hours, and he became satisfied when some of the bold civilians on the ground began to slowly resume their construction projects in the areas surrounding the two colony ships.

Tinek centered himself; he had another task to attend to before he could rest and check on A'ssia. The very act that had ended the standoff was done without orders and in an audacious act of violence. It had caused the death of hundreds and ended with the death of a member of the council. Tinek didn't know if James's actions fell under those of murder, political assassination, an act of war, or a justified execution.

He had already called the council to discuss the problem and was only waiting for James to finish making his way through the ship to rejoin Tinek on the command deck. Fortunately, he didn't have to wait long. James came through the entryway with the nineteen other members of his assault force. All of them were covered in scorch marks, dents, divots, and heavy gouges. Some leaked blood and other liquids from their cybernetic suits, but all of them had returned and now stood before the emperor. James walked forward. His men snapped into formation behind him, and in unison, they gave the emperor the salute of the Imperial Hammer. Coming up from his salute, James began to speak. "I have followed your orders, Tinek. For refusing the ultimatum, the traitors have died as you commanded after their assassination attempt. I only regret that it took us so long. Please forgive us."

Tinek was speechless; he didn't understand what had just happened. For a long time he stood, stunned. "That was not your failing. You should have confirmed my orders before you attacked. Your men are dismissed, but you must come to a meeting of the council. Unfortunately, we must find a way to solve a new problem."

The council room was dimly lit. It held twelve members seated around a huge wooden desk, one of the last made from Earth-grown wood. Admiral Hancock took the thirteenth council seat as the warrior-cast representative. He was clearly not happy. Hancock stood after Tinek had taken a seat and walked over to the front of the table. James, for his part, stood motionless behind Tinek's seat.

"As head of the military, it is my responsibility to begin court-martial proceedings for the actions of the leader of the Imperial Hammer, James Arellius Ursidae, for his instigation of actions without orders. I hope this will please the council and prevent any further fracturing of the fleet."

An angry murmur sounded throughout the room. One of the youngest members of the council rose with fire in his eyes. "Are you asking me to believe that you wish to punish this man for his actions? In no uncertain terms, he prevented even greater bloodshed."

The admiral closed his eyes, trying to suppress his anger and frustration. "He was in clear violation of both protocol and orders; he went completely around the chain of command."

"Actually," Tinek interrupted, "he was not, and did not." A new wave of understanding and a cool calculation came through the emperor's mind. Maybe he could turn this to some additional good. "As the commander of the Imperial Hammer, James is no longer responsible to the normal military hierarchy. If you remember the constitution, which you all signed, the emperor's personal force has complete autonomy from everyone—so long as it does not violate the lives of citizens—to execute the commands of the emperor." James was using every vestige of his self-control to keep from interjecting. Tinek whispered something into a communication tab on his arm as a low discussion pulsed through the room.

The conversations came to a halt as the area above the table opened into a holo-recording of Tinek's commands immediately after the assassination attempt. The recorded image of Tinek roared. "He comes to account for his action or he dies!" Tinek turned to the council. "James carried out my command. Besides, this council—your own selves—voted to employ full military response against rebel citizens before his attack, validating his actions from two completely lawful sources. The constitutional charter for what is now called the Imperial Hammer is there to streamline and enhance the protection of the empire and the emperor; the Hammer cannot be expected to double-check every action. Should Hammer Ursidae be forced to check with both the council and myself before stopping an assassination attempt? Should he double-check his orders before attacking an eminent threat? No! If you condemn his actions as invalid, you condemn the constitution you ratified as invalid. You will become nothing better than those who rebelled against the empire." Shock reverberated through the council, followed by both angry and agreeing voices.

James felt full of pride and loyalty as he watched Tinek transform his actions into a play for additional power. "If anyone has the audacity to claim the authority to surpass mine in condemning my personal warriors, speak now. To do so at any other time, you will be declared to be in rebellion against the throne and an enemy of the empire. These are my men; if you have a problem with their actions, then you have a problem with me!" Tinek waited a moment for his words to sink in before continuing. "Now, does anyone have a problem with the way I have solved the crisis on the planet?"

The room was silent. "Is there any other business to attend?" Again, the room was silent. "Admiral?"

Inclining his head to acknowledge Tinek, Hancock cautiously brought the meeting to a close. Doubts circled darkly through the old man's mind.

As the council members filed out of the room, James stayed behind. He joined Tinek, who was lost in thought. The emperor was reflecting upon whether he had just proven Austin's initial concerns correct. Tinek hoped that he was not becoming a dictator. He hoped that he was not alienating the council, and he hoped that he had not lost the loyalty of or friendship of Hancock. James and Tinek left the room, making their way through the length of the ship to his personal office. James, for his part, was thinking that it had been twenty-four hours since the emperor last had slept, and that it was showing...

They entered Tinek's personal office. Even though the emperor had defended James in the council meeting, he was still not happy with the young leader of warriors. He didn't, however, know how James would respond to him once they were alone. As the door slid shut behind them, silence permeated the room. "Why did you do it?" Tinek finally asked.

"Because it was right; because you ordered me to."

Tinek sighed wearily as he walked around to the chair behind the desk. "No...that's why you acted. I want to know why you went behind my back, why you didn't trust me to do what's right, why you didn't even let Hancock know. Hell, we could have helped you. I know you didn't need it, but why didn't you trust me, James?" The hurt in Tinek's eyes was deep, and for the first time in years, James almost regretted killing.

He didn't answer immediately; instead he stared at the floor. Slowly his breathing increased, becoming choppy with emotion. "Because they killed my people, just like back home. They killed people, and I couldn't protect them. They are monsters! He was human but he killed people for his personal gain just like the Harvesters." James seethed through clenched teeth. "And then—" he paused, choking on his own air and emotion. "And they...they tried to kill you, and I failed. I couldn't protect you. I didn't even see the second assassin. You worked so hard to build a way to protect us, and he had to try to kill it. And he almost killed A'ssia. It could have been Jessica there. I can't imagine losing Jessica, and you almost lost A'ssia."

James closed his eyes and clenched his teeth and fists, trying his hardest not to lose control of his emotions. "I saw his men kill children through my links, as if I was standing right there, and I couldn't do anything. I could see the smallest things. I was helpless as his men killed a little girl with a stick. A simple stick, and I couldn't protect her! Just like with my sister. Now I have all this power," James said, as he raised his hand to look at it. He turned the back of his hand toward himself and squeezed, the mechanical pressure creating a grating sound as he applied more than a ton of pressure. "And just like my sister, I was helpless!" James turned to Tinek, tears streaming down the side of his scarred and bleeding face.

"What sort of person does that? I had to do something. I had to kill him!" James met Tinek's eyes. "It felt good." Tinek saw fear cross James's eyes for the first time. The Illani wondered if it was for the first time since his family died. "What does that mean?" James asked. "Am I a monster? I can't tell anymore." Slumping down into one of the two chairs opposite Tinek's desk, James put his hands over his face and his elbows on his knee as he stared into the blackness of his palms.

Tinek didn't know how to respond. He had lost his family as well, but he hadn't been present when it had happened. And being a grown man, he hadn't been close to them at the time.

"What am I?" James asked, his voice betraying that he already knew the answer but didn't really want to hear it. James looked at his hand; the dried blood on it from the battle had begun to flake off a little from the wetness of his tears, leaving smudges of blood on his face.

"My friend," Tinek said, his voice directly next to James. Tinek had silently moved to the chair next to James, and he now sat staring the young warrior straight in the eyes. "You are my friend, and you are the head of my personal guard." Tinek waited a moment for his words to sink in. "But you are more than that. You are the conscience of a people. What you did on the planet is what needed to be done, the just thing to do.

"I couldn't do it, the admiral couldn't do it, the council couldn't do it. Your way was the only way to end it. I wish it didn't have to be that way, but it was. They almost killed A'ssia, and if I could have bombed his entire rebellion, I would have, but that is not what a leader does. If I had ordered your strike, I would have proven Austin right. You need to be my conscience. Justice drives you, and you did what was right. Don't worry. You aren't a monster, you are the one who keeps the monsters out."

Tinek walked back around his desk and hit a button to open the door, letting Jessica and several of the black warriors of the Hammer into the room. All but two of the men filed into the room and took up assigned guard positions. The faceplates of the other two retracted to reveal Sam and Rick, who both walked over to help James to his feet. Before they reached him, Jessica rushed between them to him. Waving the two big men aside, she leveraged herself under James's arm and helped him to his feet. The armor on his legs made it unnecessary, but her closeness was reassuring as the four left the room for a transport back to the planet.

Tinek watched them leave, his anger subdued by James's emotional breakdown. He stared at the display in the center of his desk, full of requests and messages from the fleet. All of them pertained to the recent incident, and he didn't want to address anyone with his current lack of sleep. He simply hit the save button on his desk and went to his bedroom, which was connected by an armored door. "Wake me in six hours," he told the lieutenant at the door, and he fell asleep on contact with his sheets.

Hancock stopped by the medical deck on his way to the hangar. A'ssia was awake and talking with her XO. She was less pale than earlier, and by the look of the equipment sitting next to her bed, she had already undergone several tissue regeneration treatments. "How are you feeling?" he asked.

"Oh, a little like a stuck pig, but other than that, fine," she chirped in a humorous tone. "The docs said I should be back on my feet by tomorrow. I hear James did something…out of the ordinary while I was out of commission."

Hancock's features turned a little more solemn as he thought of the recent meeting. "Yes, I'm not sure I agree with the way Tinek handled it, but he was right. James can't legally be punished for what he did."

A'ssia smiled in mock surprise. "Oh," she said. "You mean this?" She held up a data pad with a newsfeed of Tinek's statements in defense of James. "I love this full disclosure clause in Tinek's constitution. Besides, I think it was the right thing to do. Who cares if it was harsh and violent? We are in the military of an exiled fleet that is trying to create an empire and expel invaders from an allied alien world. We can't be all love and roses to every problem that comes up."

Hancock responded with a disgruntled "humph," his frustration, disagreement, and doubt evident on his weathered features. "What else would you have had them do?" A'ssia asked. After a moment of silence, she goaded him with an elongated "Hmm?"

"I don't know," he responded after a long pause. "Maybe I just don't like being left out of the loop. Maybe I'm scared of what I've helped create. I'm not sure I trust Tinek anymore. This wasn't supposed to be an empire, and I don't like secret military arms. It's wrong that they aren't responsible to the normal chain of command."

A'ssia snapped him a fierce glare. "Do you mean you? You are the chain of command." A'ssia tapped a few buttons on her panel and spun it outward to him. "It seems that the fleet doesn't agree."

The screen displayed a series of political discussions by political analysts that had surfaced throughout the fleet. Several fledgling news groups had been organized since the fleet had entered the system, and there was no shortage of opinions for them to cover about the recent events. One of the political gurus who liked Tinek and James had suggested that the people start a referendum to give James a medal for ending the rebellion. Someone had taken him seriously, and the initiative had snowballed from there. By now half the fleet was demanding a vote. Of course, most of them thought that James had been acting under Tinek's orders, and only a few had a problem with his tactics, but most of them were mad as all hell at Austin and were glad to see him die.

Hancock held the data pad with a look of unequivocal shock written all over his features. Had the exile and rebellion really changed people's sense of justice? History was full of outrage whenever anyone did something like this. Maybe things were different now. What kind of reality was he in now? He didn't know. He was tired, and he was terrified of what the answer could be. Without another word, the admiral returned the data pad to A'ssia and left for the Cerberus to get some rest.

2/4/2454

It had been a week since the end of the rebellion, and the fleet had become much more ordered and stable. James stood on the bridge of the Legatus with Tinek and A'ssia; the black warriors of the Hammer lined the back of the room. An image of the juggernaut James had captured before the rebellion spun in the holo-display as white-clad scientist from the Princeps scurried about the room, getting ready to explain their research. "As you can see," the squat man stated, "the stealth properties of the alien shields seem to be more of a beneficial byproduct of their sheering nature, rather than the intended effect. Simply stated, the shields attempt to shed all incoming material—matter, energy, light, all of it—into a vertical line along its axis. Somehow their gravity drives interact with the field and the ships' gravimetric signature is masked. Now this defies all known scientific laws. Such interaction should not nullify the gravity of the craft, but we think it harmonizes the craft with the largest object in the solar system—namely the star—thereby blending into the background signatures of its immediate area. The fact that the device shows no visible methods of fine-tuning this effect, or transferring its energy to more defensive means, has led us to believe that the Tarin'Tal don't fully understand its effects either." The man cleared his throat, and the holo-display shifted to a schematic of the Imperial shield grid.

"We are hopeful that, using our superior gravity tech and shield-manufacturing capabilities, we can create a device capable of cloaking a ship from the visible and gravity spectrum, rendering the craft invisible in both long-range and close engagements." The group watched, not fully understanding the physics, but fully comprehending the tactical applications of such technology.

"Applications?" Tinek asked.

"Ah, yes," the scientist said, as he flipped the display to several individual devices. "Here we have several versions of new sensor systems that may prove capable of detecting the alien ships with this version of the cloaking technology. Separate, they were unsuccessful at detecting them. Together, however, we were able to detect a minute variance in the background radiation that gives the location away. Once identified, the sensors can image the vessel by means of a gravity pulse, similar to ancient radar. While the device seems to mask the craft's own gravity, it cannot prevent the pulse from identifying its actual gravity." The scientist looked like he could continue for many mind-numbing hours. He was highly proud of his invention.

"So we can see them?" Tinek interrupted, saving himself and his friends from the impending doom of droning science.

"Uh…yes, we can in theory. The device is being integrated in the Cerberus's sensors as we speak. We should be able to activate it…"

The scientist stared down at his pad, waiting for confirmation before tapping it one last time and triumphantly announcing, "Now!" The little man hit a command sequence, and the display morphed into a three-dimensional diagram of the solar system. The primary habitable world, Lintalla, had many signatures in red surrounding it, marking gravity signatures that were so large they could not be masked. They were known enemy vessels. It also had a yellow number next to the Illani home world and the far side of the Gas Giant that Sh'in orbited, indicating possible numbers of unknown enemy forces.

The screen flickered, and an explosion of red washed over it. "Oh, hell no!" James said.

"I agree," stated Tinek. Even more ominous than the swath of red that had appeared behind the Gas Giant, flanking the human fleet protecting the prairie moon, was the sea of crimson surrounding Lintalla.

"How the hell do we fight that?" A'ssia whispered.

Tinek watched the screen, the more imminent threat of the craft surrounding the Gas Giant buzzing around each other. "I don't know," he said, "but we don't have a choice."

Meetings and military planning consumed the next several hours. After the creation of several contingency plans, a date was set for a preemptive strike on each force. James, having been promoted and given access to council and military meetings as Tinek's personal adviser, sat in his seat long after the meeting was over. He wore a pitch-black military suit, its angles sharp and cleanly pressed. The only color was the imperial seal on his chest and a white collar. It was a new dress uniform created specifically for the Imperial Hammer. Tinek sat in the seat next to James, his uniform exactly the same except that the black and white were reversed, with a white base and black collar.

"Now this is scary," Tinek stated, clearly uncomfortable. "You're telling me!" James responded. "Compared to a stare-down with a posse of Tarin'Tal, this is a relaxing day at the park." Both men swallowed, pawing at their constricting collars. They sat staring at the clock in the far corner. It ticked the seconds away far too fast for their comfort.

After fifteen minutes of building tension, Tinek finally spoke. "I think the human term for this would be 'time to face the music.'" James slowly stood, signaling the black warriors by the door to make way.

"Indeed it would," he stated at length. "Emperors, women, and children first," James goaded.

"Very funny," Tinek said.

As James and Tinek gathered their courage, Vilnir burst through the towering ranks of the Imperial Hammer. "It's time! It's time! Please, Majesty, the setting is ready. I don't know how well the humans will respond to delayed ceremonies!" Tinek and James eyed each other and exhaled simultaneously. Following the little Illani, they made their way to the Legatus's command deck. As they walked through the doors, they were presented with a view of every official from the fleet. Admiral Hancock and a priest stood before the holo-display, which now showed a brilliantly huge image of a Celtic cross. It was a double wedding, but the stress wafting off the two grooms made it feel more like a double hanging. They didn't fear the commitment or their future wives, but the spectacle they had become.

Although Tinek had fallen in love with A'ssia Harrington over the short time they had been together and their marriage was a great political opportunity to combine the authority of the two races, he was still too nervous to go through with it by himself. He had watched James and Jessica's interaction and had prodded him about when he would propose himself. James had been shocked—first that someone would ask such a question, and second that he hadn't considered asking Jessica to marry him.

It was a politically perfect arrangement. It unified the fleet, and it was a welcome distraction from rebellion and the approaching alien forces. It gave them something to celebrate, changing the entire mood of the exiled civilization. The council had declared it a national holiday. The fleet had been prepared as much of a feast as it could on its limited supply, while still remaining vigilant against the fleet looming around the Gas Giant. Even though the Illani had a deeply seated religion of their own, Tinek found the Christiany, the dominant religion in the exiled fleet, to be highly interesting and agreed to have the ceremony preformed in the human fashion with a Christian leader. He had also requested that it be combined with a military ceremony.

Every aspect of the ceremony was beautiful. It went flawlessly, and the stress of the two men evaporated when they saw their future wives. The only ire in the room came from Jessica, whose crooked smile demanded to know why they didn't do this earlier. The ceremony came to a close with the priest stating, "By the power vested in me by God—"

Hancock interjected his planned addition: "And in me by the fleet and the empire."

The priest once again took over. "I now pronounce you, Tinek Illan Xalion, and you, A'ssia Harrington, to be man and wife. I also pronounce you, James Arellius Ursidae, and you, Jessica Obsianus Miller, to be man and wife!" As the two patriarchs kissed their brides, the entire fleet celebrated.

Hours later the four newlyweds were still being congratulated by influential members of the new empire. The feast had been made of the basic ingredients found on the planet, but it had been excellently prepared. The celebration had moved down to the planet after the ceremonies, where massive tables were set up outside New Carson by the main river. The tables were made from a large local tree, which although rare on the planet, closely resembled oak in its usefulness. The food had been prepared in gigantic open pits by the local entrepreneurs in the food industry. Most of them had worked as chefs or at other jobs related to food before the exile, and all of them had taken an incredible amount of ingenuity to the food of the new planet. The celebration went on well past the planet's long dawn and through its shorter day. As the sun began to set on the prairie planet, the four newlyweds were surprised by a very unexpected wedding present.

In the waning light and cooling breeze of the evening, Sergey, the former captain of the Explorator and now the mayor of New Carson, escorted a plump, bearded Irishman and a handful of other men carrying large barrels. "This is Brewmaster Torry and his men. They have a present for the wedding table."

The round man ducked his way around the mayor and shuffled his way over to Tinek and James. "Ah wanted to personally congratulate ye," he said in a thick accent. "Mah boys and I have a present for ye. We've been keepen most 'o it for a special occasion, and ah think this fits te bill." The men rolled the barrels over and cracked their seals, ramming spikes into them. The bearded man snatched a large mug from a crate his men brought up and filled it with the dark liquid from inside. "Genuine Guinness, the real deal!"

The crowd sucked the air out of the area with an audible whoosh. None of them had seen alcohol since before the exile. Tinek, however, looked more confused than impressed. He leaned over to James and quietly asked, "Uh…what's Guinness?"

"It's alcohol with hops and such—really good stuff, some say the best." To prove his point, James walked over to the barrels, took a mug, and filled it. With the thrust of a barbarian, he drank the whole mug in one go. "He's not lying!" James called. "It's the good stuff. Come on, try it."

Before he could muster the courage, A'ssia leaned over and whispered in his ear, "That is if I don't beat you to it." For a moment, the whole table stopped being dignitaries, stopped being exiles, and became people again. The barriers and tension that had been slowly torn down during the celebration finally fell in one massive movement as everyone rushed to try the beer, only waiting for the newlyweds to fill their cups first. Everyone was equal for a few happy hours. No one had to fight to live, and all they had to do was enjoy life. It was only a moment, but it was something. Something that the beleaguered leaders and people needed in order to restore the resolve and energy for the tasks upon which they were about to embark in the effort to retake Lintalla.

2/12/2454

"Status of the enemy fleet?" A'ssia demanded. A sensors technician swiveled in his seat, spinning a smaller holo-display to examine the detailed information.

"Their advance has not deviated. They are continuing to approach from both sides of the planet. Estimates still indicate their numbers to be five to six spire ships and a similar number of support vessels for each as per our last engagement. It does not appear that they have noticed our preparations."

A'ssia put her hands behind her back as she began to pace. "Good, update us if anything changes." James had two full squads in the room—all in complete battle armor, all of them his best warriors. They were the same ones that had attacked the rebels with him.

Tinek sat in one of the command chairs, watching the rotating display with calculating eyes. "How are your preparations on the ground?" Tinek asked, never taking his eyes off the display.

"Ready. The civilians in both the new colony and New Carson are in the bunkers, and the decoys are in place. We have twenty divisions in each city and another fifteen in orbital reserve for situational deployment. The rest are distributed throughout the fleet to defend against boarding parties. Cormac says that his divisions are primed and ready to defend New Carson and all of mine but your guards are in the new colony. We'll give them a hell they've never experienced. If they behave anything like they did on Lintalla and their first attack, they have already sealed their own fate,"

Tinek grunted. "Good. Don't leave any alive. We don't need prisoners."

James saluted. "There will be no survivors," he stated as he walked out of the room. An airlock with a series of pods had been installed just outside of the massive assault doors to the command deck for James and his warriors to use in coming and going from the imperial flagship. He entered one specifically designed for him and his cybernetic interphase. The pod mostly guided itself but could be controlled by the occupant if he or she so desired. In a flare of gas and propellant, James sped toward the planet, slipping through its atmospheric burn zone with only the shortest of flare as he plummeted toward the two landed colony ships.

Admiral Hancock watched his arrayed fleet on the holo-display. Masses of destroyers and frigates buzzed around the Cerberus and the cruiser Leviathan. Fighters were everywhere. They blanketed the sides of the massive capital ships, they filled every connection on the destroyers, and still they flooded the space surrounding his fleet. Mercenary ships and combat mules were interspersed with the more powerful military vessels. There were thousands of them all running on their lowest power, masking their signatures to the greatest possible extent. The civilian ships—those who had not landed on the planet—had hidden among a dense asteroid field in orbit around the planetoid moon, possibly the remains of a secondary moon shattered long ago. Defending them was the Princeps, the Legatus, and thousands of fighters, which could be called into battle at any moment. Everywhere, the humans waited.

The Tarin'Tal fleet continued its languishingly slow advance, believing themselves undetected. As the alien ships closed, they entered the outer range of the human's regular sensors, and still their pace remained unchanged. "Sir! They are in range of the antimatter cannons."

The admiral waved his hand. "Hold. Wait till they are in range of the artillery." Hancock watched the distance between his fleet and the aliens tick down. "Fire!" the admiral bellowed. "All craft, advance, capital line full assault."

The space between the ships lit up brighter than a desert day on Sh'in as the fleet unleashed its deadly power. The alien fleet had a fraction of a second's warning before the reaction of matter and antimatter obliterated their front ranks.

Instead of breaking away from the onslaught like the last engagement the Tarin'Tal leaped forward, undeterred by their unexpected casualties. With the capital ships forming a shield barrier for the remainder of the ships, the fleet began its barrage. Surging forward, following the massive antimatter cannons on the Cerberus and the Leviathan, the human fleet began firing every weapon they had. Their fire did not go unanswered. The mass of Tarin'Tal ships began pouring their weaponry at the humans. Unfortunately for the aliens, the human fleet's numbers and their own were equal, allowing the technological superiority of mankind to tip the scales of combat.

They assaulted the human ships directly, wasting their weapons on their unyielding shields. Each attack hurt the human forces less and cost the 'Tal more. Finally after four bloody assaults, the alien fleet attempted to break around the human fleet. They sluiced over it like sand falling on rock in a desperate attempt to get around the human shield wall, carpeting the exterior of the fleet in a blanket of ships and fire. They failed. The fighters, still waiting in the rear of the fleet and on the side of the ships, launched their attack. They carpeted the flanking ships with deadly Gatling fire. Thousands of fighters punched through the gunships and juggernauts with resistless speed, sweeping across the ships-cum-debris like a column of angry rivers.

The spire ships found themselves nearly defenseless as two-thirds of their escorts vaporized in fire and shrapnel, only to be replaced by the angry forms of human Peregrine fighters. They tried to run toward the other fleet that had been attempting to outflank the humans under the assumption that they were ignorant of their presence. The humans didn't give them the chance. "All batteries set up a barrier between those forces! All antimatter cannons, take their shields from them."

The fleet spun apart to intercept the retreating forces. A pulse of explosions intercepted the retreating ships, spreading a blue haze in front of them. They tried to avoid the quicksand, but only one of the five did, and that one was ripped apart by four of the Cerberus's and Leviathan's antimatter cannons. The dead hulk floated aimlessly away from the doomed ships trapped by the quicksand. The military ships in the human fleet ignored the doomed craft. They left them to their fates at the hands of the mercenary ships and battle mules of the human forces. Their deaths were slow and brutal as the less powerful ships slowly carved them up like a burnt roast. With the least powerful crafts in the fleet occupied, the remaining warships turned to the quickly approaching secondary fleet to meet them in battle.

The humans had eradicated the first wave of Tarin'Tal, but they had failed to do so before several craft had broken away from their fleet and headed toward the planet. The land craft's shields were superior to those used by their space-borne cousins, and they easily ignored the few flights of Peregrines that were able to break from the engagement to intercept them. James watched from his command base in the same courtyard he had found himself assaulting just a few days earlier. He only had a moment to consider the irony before the enemy craft appeared on his holo-display. There were too many for him to count, but that didn't matter. The only ones that James cared about were the ones that had separated from the others and were headed toward the planet.

James turned to the three hundred men in the courtyard. He raised his sword into the air and his faceplate closed, replacing his face with white metal. "They come!"

The men beat their chests, chanting, "Hu-yuh hu-yuh hu-yuh!"

James stabbed his sword into the ground and grabbed one of the flags. "We fight for the emperor, we die for the emperor."

"We claim victory for the emperor!" his men finished, unsheathing their swords.

"Now we fight!" James commanded, as he slammed the pole into a wall, the flag draping over the doorway. "To your positions!"

"Sir!" his men shouted as they scattered to their position.

James sat down in a huge chair, mirroring a throne on the awning of the courtyard. The ground sloped down to the maze of pathways and construction sites that dominated the valley floor. James watched the skies; the sensors in his helmet magnified the flaming forms of the descending Tarin'Tal troopships as they made their way to the two population centers on the planet. The entirety of the alien space force was tied up in the battle above; they had no power to barrage the colony before their landing. Three of the bulky, ugly ships landed on the outskirts of the city and began pouring out troops.

The screeches and roars of the aliens' anticipation for battle filled the air. They were angry, and they were here to kill, maim, and destroy. As James sat watching the invasion from his high vantage point, he turned his suit dormant, reducing his energy signature to appear nothing more than an ornamental statue; he only left his sensors on. The aliens swarmed to the outskirts of the city, and he watched. The aliens swarmed through rows and rows of new homes—homes that represented the hopes of his people—and he watched. The aliens swarmed through the construction sites before him, and still he watched. James watched the confusion on the grotesque faces of the Tarin'Tal as they walked up the pathway to the courtyard. They had found no enemies, no civilians, nothing but empty streets and dark buildings, and they were confused. Not even on the most desolate planets they had conquered had there been no one willing to oppose them.

As they reached the top of the courtyard and began filing past James, one particularly large beast, with a spark of intelligence in his eye, walked right up to him. James looked like a statue, but the Tarin'Tal didn't trust anything on the planet.

In one concerted command, every squad's controller followed Jessica's example as she reacted to James restarting his suit. "Activate commands!" she demanded. In a blinding flash of hundreds of grenades, the Imperial Hammer attacked the interlopers. James blurred into motion, reaching up with his powerful armor-encrusted hand and gripping the Tarin'Tal across the bridge of its nasal cavities between its eyes. He clamped down on them, cracking the bone and cartilage beneath in a spray of blood. With a gut-wrenching force, he yanked the beast's face down on the corner of his chair, crushing its brain as the front half of its head disappeared.

Using the leverage he gained from his attack, James vaulted into the air, pulling out both his rifle and sword, laying waste with the first as he fell to use the latter. His plasma rounds exploded in a sea of superheated material that cooked and cleared the ground on which he landed. The space where James now stood was surrounded by a ring of Tarin'Tal still recovering from the shock of the initial attack. As they recovered, they heard the sounds of battle from throughout the city. Their agitation grew. None yet ventured to attack the bizarre titan standing on the scorched ground. James stood motionless, waiting for his monstrous opponents to make the first move. He held both his rifle and sword out from him along his sides. In an echoing bellow, one of the larger aliens attacked, and the fighting began.

With a spray of fire in the opposite direction, James hurled himself at the Tarin'Tal who attempted to burn him with its kinetic weapon. Twisting himself out of the beam's path, James rotated his body in a complete spin, all the while maintaining his forward momentum. He slammed into the beast with his sword in its shoulder. The impact robbed James of his rifle, which he dropped as he grabbed the shield from over his back, activating it a moment before the monster's talon-like sword could pierce his exposed back. The blue of the shield flared with a cracking hiss as the metal struck it. Allowing himself to be moved by the strike, James yanked his sword from the Tarin'Tal's shoulder as new momentum moved him further under the beast, while dragging his sword across its chest.

The wound in the beast's chest poured its inner filth on his shields to burn in the unyielding energy of the device. Pulling his weapons toward himself, James rolled out from under the Tarin'Tal, jumping up at another beast as it tried to impale the human warrior. In an explosion of power from his suit, James rolled over the strike, spinning his feet behind and over himself in a summersault, ending with his metal feet sinking into the alien's face.

Moving through the attack, he hit another one as it attempted to burn him with its weapon. With a sidespin carried into a crescent kick, James broke the beast's weapon in half as he advanced behind the enemy. Reversing his direction by planting his foot and rebounding, James gained the back of the creature, plunging his sword in the beast's neck along its spine. With inhuman speed, James avoided the inevitable spray of gore as he tore the sword free by attacking his next opponent. Even with his advanced speed, the creature was too far away for James to close before it could blast him with its weapon.

Rolling along the path of bodies he had left, James absorbed the majority of the blast on his shield. A searing pain burned along his left shoulder, and he glanced at himself to see scorched metal. Using his onboard computer and targeting system, James knew exactly where he had dropped his rifle, and he snatched it before a 'Tal fell on top of it.

In a backward flip, James spun his legs around and landed behind the body of one of the aliens he had killed as it burst into flames. He gripped his rifle and spun to the attacking beast and unleashed a torrent of fragmentation rounds, tearing the flesh from its insides as they ripped massive exit wounds in its back. As James turned to engage the next alien, his computer informed him that all the attacking beasts had been slain. James spun to confirm the computer's statements to see a neat ring of dead Tarin'Tals at his feet, their gore wetting the burnt cement beneath him. He prepared himself for another wave of warriors, but when it didn't come, he surveyed the battlefield and accessed statistics through Jessica. After the initial assault by the Imperial Hammer, thousands of regular troops entered the battle, the confused and fractured alien forces falling in waves before their rows of blazing weapons and shield walls.

With their momentum gone and their organization shattered, the Tarin'Tal lost the advantage of strength and maneuverability they had experienced during their previous land engagement and were forced to fight the human troops weapon to weapon. The humans' superior rifles reaped a devastating toll among the Tarin'Tal, the force rending flesh and shattering bone, while the aliens' less powerful kinetic weapons were harmlessly absorbed by the rows of human shields. The black warriors of the Hammer still engaged the disorganized aliens, continuing the undulating slaughter among their confused ranks.

James turned as the alien forces remounted their attack on the courtyard. He stood alone on the crest of the hill as the aliens charged, hell-bent on tearing him open. In the face of the oncoming horde, James braced himself, held his sword out in front of himself, and bellowed, "You die here!" Crushing the pavement with the force of his leap, James rocketed forward toward the aliens. He lashed out at the aliens on his right with his sword and blasted those on his left with his rifle, while spinning, contorting, and swerving around the alien's counterattacks. The leader of the Imperial Hammer disappeared into the mass of aliens amid a roar, both his own and from alien throats. The sounds of the battle rose above even the larger conflict occurring below in the construction fields. Then in an explosion and corona of flame, James came out the other side of the attack, his suit covered in blood, scorch marks, dents, and gouges. He staggered to regain his balance and strength.

He turned to face the aliens he had passed through. Far fewer remained than he had expected; most of the others lay dead and dying with grievous wounds. As James took up a defensive posture to take the assault, his eyes reflected black and locked to his screen as he watched the Tarin'Tal soldiers as they charged. Standing his ground, James was shocked when they simply ran past him toward the pathway to their ships. The black pulsating in his eyes and veins rekindled with battle lust as he turned to pursue his retreating enemies. The Tarin'Tal ran, but James was faster. He tore them down as they fled.

The remaining aliens hit their own ranks in their growing terror followed closely by James's armored form going at full speed. The impact toppled several of the densely packed beasts in a domino effect. Already shaky and uncertain from the sudden assault and impenetrable walls of shield and guns, the Tarin'Tal forces broke. In one teaming mass, they ran. James remembered Tinek's command that none should survive; he was going to ensure that would be the case. Continuing his attack, the battle turned into an all-out rout as his men rallied with him to pursue the Tarin'Tal. The regular troops began wiping out the forces that James and his men missed as they ran down the retreating aliens, spilling blood and guts as they plowed through them.

Noticing that the aliens were approaching the end of the long road out of the city, James activated a series of commands for a squad of black warriors and regulars he had lying in wait. A series of explosions rocked the front ranks of retreating Tarin'Tal as they were hit by a barrage from the new force. The front ranks halted their momentum as their terror levels reached insanity. The enemy behind became the enemy in front. Enhancing the terror of their fleeing enemies, James activated another command that launched an artillery barrage against the landed transports, tearing their shields down and allowing the Peregrine fighters to destroy them in a pulse of incendiary rounds. The Tarin'Tals trampled each other as they fled. It was one tangled mess that was attacked simultaneously from both sides. The slaughter was complete; everything had died.

James stood before the mound of dead Tarin'Tal while his men milled around and sat down in utter confusion. He began to receive reports from his men and the regulars. As the madness passed, James felt his energy leave him, and all the pains and injuries he had sustained in the battle rushed into his senses. "Ah!" he moaned in agony as he slumped toward a nearby wall. He slid down the wall with his back against it, the world spinning as his body reacted to having his muscles and bones forced to act far beyond their natural abilities. *Don't pass out…don't pass out. You've still got work to do!* he thought as the world slowed and eventually stopped its counterintuitive rotation. James slowly pulled himself back up as he began receiving reports from his men and security patrols. "Now," he said to Jessica, "what's happening above? Can we help?"

In orbit the remaining five spire ships and their swarming escorts prepared to engage the human forces, fresh from defeating the aliens' first fleet. Using pulsating cannon fire, the human ships attempted to corral the oncoming fleet with quicksand charges. Not to be caught off guard like their unfortunate allies, the Tarin'Tal fleet launched a series of guided missiles of their own, deflecting the exploding charges away from their fleet in an expanding ring. As the fleets closed, the humans moved to create their impenetrable shield wall. The Tarin'Tal, unlike previous engagements, pulled their forces into a tight line, accelerating undaunted toward the human fleet. A sphere of juggernauts formed in front of the lead spire ship with gunships filling the gaps between them. The aliens tightened their ranks until almost no space remained between their lead ships as they screamed toward the human fleet. With the barrage of antimatter, plasma and piercing metal, the Tarin'Tal closed their ranks with fresh ships, completely ignoring the human weapons. Round after round blasted from the Cerberus and the human fleet— nothing slowed the oncoming vessels. Every time the assault ripped a ship from space, it was replaced with others willing to die.

Hancock stood behind his chair, gripping its back as he commanded his ships on the holographic display. "Fallen Earth!" he said, not trying to hide his distress. "They are going to pierce the capital shield! All ships, split apart; all alpha groups, follow the Leviathan, all beta groups, follow the Cerberus. Send fifty fighter groups and fifty frigates down their throats. Execute the Shanghai maneuver! Pull all other light craft around the exterior of the capital ships." The human battle lines cracked down its center, and the shield wall fell seconds before the Tarin'Tal hit with it. "They are willing to sacrifice half their fleet to deprive us of our shields. Execute Shanghai!"

The ships pulled apart just in time to avoid the suicidal onslaught of the alien crafts. In under a second, the two separated parts of the human fleet opened fire toward each other, knowing that the speed of the enemy fleet would carry them into the crisscrossing wall of death. As the fighters and frigates unleashed their weapons before veering out, the Tarin'Tal fleet arrived. Trying to avoid the rain of death, they swerved, they reversed, they dove, and climbed, but not in time. The explosion was greater than anything either fleet had ever experienced. Four antimatter rounds and more than four thousand plasma rounds detonated at point blank range between fleet segments.

The battlefield was chaos; both fleets recoiled from the explosion, mixing together in an uncontrolled mess. Peregrines ricocheted off gunships, frigates slammed into juggernauts, and spire ships spun out of control. Rotating with the force of the explosions, the Cerberus blasted a spire ship in two as it was about to collide with the warship's forward compartments. The Leviathan spun as a spire ship and a juggernaut collided and sent a shockwave across her elongated sides. The battle raged as captains and pilots began to gain control of their crews and craft. It went from chaotic to deathly brutal as both fractured fleets tore into each other. The Cerberus went after a group of juggernauts as they attempted to corner the Leviathan with a flight of gunships. In a multi-gun burst of antimatter, they were vaporized. Two of the remaining spire ships, however, had been thrown under the battleship as well. They turned on the massive warship, their towering lengths rising on either side of the now exposed capital ship.

"All hands brace for impact," an officer screamed into a communiqué, as the two ships opened fire with kinetic weapons and missiles. Their attack didn't go unchallenged as the Cerberus unleashed its massive side plasma cannons on the two ships; but outnumbered and outflanked, there was little hope that the Cerberus could bring her capital cannons to bear before she lost shields and was torn apart by the Tarin'Tal's burning weapons. As the craft rocked and Hancock shouted orders to his men to rotate out from between the two ships, an explosion knocked him off his feet.

"Sir! We've lost shield eight, and nine is almost fried."

The captain's display switched to his own ship, the damaged areas pulsing red and text scrolling by, describing the damage. "Use both top and bottom shields sixteen and twenty-four to compensate." The shields rotated, slightly exposing the ship's upper and lower sections but filling the gap just in time as another sheet of fire from the spire ship struck the ship.

"Sir, we have multiple contacts closing on us: thirteen juggernauts and an unknown number of gunships. We can't get out!" The officer began to panic.

"Damn!" cursed Hancock. "Prepare the trireme device, activate on my command. Switch to concussion rounds. See how long you can keep their maneuverable craft off our backs." The ship continued to twist along multiple axes, attempting to get away from the Tarin'Tal, but the spire ships matched her every move.

"All shields critical!" the officer shouted. "Orders?"

Hancock stood motionless, uncertain about his next course of action. And then the decision was made for him. The spire ship assaulting the Cerberus's port side shuddered and was pierced by a thousand streams of fire followed closely by a secondary antimatter explosion. The ship shattered like a pane of glass.

Tinek stood on the bridge of the Legatus. "Excellent!" he shouted.

A'ssia spun the image and commanded the fighters to their next target. "Clear those gunships. Weapons full barrage on the juggernauts and start drilling the other spire ship with the main cannon!"

"Yes, sir!" the officer shouted, the excitement of battle clear in his voice. The Legatus burst through the dead spire ship's debris cloud as she began pummeling the ships attacking the Cerberus. Fighters blanketed the entire space, surrounding her like an angry nest of hornets. As the Cerberus turned on her second attacker, freed from the trap of the two rotating ships, the mercenary and battle mules returned from their lighter engagement with the disabled ships in the quicksand.

In as much time as it had taken the Legatus to join the battle, the conflict was over. The human ships began routing the Tarin'Tal; each ship they destroyed freed more ships to turn on those still living. Within a matter of minutes, the sky was filled with nothing but burning hulks and battle-scared human warships filled with exhausted people.

"Sorry, Admiral," A'ssia said into her communications panel. "I just couldn't help myself…and it doesn't hurt to have an order from an emperor to override an admiral's."

The sound of a relieved chuckle came back through the device. "Fine by me. Thanks for that little maneuver back there. You really pulled us out of the fire."

The ships began spreading out and scanning for survivors as the civilian fleet moved out of hiding and began helping with the triage efforts after the battle. The scene was devastating, but mankind and the empire had won and had suffered comparatively few losses during the conflict. The carnage, however, had been anything but one-sided; there were masses of wrecked ships tangled together in one floating graveyard. "Get the MIC and Princeps on the line," the admiral commanded. "We need the fleet battle ready again by tomorrow."

2/20/2454

The fleet circled the civilians like an ancient wagon train under attack. Even though the Tarin'Tal fleet had lost all its spire ships, several hundred gunships and several juggernauts had escaped, and they were attempting hit-and-run missions on the fleet as they attempted to repair and refit from the encounter. After five days the attacks had died to nothing, and the guard the fleet kept up at this point was merely precautionary. Even though the fleet analysts had assured him that all Tarin'Tal forces had been destroyed, Hancock still remained cautious. Almost all the damage incurred by the fleet, besides those ships destroyed, had been restored, and they were ready for the next stage of the war. James sat in the maintenance building, which housed both the Imperial Hammer and the divisions under Cormac's command. He was finishing some work on one of his suit's more complex circuits that had been damaged during the recent battle. The suit had, however, been pounded, welded, cleaned, and generally mended by the division's now permanent mechanics who had volunteered to serve the now legendary division with their own skills. Unfortunately, James never found their work up to his personal requirements. It was passable, but lacked the years of experience of an actual cyborg whose life depended on the machines he maintained.

He didn't hold their work against them. It was excellent by normal standards, and it kept his men's suits in operating order while most of the warriors were still learning the basics of posatronic interphase adaptation. Eventually, he planned to have high-level cybernetic suit maintenance and reconstruction a requirement for entry into the Imperial Hammer. "Still fixing what ain't broke?" Cormac's voice came from around the corner as his footsteps became audible.

"I think the fact that I'm fixing it means it isn't broken anymore," James replied in quick succession. The younger man leaned back in his chair, setting the object to the side of his specially designed workspace with a simultaneous yawn and stretch. "It's nice to fix things; it's just intensive enough to keep my mind from wandering to places I don't want it to go and doesn't take much effort or energy."

Cormac looked at the components strewn on the table and then back to James. He cocked an eye, plopping down in one of the other chairs strewn about the large room. "You do realize that those are some of the most advanced pieces of robotic and cybernetic technology that you have integrated into a seamless killing machine, that you are working on one of the most advanced parts of that machine, that this technology wasn't even in the theoretical stages. Just thinking about it gave some of the best scientists that we have left a week-long headache, and you just called it mind-numbing."

James looked at Cormac and then at his machines with an innocent expression. "I guess this means we need better scientists," James quipped with a smirk. Cormac laughed at their somewhat morbid joke about the state of humanity.

Cormac pulled two small bottles out of his pocket and tossed one to James. "Lax whiskey," Cormac said as he popped the top off his bottle with a quick twist of his wrist. "That brew master held out on us; he had a set of bio-pods on his ship. You know the ones that they're using to mature the animals in stasis?" James nodded as he removed his lid and took a sniff of the blackish liquid inside. "Turns out he used it to speed up the fermentation of his alcohol. He doesn't have a harvest of hops yet, so he tried to use the local vegetation, and this is what he got. Said that this is only about half as good as the stuff would be if he had time to brew it normally, something about funky growth speed of microorganisms in the pods." James took another whiff of the liquid and then took a swig. Almost spewing the liquid out of his mouth, James started coughing heavily after swallowing the whiskey.

"Ha ha ha!" Cormac laughed. "Strong as hell, ain't it?"

James blinked water out of his eyes. "Yeah!" he rasped, taking another, infinitely smaller, sip. "It's like twice the punch of anything I've ever had."

The two sat enjoying their drinks; there wasn't much, and the fleet was trying to spread as much of it around as possible to improve morale. "I hear you did well in the new colony," Cormac said after a long time. "I heard nothing survived."

James swirled his bottle around and peered into it to see if anything was left. "Yep. Sent the devil's spawn back to hell. You didn't do so bad yourself. You wiped yours out faster than I did." A hint of envy was detectable in James's voice.

"It's not a contest," Cormac said almost, like a father. "I just did my job…Besides, I had three times the armored troops you did. It's only expected that I would finish a little quicker."

"Thanks, Dad," James responded with sarcasm. "I don't need a pep talk, but thanks anyway." This time his voice was serious, and Cormac could tell that he meant it.

Cormac set his empty bottle down and picked up one of the devices James had been working on. "So how do you like being the big cheese? You didn't get much practice at lieutenant before you got the job."

James thought for a moment, not quite sure how to answer. "Well, to tell you the truth, I haven't had any time to like it or dislike it. I haven't really thought about it. I guess that means it's going well. I like my men, I like picking where, when, and how to fight, and my men don't seem to have any real problem with my leadership. So, yeah," James said, having led himself to a conclusion. "I like it."

Cormac chuckled, almost inaudible, and then became serious. "You don't even notice, do you?" Cormac asked.

Looking up James responded. "Well, you think I haven't since you asked. What don't I notice?"

"How your men respond to you, how they mimic you, how they try to be you. Don't you find that strange? That's not how people act—not all them, anyway—and it's definitely not how men usually view their commander. Look at my men."

James looked straight through Cormac. "They respected you; we wanted to be you."

"No," Cormac stated emphatically. "The men may have respected me, maybe for my fighting or something else, but they never wanted to be me. They wanted to fight like me, act like me, have a command like me, but you…they don't simply want to follow you or act like you; they want to be you. They take your ways and make them their own. It's kinda creepy. You're making yourself your own clan, a berserker clan."

James thought about what his mentor had just told him, finally realizing the ramifications. "Fallen Earth!" James finally said. "What does the fleet…how…no? Uh…is this hurting Tinek's image?"

Cormac whistled. "James, for someone so smart, you are so dumb and unobservant sometimes. The fleet loves it. They idolize your Imperial Hammer in a cultish sense, like they are warriors from God. Not only do your men want to be you, but the fleet wants to be your men. Every division is demanding armor suits, and ships are requesting attachment to the Hammer. Have you even checked your transfer applications?"

James looked a little embarrassed for a moment, like a kid who forgot his homework. "Uh…no. I was full. I don't need anyone, so I haven't checked."

Cormac grabbed his pad, punched a few panels, and tossed it to James. "Oh, man!" James exclaimed as he scanned the lists of people who wanted transfers into his division. "I can't count them all. There must be thousands!"

"And more by the minute," Cormac added. "It seems that the fleet reached a breaking point with the rebellion and found itself at a crossroads. They needed something to latch onto, something to give them hope. Some wanted justice, some wanted victory, some just wanted a home, and some…well, I don't know what they want, but all of them saw you and your men and what you did. They see that hope in you, James. You appear invincible, like the hand of God, and they love it. Humanity's attitude is fundamentally different, and they see you as the expression of their new outlook."

James tried to take in the significance of what Cormac had told him. His thoughts began to swirl almost out of focus. He had always known this was happening; he just hadn't paid attention. His anger and determination had guided his focus so entirely that even though he saw what had gone on around him, he hadn't truly realized it. "I…I can't be that person. I'm not a role model," James said, as he looked down at his arms, covered in scars that were still bright pink. He said the scars represented both his own blood and the blood of everyone and everything he had killed. And then he saw his sister and had to force himself back to reality before his emotions claimed him again. "I'm not a good person; they need a good person, not me."

"Then who is?"

James jerked his head to look at Cormac. "I don't know...not me!" James shouted, beginning to lose focus in a growing emotion of fear, anger, and panic.

"No one," Cormac answered for him. "No one can be that person." In a burst of speed and power, Cormac covered the distance between the two men, seeing the growing state of the younger man and knowing the only action that could keep the warrior in balance. The large man grabbed James by his shirt and jacket. Twisting and yanking, Cormac pulled James down to his knee and stared into his face. James countered by reflex, grabbing the other man's shoulder and cocking his other arm to strike, forcing the older man to release him. The young warrior's pupils pulsed with a surge of adrenaline as his body began to wake its darker aspects.

"No one! Especially not you!" Cormac bellowed. The two men stared into each other's faces—Cormac with grim resolve and James with anger and uncertainty. "No one can fulfill that role. But it must be filled! Tinek can't do it, he's the Emperor; neither can Hancock, Cho, or even Karen. It doesn't matter what or who you really are!" James tried to jerk away from his older friend, his madness dying as he comprehended that he wasn't angry at Cormac, just at the reality of the situation.

"Yes, it does! What's real always matters!"

Cormac shook James, both men still locked, ready to strike. "They need a bloody hero! Damn it, James, it doesn't matter if you are one or not! They need one, and you need to act like one." *Crap*, Cormac thought, *I should never have brought this up!*

"I'm not a hero! I kill. It's the only thing I'm good at!"

Trying a different approach, Cormac tore one of the components from the table and shoved it into James's face. "This isn't death!"

James grabbed it before it hit him and spun it around as the two broke free of each other. James hit a button, and his hacking spikes extended from it. "This is a weapon."

Cormac sat back down in the big chair. "Yes," he said. "It is. And that is why you must be the hero. No one really knows much about you other than Jessica, Tinek, myself, and your best men. Hancock and his PR aids have come to a conclusion after examining the news feeds on you, and they want to build your image into a legend, an Imperial Hero." James slumped back into his chair, his anger leaving him, only exhaustion remaining.

"But I'm not," he said.

"It doesn't matter," Cormac responded. "I won't be a part of this," James demanded.

"I know," Cormac said, understanding. "I told them as much, but they said the decision isn't yours. I took it to Tinek, and he demanded that you agree before they proceed."

"I won't be strutted in front of people as something I'm not."

"You won't," Cormac replied. "They are just going to feed the press what they need, what they want. It's really out of our hands already; the press has been having a heyday without anything from you or the government. It wasn't really a decision other than keeping them from anything subversive, but we can't demand they stop. Freedom of expression and press and all, but we can temper it with information. Sorry, bud, but like it or not, you're a hero."

James sat silent again, finally tossing his hacking spikes back onto the table. "Crap!" he exclaimed. "All I want to do is protect Jessica and everyone, and I get turned into something I'm not."

"I know, James, I know. We'll try to contain it and keep it from getting out of hand. All you have to do is what you've been doing; stay out of the public eye and leave the damage control to the PR guys."

2/22/2454

The fleet held position behind the moon Sa'ber as it spun in its slow orbit around Lintalla. Admiral Hancock paced in front of his holo-display as he watched his orders carried out. The fleet was running dark, but there was no way for them to mask the energy signature of every ship. They waited and watched as the Tarin'Tal fleet lethargically flowed in and around their massive GravityPort and the Commune Spire, a ship so large its shadow easily dwarfed that of the Princeps. Every soldier, pilot, and officer in the fleet stood ready, watching and waiting for the battle to begin. Fleet scientists and strategists had determined that the GravityPort must be destroyed before the attack could begin. Otherwise the Tarin'Tal could call for reinforcements, which would arrive far before the humans and Illani could build up enough strength to resist another fleet of equal or greater strength. The battle had to be decisive to ensure any hope of security. Everyone had been pumped full of stimulants, and the seconds seamed like hours as the fleet waited for the portal to be disabled. It hadn't been used yet, but the scientists said that its gravity signature indicated that it was at least partially operational, and that couldn't be allowed. The confusion that would be generated by a sudden loss of the massive structure would also provide the humans with an excellent window of opportunity to attack the alien forces. It was the linchpin of the entire operation. Everyone in the fleet waited on the success of James and Cormac as they each led a division of armored soldiers through the fleet in the captured juggernaut. The shields on the ship had been modified to enhance and amplify their cloaking elements, allowing them to slip into and around the Tarin'Tal fleet unnoticed and undetected unless someone were actively looking for them.

In the silence of space surrounded by several million hostile aliens, James sat restlessly in his armor. The Imperial Hammer and Cormac's elite division were both attached to the sides of the juggernaut as it coasted toward the GravityPort using barely any power. The six hundred warriors had nothing to do until they hit the complex other than watch the seconds tick by on the insides of their helmets at an agonizingly slow rate. But in the silence, James was not alone. Jessica was in the craft as well, and their close proximity allowed them to communicate cybernetically. Neither of them could think of anything to say; they were content with the presence of each other's minds. All controllers for both divisions had been loaded into the assault vessels so that they could aid the troops without betraying the location of the fleet with the strong communication signals the suits would require over such great distance.

James and Jessica listened to the seconds tick by. Tick, ten miles to separation. Tick, tick, tick, nine miles. Tick, tick, eight miles.

Tick, seven miles. Tick, five miles. Tick, two miles—separation. In a jolt of energy coursing through their suits, the Imperial Hammer powered up. As their assault craft launched themselves from the sides of the juggernaut, the space around them filled with fire as they accelerated even faster toward the massive structure. Again they waited for impact. Tick, two miles to impact. Tick, one mile to impact. Ti—slam! The metallic vibration and gut-wrenching violence of the Landers slamming into the metal port reverberated through the warriors. The sound of metal tearing through metal tore at their ears even through the insulation of their suits as the ship came to a grinding halt. The only force keeping the men and their controllers from becoming plastered to the inside of the craft by the magnitude of the impact was the ship's inertial G-force negation technology.

James didn't try to reassure his warriors. They had strength of their own, and he wouldn't take that from them. He watched them and realized that what Cormac had told him the other day wasn't true. His men didn't want to become him, they *were* becoming him. In the opening of their suit's visors, James saw a fledging battle lust in even his most inexperienced men. His veteran warriors exhibited a disturbing desire for bloodshed. *This isn't how it should be*, he thought. The old saying, "War is hell," came to his mind. Even in truth it didn't seem right that these men sought battle; he fought for unique reasons that ended with him enjoying battle, and now others were as well.

In a mix of horror, pride, and commanding confidence, James watched his own desire for combat enflame through his men. Each had their own way of expressing their berserk intents. Some did it through their religion, praying and chanting as adrenaline and endorphins coursed through their veins. Some latched onto their mission, their muscles twisting and filling with blood and chemicals as they set their minds on their bloody objective. Others did it through the pure enjoyment of killing—these were the dangerous ones, the ones who had begun to lose their sanity and become the essence of the berserker. Still more had taken the essence of James's will to fight: they warred for ideals, they warred for revenge, they warred for their people, and like James, they lusted for battle through every reason mentioned and otherwise.

These, James knew, would be the true forces to be reckoned with. They were the ones who had broken their own minds in exchange for a new mentality. They had, just like James, unleashed the demons of their souls; their minds had become both broken and complete through the strain. In understanding his men, James finally saw what he had been searching for since the death of his family: a force that would never stop, never rest, and take an unyielding, unsatisfied, unmerciful vengeance for any harm that came to the people he cared about. He was satisfied. Tinek would guide his people, and these men—these men were the summation of everything he had worked for in his entire life, and they would be the unstoppable Hammer defending those people.

A jolt rocked James back from his thoughts, returning him to the moment and the imminent attack. James closed his visor and activated a communication to his men. "Ready arms! Seal armor! Prepare for the battle that awaits us!"

The men responded with their signature chanting, as weapons unlocked and armor closed and sealed.

"We are the Hammer, we cannot allow any ship to escape. Our victory and the survival of our race depend on this. Do not fail!"

The men slammed their weapons into their chests as they prepared for battle. With the hiss of escaping gasses, the doors to the assault vessel opened to expose the insides of the massive station as it tried to regain pressure after the impact.

They attacked with a deafening roar enhanced by cybernetic speakers and the blasting of rifles.

Once the ships separated from the speeding juggernaut, the juggernaut lost its cloaking shield and activated the new fleet shields it had been fitted with. The surrounding Tarin'Tal forces were both surprised and confused when one of their own ships materialized so close to the center of their fleet and at first did nothing but watch. They realized the intent of the human warriors too late. As they opened fire on the transports, a series of quicksand charges the juggernaut had deployed on its approach detonated, leaving the troopships mostly obscured by the cloud on one side and the massive structure on the other. The tactic, however, wasn't perfect; there was still a large gap between the two, and streams of Tarin'Tal weapons began to pour through. Swinging itself around, the human-controlled juggernaut took the full force of the impact, planting itself squarely between the now attached human troopships and the deadly streams of fire. The sides of the ship lit aflame as the retrofitted ship attempted to absorb the impact of an attack from dozens of sources.

The initiation of combat had been the signal the fleet had been waiting for, and Hancock ordered the entirety of the human armada into the engagement. Virtually the whole Tarin'Tal fleet was gathered around the port as it was about to become operational, wisely protecting it from the human threat. With pulsating blasts, all three of the human capital ships unleashed their antimatter cannons as they raced toward the alien fleet. The smaller ships poured their long-range weapons after the antimatter warheads, blanketing the space above Lintalla in an enveloping shroud of fire and plasma. The resulting impacts expunged an entire spire ship and all her escorts from space before they knew they were under attack.

The result throughout the expansive Tarin'Tal fleet was unimaginable. Space literally writhed with activity as thousands upon thousands of warships raced to battle. Hancock attempted to pull his forces into a tighter capital line as they approached the enemy forces at breathtaking speed. In a wave of destruction, the human and Tarin'Tal fleets met each other in a final battle to decide the fate of Lintalla and both the human and Illani races.

Aboard the GravityPort, James and Cormac's men slaughtered their way through the Tarin'Tal, defending the station. Most were construction workers and scientists; few were warriors. All died. Blasting, slashing, and tearing their way through the enemy, James and his elite warriors battled through the teaming masses of aliens as they forced their way to one of the main nodes they had detected. Nothing stood in the way of the human advance; the men of the Imperial Hammer fought with the ferocity of deranged animals and the skill of warrior angels as they obliterated all Tarin'Tal that stood between them and their objective. With the grating of twisted metal, two of James's personal squad tore the door off the node's hinges, entering the large command room in an arterial spray of blood as they tore its occupants from the living. Walking up to the banks of computers and displays, James extended his hacking spikes and inserted them into the electronics, resulting in the same electrical surges as before.

But unlike before, James couldn't see the entire ship. It was too big; there was too much information. His eyes rolled back into his head as his consciousness focused entirely on attacking the artificial intelligence of the massive structure while still protecting the pathways back into his own mind. It wasn't enough. He was only able to see through the ship's sensors, and even then, only for a moment before the weight of the ships computers forced him out. James was forced to break his connection with the machinery to protect his own mind from the overwhelming weight of the network. But he had seen something, something that was more important to him than the conquest of the massive structure's computer.

A concentrated barrage from three spire ships had vaporized a column of quicksand large enough for a juggernaut to pass through, and one was making its way to the port, which had been activated. Running back through the carnage of battle, James made his way to the troopship and its massive engines. If he could ram the juggernaut, he could block the entrance to the portal and stop the alien from warning the rest of their dominions. Without his armor to guide him, James would have slipped on the bodies and gore over which he traveled; instead he sped over them.

"James to all personnel, vacate the troopship! Vacate the troo—!" An enormous explosion rocked the complex before he could finish his statement. The defending juggernaut had been forced into the complex and had crushed his troopship.

James was paralyzed momentarily. Panicking, he tried to contact Jessica—nothing. Again he tried calling on their cybernetic link. Again nothing. James's mind and body fell out from under him. She was gone. Whereas he had been on the edge of going berserk throughout the battle, he now fell further into madness than any human could ever fathom. "Nooo!" James bellowed as he charged forward, tearing door after door from the ship's pathways. In a final burst of power, he ripped the last hatchway apart between him and the remains of the troop ship; there was nothing but fiery twisted metal, and his sensors confirmed his worst fears. No one was alive onboard the ship. "Damn them! Damn their godless, inhuman, murdering race!"

The air from the hatchway he had opened rushed by him, trying to pull him out of the ship, and he let it. He was flung from the station toward the juggernaut, which listed on its side. The crew must have been stunned by the impact. Several other juggernauts and flights of gunships still hammered at the ship's shields, which grew brightly as it attempted to absorb the destructive energy. As he approached the ship's shields, James activated his own shield, which interacted with that of the ship. Twisting himself between the ship and his own shield, James slipped through as the huge shield connected with his small device, temporarily jumping over him to the small emitter. The space between the shield and the ship was covered in a heartbeat, and with a metallic clang, James slammed into the ship's side. Shortly after wrenching open an exterior port, another series of clangs sounded through the metal.

James took a second to glance at their source and saw half of his personal squad scrambling over the hull toward him. *Idiots!* James thought. *No one will survive this.*

Ignoring the men as they raced toward him, James hurled himself through the opening and into the ship. Punching handholds in the hallway as he entered, James made short work of the opposing force of the atmosphere leaving the ship, entering a secondary compartment with his men in mere moments.

Even before the hissing of escaping air stopped behind the closing doors, James had taken off down the corridor at full speed. The urgency and wrath of his advance caused him to force every ounce of both his own and his suit's strength into speed, leaving deep gouges in the floor where his boots had dented it through sheer force. The halls were mostly empty of personnel as only a skeleton crew of men who could figure out how to operate the alien technology manned the ship. It didn't take long for James to reach the bridge. What he found on the command deck would have horrified him if he had any humanity in him left to horrify. The ship had lost its inertial dampening systems, and the crew had been dashed apart when it had struck the lander and Gravity Port. The deck had also lost its gravity control, and bits of people drifted aimlessly in the now weightless environment.

As James had left the alien port, Hancock had been forced to pull the fleet back from the engagement, the capital line reversing even as they continued to pour endless rounds of plasma and antimatter into the vast ranks of Tarin'Tal. Thousands of gunships poured through the tangled masses of spire ships and juggernauts to drill the human force with their missiles and kinetic beams. Even under the constant barrage, the shields protecting the fleet held, shimmering their brilliance as they absorbed the malicious energy. No matter how much force the aliens threw at the line, they could not break it. But repeatedly, they threw themselves at it, knowing that the human technology could only last so long against such vastly superior numbers. The reversal of the fleet's momentum away from the enemy onslaught was the only thing keeping the aliens from swarming the humans and obliterating the shield wall.

Aboard the juggernaut, James took control of the large ship with his hacking spikes. Although damaged from his attempt at the GravityPort, they were still strong enough to command the weak computers on the smaller craft. Most of the ship's systems still worked, surviving the grueling barrage it even now sustained from the Tarin'Tal fleet's attempt to save their massive construct. In his rage, James opened every last battery of weapons on the offending juggernaut as it attempted to pass through the gravity gate, but to little effect. The ship would make it through. James slammed his ship's acceleration controls with his mind, but it still moved too slowly. James stopped firing and diverted everything to the engines. He took away life support, sensors, and shields to force the ship to accelerate far beyond what it was designed to endure, and it worked.

With unreal speed, the ship shot forward, its engines boiling with effort and its hull blazing with flame. The alien weapons now had nothing standing between them and the exposed ship. Even as the juggernaut shot toward the other, it burst into flames as panels and large chunks of metal wrenched from their positions to fall into space, spouting flames and charred bodies as the atmosphere inside the vessel was ignited by the brutal alien kinetic weapons.

James turned to the men that had followed him and snarled, "Get out."

His men tried to protest. "Sir, we follow you till death!" James turned on them, and even with his arm still locked into the console and his mind's eye still consumed with controlling the ship, he latched onto Tom's faceplate. He began to squeeze, the creaks and groans of straining metal forced his point home to the men.

"Get the hell out!" he screamed. "I'm doing this! They've taken her from me! She's gone!" James's scream echoed throughout the burning ship and rang the metal that still stood intact. The microphones on the men's suits popped and died under the mass of incoming noise. His men saluted and left, punching through to space just outside the command deck's door as it closed behind them.

As he allowed the depressurizing atmosphere to carry him out and away from the ship, Thomas was sure that he was leaving his leader's self-imposed funeral pyre. He turned, and in the silence and cold of space, he watched his fears become reality.

James had left only the ship's navigational sensors active aside from its engines. Even through the static and distortion of battle and the GravityPort, James focused only on the other ship as it attempted to warn their dominion. His mind's eye was fixated on the other ship's bridge through the sensors, but what he saw was not reality. He had lost reality when his sister died. He now lost the facsimile of reality he had held only through Jessica. What he saw was not Tarin'Tal; it was the Harvesters. It was the Death. It was everything that had ever hurt anyone he cared about, and he would kill it. He looked through the twisted wreckage flying off his ship through the billows of flame and weapon fire and into the other ship's command deck. He saw a Harvester, a Harvester with the blood of his sister dripping from its grotesque tail, claws, and mouth. His eyes lost in blackness, his veins tight with blood and rage, James let his anger, his rage, his guilt, his remorse flow out, and in one final moment, he finally saw himself. And then he struck.

Just before the juggernaut could enter the gravity well of the port, the two ships collided. The front of the ship crumpled. The engines finally gave into the strain of the bombardment they had been enduring and exploded, buckling halfway down the length of the ship as it shattered. The other ship spun with its side crushed. With parts flying everywhere, it slammed into the side of the port. In a blinding display, the side of the port buckled, and in unison, all three alien constructs were enveloped in fire and death.

All that remained was the lightless hulk of the port with a massive chunk missing where the juggernaut had struck it and a field of shattered shards of ship.

Aboard an escape vessel from the troopship, Jessica attempted to reconnect with James's squad. She had been unconscious for only a moment. She had tried to contact James's cybernetics, but when she did, all she could hear was pain—and it was driving her mad. After only a second, she contacted Thomas. "Need pickup immediately," the man demanded. "James is on the—Oh, NO!" the officer exclaimed as the massive explosion rippled space too close for his or the remaining warriors' safety. Jessica's mind went numb. She simultaneously screamed into her communications device and mentally through her cybernetics, trying to contact James. No one answered. It wasn't a second, it wasn't even time, it wasn't even truly real. In that moment she knew James was gone. Her pain was inhuman.

She screamed.

She screamed so loud that all the mikes in the pod buzzed in protest. She screamed mentally, physically, spiritually, and cybernetically. It reverberated through everything; the rage she felt permeated all her technology and flowed into that of the pod's, through its communications channels and into every ship in the fleet. It flowed through security lockouts, through fighter and troop commands, and into the ears and minds of every last person of the fleet. In that moment, everyone knew who had fallen: the Hero of Sh'in; the Hero of the Empire was dead.

Jessica's rage was not equaled, but it was not alone.

The fleet fed off her hatred and her wrathful screams of sorrow and defiance of reality. He was gone, and humanity would have its revenge. In an unprecedented unanimity of movement, the entire human fleet stopped retreating. No commander had any taste for retreat, no warrior had room for surrender, and no human had any mercy left for the incalculably numerous foe. As Jessica's scream died, so did any reservations about full-on battle. Even though they were vastly outnumbered and had almost no chance at victory, the last of mankind charged as one.

The Tarin'Tal tried to meet them head on, but they failed; they died. In blinding sheets of flame that mirrored their rage, the Imperial fleet hit the alien lines and broke through them to the unorganized ranks behind. They no longer saw battle for its strategic sake, or even survival; this had become a battle of vengeance.

Against the Tarin'Tal armada, the exiles unleashed all their sorrow for Earth and every human that had died at the hands of the Harvesters, the Death, and the Tarin'Tal themselves. Their wrath was invincible. With a word, Hancock loosed every last fighter from the fleet's reserve. At another word, the Princeps, all her escorts, and thousands upon thousands of fighters entered the battle from the other side of the moon, flanking the teaming Tarin'Tal with unfathomable ferocity.

Tinek brought the Legatus and her escort of destroyers and frigates into the full engagement.

It was no longer a fleet, it was Mankind. Humanity fought as if their soul had been stolen, and they raged in a futile hope of having it returned. They knew the loss of the moment as a key to unleashing the entirety of the losses they had endured as a race.

Against odds greater than any a human military had ever faced, they cracked the alien forces. No one knew if it was the ferocity of their charge, the sudden change in tactics, their technological superiority, or their pure rage that turned the tide. Maybe it was none of these. Maybe it was all. But the battle turned.

When the first spire ship shattered under the weight of the human assault, the wave of destruction spread throughout the alien fleet like a chain of dominoes. The human shields were far superior at deflecting the resulting debris and their fighters far more capable of dodging the fires and spinning hulks. With the chaos of destruction leading their way, the human armada continued their assault through the masses of vicious aliens.

Even though the battle turned to a one-sided affair, it was not without loss. As ships swarmed the Cerberus and the cruisers, a hail of death was brought against them from a dozen spire ships apiece. Never ceasing, the human forces responded by riding the pulsations of destruction even harder as it hit them with tidal power. Debris, plasma, kinetic fire, missiles, and antimatter were everywhere. Sensors became useless, and pilots were forced to rely on their eyes alone. Flights of Peregrine flowed through the battle like a thousand veins of deadly blood that burned all it touched. Nothing stood in their way for long.

Still the alien forces retaliated. They fought, but now only for their survival. In a surprise maneuver, six spire ships descended on the Legatus and began pounding her forward shields as the wave of destruction abated. Now the forces in the battle were equal, and now humanity had hope. But not the Legatus. In a cascading effect, she lost her shield emitters, sensors, and engines. She was dead in space. A second wave of fire descended as Tinek and A'ssia watched their doom fall upon them. With a glance, Tinek told A'ssia to activate the massive ship's trireme device. She didn't get the chance.

The first of the new volley hit the ship, rocking everyone off their feet as the inertial dampeners began to fail. As the remainder of the assault burned its way through space, the kinetic weapons, glowing as they traveled, and the missiles leaving ugly trails of smoke, were obscured in one single moment by the Leviathan. As the side of the cruiser took the swath of devastation meant for the imperial flagship, the Legatus received a single broken transmission— "Hail...ek, Lo...live th'Empire!"—and then her side shattered under the strain. Her engines, however, still burned, and she rocketed toward their ultimate target—the Tarin'Tal Commune Spire.

It was the alien's doom, and they knew it. Every ship in the alien fleet descended on the Leviathan as it advanced, unrelenting, toward their prime vessel. Every last human ship fought to give her cover and allow her to complete her noble sacrifice. Alien ships began to slam into the doomed cruiser as it approached its target. Gunships and juggernauts alike took chunks out of the craft, only partly redirected by the ship's cannons and failing shields. In a desperate move, an entire spire ship plowed into the Leviathan, sending the burning wreck from its path and tearing its engines apart. But it wasn't in time. As it was torn apart, it was still able to detonate its trireme.

Along with the ship's antimatter and fusion drives, the cruiser's trireme carried an untested weapon. A gravity bomb. First detonating in pure energy, the ship tore through space. Following the first wave of death was a second, more powerful pulsation destruction. Human and Tarin'Tal alike, they fled. The pulsating ribbons of gravity tried to both expand and contract on itself as they rippled across space. Anything caught in its path was simultaneously pulled in on itself and forced away from the detonation's epicenter in violently opposing gravity and antigravity. The humans were farther from the detonation point and faster; most survived. The Tarin'Tal were not so lucky. They died in agony as they tried to run in terror. The pain they had inflicted on human and Illani alike was returned to them a hundredfold as their ships were cracked apart to leave them dying in the icy cold of space. Some lucky warriors were killed by their craft's cores and engines buckling and exploding before they could be expelled into space; most were denied that luxury. All died.

The tattered human armada sat drifting in space, too shocked by the battle's ending to search for remaining Tarin'Tal. They didn't need to. The Peregrine fighters easily mopped up the remaining wounded ships as the remainder of the fleet pulled itself out of the field of destruction to lick their wounds and take stock of the new reality. The planet still remained to be liberated, but their sensors identified very few Tarin'Tal life sign signatures, and most were concentrated around massive work camps they had forced the Illani into and would fall easily. The only problem would be how to do it without hurting the Illani they held prisoner, but that was a task to be undertaken after they had regrouped and had time to prepare.

2/23/2454

The sky rained fire as the carnage in orbit began to fall to the planet. Lintalla had been rocked by massive earthquakes that had done serious damage to the infrastructure of some of the less stable cities. Most, however, had stood. The populace was used to large tectonic movement and the gravitational shear of Lintalla's large moon. The battle above had thrown large debris and missed weapons toward the planet. The debris served as cover for the now approaching fleet of warships. Only the capital city and industrial centers had any major Tarin'Tal presence, and even then, they were concentrated in communal housing they had erected around concentration-camp-style work prisons. With expert timing and precision, virtually all the Tarin'Tal's orbital and air defenses were vaporized in a massive barrage of artillery. Lines of Peregrine fighters began to puncture the cloud layer in eddies of light that appeared almost as a network of fiery chains wrapping the sky in its burning embrace. The capital city lay dark in the valley surrounded by the black cliffs. A gushing waterfall glistened in newfound brightness as it fell behind the walls of the royal palace and flowed out through the city and into the large lake. The interim commander of the Imperial Hammer, Thomas Hilben, stood beside Tinek as the lander sped toward the dark surface, the early dawn only making the landscape visible as a sprawling specter of its true self.

Tinek turned to the new leader of his personal guard. His face was shadowed darkly with anger. "No mercy, Thomas, no mercy. I want you to do exactly what they did to my people, what they did to James. Burn them from existence with no mercy. Kill them for your people, kill them for my people, kill them for James."

His muscles tight in an anger and determination mirroring the emperor's, Hilben responded simply and forcefully. "It will be done. I swear on my life and on the lives of the entire Imperial Hammer that no Tarin'Tal will leave the palace alive." Hilben watched outside the craft on his suit's monitor as hundreds upon hundreds of similar craft to his own descended toward the Illani capital.

"You heard the emperor!" Hilben shouted to all the men in the lander through his suit. "For vengeance!" he demanded.

"For vengeance!" they echoed in a wave of sound that reverberated throughout every corner of the large craft. Only a few seconds elapsed before they hit the ground within the palace walls. Even though the troops were protected by the ship's powerful inertial dampeners, the men inside could easily tell that the craft had forced its way at least several feet into the ground. As the doors opened, the soft light of dawn crept in, shading a mass of oncoming alien warriors more as tangible specters than physical beings.

"Abominations!" Hilben accused, as he attacked. Without the overwhelming shock the Hammer normally delivered when James attacked, the aliens didn't break at first. The pure power and skill of the human warriors only took a second to overwhelm the Tarin'Tal with both firepower and blades. The battle was quick as the humans poured out of their craft, every new armored warrior tilting the balance of battle heavily in their own favor. An entire second division of Cormac's forces had been devoted to the attack as well, having been mixed throughout the thousands of regulars to prevent the aliens from tearing the unarmored forces to pieces. The ending result was not so much a battle as an execution; the most violent execution imaginable.

The Imperial Hammer, Cormac's divisions, the regulars, the fleet, everyone had taken the death of James, the Imperial Hammer and Hero, as a personal offense. They took their anger out on the abandoned Tarin'Tal. The slaughter went on for hours; almost no Tarin'Tal tried to surrender, and even when they did, they were seldom given any quarter, and true to his word, Hilben and the Imperial Hammer gave none within the walls of the palace. Some would call it brutal and an inhuman display of violence and rage. Others would call it perfectly human, a reaction to the death of a leader, but no one disputed that the Tarin'Tal deserved every last bit of the destruction they received.

The Imperial Hammer had reformed around the lander after destroying all the Tarin'Tal they could find. As they all took defensive positions, another armored suit came out of the lander. The black and white of the suit, however, had been reversed, and the deep black of its faceplate somehow seemed to reflect more light than the white of his suit. "We are ready to take the throne room," Hilben informed the emperor. "The only Tarin'Tal registering on sensors are inside, two dozen total."

"Good," Tinek stated, the anger in his voice no less than when the invasion had begun.

"I beg you to reconsider; you are too valuable to be in combat, and you haven't been trained beyond the suit's operational basics."

"No...no," Tinek yelled but quickly controlled himself. "I need to be there when we retake the seat of power. This is how it has always been. This is how my people think; this is how we live."

"Yes, sir," Hilben assented, and the division moved out. In a column, the troops reached the massive doors and fanned slightly to the sides as Tinek made his way through the men.

The emperor put his palm on the door, taking a long moment to inhale a single breath of air. The air in the room seemed to change as if he were drawing all the pain from both their races into himself and into that room. Putting all his suit's power behind a single concentrated push, the doors cracked along their seams that had been sealed by the Tarin'Tal and slammed open. The change in air pressure rushed past the black warriors as they entered the room in a burst of speed. Before the dust could settle, the Imperial Hammer had obliterated all the aliens in the room but one. They hadn't been affected by the noise, dust, or light—their suits had cut through all distractions as if they were a fading wisp of nothing. As the bodies hit the floor, Tinek walked into the room. The dust settled behind him, allowing light to stream over his white and black armor as the sun finally broke the horizon directly behind him.

Tinek stopped before the throne and pointed accusingly at the large beast sitting hunched in the human and Illani-sized seat. "I thought your race killed the disproportionate!" he said mockingly.

The beast snarled a reply: "A polluted biped cannot understand The Will. It can only serve or die before it." With a lurch, the beast launched itself at Tinek. It pulled both its kinetic weapon and hooked sword from its belt and leveled both at Tinek. It fired. The blast impacted the unison of six shields as half a dozen of the Hammer rushed between the alien and their emperor with speed bordering that of light. With unsaid orders, another dozen warriors attacked the alien war chief. Its sword blazed toward the first warrior who deflected it easily. In a spray of gore, all twelve men struck in harmony, spreading the beast across the entire throne room.

Tinek walked up to the throne. The armor on his hand unscrewed and hissed as it came apart and retracted up his arm. His hand shaking slightly, Tinek ran his fingers across the throne's arm and stared at them, now covered in the blood of the Tarin'Tal, whose head lay at his feet. "Washed in the blood of our enemies," Tinek mused. "James would be pleased." Turning to his men, the emperor sat on the bloodstained throne. "We've won. Welcome home," he said to the two and a half hundred men in the room.

The black warriors saluted him and shouted, "Hail Tinek!"

27 >> Life

2/4/2454

The leaders of the empire stood in the spire of the now Imperial Palace, watching the broadcast of the address Tinek and the council had prepared before the invasion broadcast throughout the planet. They were informed of the new government and told about their liberators and about what they already were experiencing: their returned freedom. No one knew what the reaction would be as the leaders looked out over the city as it slowly came back to life. The populace was freed from the work camps to return to their old homes. Their broadcast network was primitive by comparison to the technology the humans were accustomed to, but relatively consistent with that used by twenty-first-century Earth. Most of the freed Illani had found their way back to their homes. Having been of little importance to the Tarin'Tal, they had been relatively untouched. It was the Lintallan equivalent of fall in the capital city, and the long drizzly day was relatively undisturbed by either Illani or human; both were recovering from their own ordeals.

Even when the announcements began to broadcast, there wasn't much stir. The Illani weren't used to change, but to them this wasn't much of a change. Most had seen the bottom-up segment of society as an allowance for the humans with whom they now found themselves joined.

They were correct in part. The constitution didn't demand for the election of mayors and councils, but it did give them power when elected. Many Illani provinces wouldn't elect them at first, but over time they would come to embrace the benefits of representation, both at the local and national levels of society. They had been comfortable with their old society, and the topdown control from the emperor restricted by the human-style constitution mirrored it well. At least while they recovered from both war and enslavement, they would find solace in an old system before experimenting with the new.

The reaction to the announcement would have been subtle even if they had not been recovering, but with their turmoil fresh in the Illani's minds and bodies, there was barely more than a whisper. Tinek and A'ssia stood on the tower long after the remaining officials had returned to their ships and craft. They stood looking over the capital city as it slumbered and watched. It hadn't been disappointing that there was virtually no reaction to the reconstitution of their society.

It had been almost a shock to the humans, while Tinek was more pleased than anything. He knew the temperament of his people. The imperial government protected what they wanted to be protected, and that was enough for them. When combined with their liberation, Tinek knew the humans and government would be welcomed; maybe not with open arms, but welcomed, nonetheless.

A day later, Hancock stood on his command deck, watching the two remaining colony ships descend toward the new home world, Lintalla. One was headed toward the planet. Like their four predecessors, they would land together. But unlike them, these ships would land on the outskirts of an already functional, although damaged, city.

"Display telemetry," Hancock ordered. The image of the ships exiting the burn zone of the atmosphere filled his screen as they began to reform themselves to land and construct new homes. As the last of the Tarin'Tal warships had gone dark in the cold of space, half the fleet had begun demanding dismissal from their military conscription. With a planet to live on and the immediate Tarin'Tal threat neutralized, Hancock had agreed. Not so fortunate was the entirety of the military fleet. While the admiral had dismissed anyone who had lost limbs or sustained serious injury, he wanted to keep the fleet at as much strength as he could. The Tarin'Tal couldn't have been a migratory race, and he feared that their gravity port had sent a signal of some kind to their kin.

The Exile Empire

The admiral, the council, and Tinek had agreed that they needed to be ready for any future attack. Inconsistent with their disposition before the invasion, many Illani had immediately enlisted in the military. Not surprisingly, however, was the fact that most of them were the children of the eliminated warrior caste. Since the Illani did not join a caste until they came of age, the caste members had been eradicated, but not the families of the caste. They had been among the remainder of the civilian population and enslaved as well.

The admiral looked at a display paralleling the image of the colony ships, now on the ground. It had only been a little more than twenty-four hours since the broadcast following the unification presentation. It had called for recruits to defend the empire against future attacks, and the enlistments had already risen to more than one hundred thousand and were still rising.

The cities, which from orbit had been dark when the fleet had arrived and fought, now glowed brightly from the planet's surface as power and basic infrastructure were restored by the large numbers of civilian mules who had quickly found entrepreneurial opportunities on the planet. Most of the military had been recalled to Sh'in for rest and repairs, leaving only the Cerberus with a few destroyers and frigates to police the civilian ships, which were still streaming down to the planet to make new lives for themselves. Most of them landed around the two colony ships; some had found other cities across the lush super-continent that many found inviting. Still others had opted to return to Sh'in to establish themselves on the arid prairie world. Compared to the chaos of the past few months, the relative mundaneness of directing and policing a tired fleet was almost intoxicating, but Hancock knew that he had to get the people to the planet soon; they were cramped, hungry, tired, and eager to start their new lives.

It had been decided that there would be an official ceremony through which the empire would transfer the seat of power from the Legatus to the Imperial Palace. After three weeks of rest and reconstruction, they had reached the set date. The sprawling courtyard was filled with newly elected representatives from across the empire. The number of human and Illani were relatively equal, most of the Illani having not got around to electing anyone yet. There were, however, masses of reporters present. The companies started on the fleet had already blossomed into major news corporations by partnering with several Illani businesses. The fledgling human news industry was nothing compared to the swarms of locals who held everything ranging from primitive visual-audio recorders to human-purchased holographic imagers. It was an enormous ceremony. The entire planet watched, either in their homes, in restaurants, or on the new community news holograms doting the city squares and anywhere humans settled.

The people within the towering walls of the palace easily counteracted the cool fall temperatures as they waited for the ceremony to begin. With clashing brass instruments, both human and Illani, the massive spectacle began. In a burst of color and sound, the Imperial Hammer appeared from various entrances to cover the steps leading to the grand white-stone throne room. Their polished metal glistened even in the low light of the cold day. The rasping of metal filled the space as they all drew their swords and turned toward a center aisle and held their position. Once they were in position, captains and commanders from throughout the fleet entered the courtyard, bringing deafening cheering from the crowd.

Over and over, the words "Xillion! Xillion!" were shouted. The words didn't translate directly into English, but their meaning wound its way through several concepts—crusader, liberator, untarnished warrior. It was the highest praise their society could deliver. The music died for a second, and the crowd fell silent. For a moment, one could hear a pin drop on the stones beneath the feet of Illani and human. The instruments resumed in a clash of sound that felt almost physical, and the emperor and empress appeared. They walked through the soldiers and officers and were joined by Hancock, Cormac, and Hilben as they walked up the steps.

They took each stair carefully and deliberately. The emperor's new white and black was worn by both Tinek and A'ssia, and their pure white cloaks billowed slightly in the breeze as they ascended toward the throne. As they reached the top where the throne sat, Jessica came out from the building to stand with them.

The cheers from human and Illani throats blended into a deafening roar as every last person celebrated their liberty and emperor. The music rose, and flight upon flight of fighters buzzed the palace. The din continued for several minutes before Tinek again rose. "My people. My friends. This day we are free because of a new unity. Mankind had found its way through the universe to our steps. Led by something greater than ourselves, their exile has ended our slavery. Together we must become strong! Illani and Mankind will be referred to as one. Together we will build freedom, prosperity, and security in our great Hyperion Empire!"

The crowd burst into the massive sounds of cheering as they mirrored the enthusiasm and strength of their emperor. Tinek turned to Hancock and drew a reddish black Illani-style sword from the side of the throne. It was curved like a katana but broader and bladed on both sides. "Immanuel Felix Hancock, for your strength in holding the exiled fleet together, and for bravery in combat, for your victory against the Tarin'Tal, I grant you the title Duke of Sa'ber and induct you into the order of the Crimson Sword."

He then continued, "I hereby bestow on you the title and role of supreme commander of the imperial forces, responsible directly to the imperial council and myself."

He turned to Cormac. "Cormac William Kincade, I appoint you Count of New Carson, your realms including the province of New Carson and all military instillations throughout the empire." Tinek pulled another sword from the throne. "I induct you into the Order of the Crimson Sword and grant you the title of imperial general in command of all ground forces responsible to the supreme commander, the council, and myself. I task you with the creation of a new breed of warriors for our new breed of empire."

Finally he turned to Jessica. "Jessica Obsianus Ursidae, I posthumously grant your husband the title of duke, lord of the imperial families' holdings and defender of the Imperial house." Tinek pulled one last sword out, still in its sheath. "I induct your family's line into the Order of the Crimson Sword. This shall remain sheathed until the title is claimed."

Jessica glanced at her belly, where James's son grew.

"Furthermore, I grant him the title of Imperial Guardian. His name shall be carved into the throne itself." Tinek turned to the people gathered, the crowd silenced by the depth of the actions taking place. "My people! These are your liberators, and your brothers!"

"Hail Tinek!" arose from the crowd in both the Illani and English languages. The noise didn't die until Tinek moved back into the Imperial Palace to begin the administration of the empire.

>> Epilogue

"That was seven years ago. Since then we have repaired all the damage the Tarin'Tal did to our cities and people. We have even added human technology to almost every aspect of our lives. But you already know that; you even have some of it inside you. But that is how your father became emperor. Now go to sleep. You have training with Hilben in the morning. He wants you to try out the miniature armor. He made it himself and is really proud of it. Jessica says he is almost as good as she is. Good night, Tellia."

The little girl pulled herself into her covers and pulled over her stuffed dragon. "Good night, Auntie. Thanks for the story. I like it best the way you tell it."

The human woman smiled and walked out of the room with a slight limp as the door slid shut behind her and the lights dimmed.

>> About the Author

Joshua Done – was born in Long Beach California and grew up in the Snoqualmie Valley of Washington State. He loves to read science fiction and urban fantasy because "science fiction allows you to approach human questions without the trappings of modern society."

Overcoming obstacles has become a big part of Josh's life. He readily responds to challenges from rock climbing (he earned his teaching credentials from Boy Scouts of America) to conquering severe food allergies by becoming a self-taught gluten free, dairy free chef. When Josh complained to his brother that science fiction lacked stories that, "follow historical trends," he was challenged to describe that world and put it in writing. Josh responded by creating the world of the Hyperion Empire and writing his first novel, *Exile Empire*.

Josh has a B.A. in Political Economy from Hillsdale College in Michigan. When not writing, Josh enjoys collecting ancient coins and his hunting and fishing expeditions into the local forest.

Made in the USA
Monee, IL
09 June 2023

35542817R00146